JOHN HERSEY

Key West Tales

John Hersey was born in Tientsin, China, in 1914 and lived there until 1925, when his family returned to the United States. He studied at Yale and Cambridge universities, served for a time as Sinclair Lewis's secretary, and then worked several years as a journalist. He had published sixteen books of fiction and nine books of reportage and essays. During the last years of his life, Mr. Hersey and his wife, Barbara, divided their time between Key West, Florida, and Martha's Vineyard. He died in 1993.

May all your
Key West dreams
come true.
Love,
Dore & Jackie
196
Chri[illegible]

BOOKS BY JOHN HERSEY

Key West Tales (1993)
Antonietta (1991)
Fling and Other Stories (1990)
Life Sketches (1989)
Blues (1987)
The Call (1985)
The Walnut Door (1977)
The President (1975)
My Petition for More Space (1974)
The Writer's Craft (1974)
The Conspiracy (1972)
Letter to the Alumni (1970)
The Algiers Motel Incident (1968)
Under the Eye of the Storm (1967)
Too Far to Walk (1966)
White Lotus (1965)
Here to Stay (1963)
The Child Buyer (1960)
The War Lover (1959)
A Single Pebble (1956)
The Marmot Drive (1953)
The Wall (1950)
Hiroshima (1946; new edition, 1985)
A Bell for Adano (1944)
Into the Valley (1943)

Key West Tales

Key West Tales

JOHN HERSEY

Vintage Books

A Division of Random House, Inc.

New York

FIRST VINTAGE BOOKS EDITION, AUGUST 1996

 Published in the United States by Vintage Books, a division of Random House, Inc., New York, and simultaneously in Canada by Random House of Canada Limited, Toronto. Originally published in hardcover by Alfred A. Knopf, Inc., New York, in 1993.

The Library of Congress has cataloged the Knopf edition as follows:
Hersey, John 1914–1993
Key West tales / by John Hersey.—1st ed.
p. cm.
ISBN 0-679-42992-1
1. Key West (Fla.)—Fiction. I. Title.
PS3515.E7715K48 1994
813'.52—dc20
93-11094
CIP
Vintage ISBN: 0-679-77263-4

Random House Web address: http://www.randomhouse.com/

Printed in the United States of America
10 9 8 7 6 5 4 3 2 1

Contents

Key West Tales

God's Hint

The preacher on this Sabbath morning is Brother Eagan. A big bear of a man, he has a chestnut beard and sideburns like huge ficus bushes sticking out on either side of his face. He is a Methodist, with embers for eyes and a whip for a tongue. Just now it is the Methodists' nine o'clock turn to hold their service in the great hall of the county courthouse in Jackson Square, which all Key West denominations use, in round-robin hours, for worship on Sundays.

Squire Eagan, as most people call the Methodist parson, is feared more than he is loved, and envied more than he is feared. He has a deadly aim, and the bull's-eye he consistently hits is his listeners' rather weak sense of having done the wrong thing. The sun shines bright and hot on Key West; this is a climate that is kind to bright-blooming greenery and to joys of the flesh—frisky trysts, rum, and rumpled bedsheets—and so it is that many of the citizens are well acquainted with mischief, but at a cost. For once a week, at Sabbath meeting, when the hot tongue of Squire Eagan is levied at them, they suffer remorse. The remorse is not extreme, and it is short-lived, but while it lasts it is most annoying, like the bite of the fire ant.

Squire Eagan is envied because he is rich. He is rich because on weekdays, instead of visiting the sick and comforting the poor, he plies the trade of an expert wrecker. He owns a swift and sea-kindly schooner, the Godspeed. *The trade that goes by the name of wrecking has brought great prosperity to our little town, which, being the most southerly place in the United States, is a port of landfall for bottoms from all over the world, laden with spirits, silks, finished articles, works of art, silverware, lace, fine furniture, and other goods and artifacts, to say nothing of bulk cargoes of lumber, sugar, fruits, and the precious bird droppings known as guano.*

Wreckers are salvors. That enormous living creature the coral barrier reef along the Keys lies in wait in all weathers for unwary ships. There is not a single lighthouse along the one hundred twenty miles of this monster from Carysfort Reef to Key West, and indeed, the influential wreckers of our town have vociferously opposed the setting out of any government lights. Some slanderers from the mainland have invented a story that Key West wreckers have actually set out a light at a place where there is no channel at all; the wreckers say to cynics who point toward a shining speck out there at night, No, no, that is just a star very low over the horizon.

At any rate, the moment the great coral beast clamps its southernmost jaws on a stray vessel, or, at the latest, at dawn the next morning, the wreck is spied from a whole series of high lookouts on the waterfront of Key West. A cry goes up, passed through all the Old Town: "Wreck ashore! Wreck ashore!" *and within minutes the streets become racecourses for crowds of men, running for the harbor. Soon scores of vessels there bend on their canvas, slip the pennants of their moorings, and crowd all sail for a race, be it in doldrums or gale winds, out to the reef. What regattas those are! The captain of the first vessel to reach the vicinity of the derelict becomes the Wrecking Master, who can then lay claim to whatever he salvages. He lays claim, too, to mean and dangerous work, which often involves skin-diving in the foulest of weather. Squire Eagan's* Godspeed, *whether with divine assistance or not, has had a way of getting there first again and again, and Eagan's house on Front Street, a three-story clapboard mansion with a widow's walk atop it, has in it, among many other treasures, a Ming dynasty coromandel screen, a silver tea service said to have been made by Paul Revere, a cloisonné tea caddy from Bombay, and a dazzling collection of South American butterflies mounted as if on the wing in a glass case lined with crimson velvet.*

Squire Eagan stands now in the raised rostrum from which, when court is in session in this room, the judge presides. On Sundays, this is the pulpit. Magisterially intimidating, this rostrum stands a full six feet higher than the floor of the hall, where the Methodists are seated. The walls of the chamber on either side have tall and wide windows, so that the eye of God has a good look at the brightly lit faces of His flock—and by the same token, the eye of God's messenger, up in the rostrum, has a fine clear view of the expanse of ocean out to the south.

The text for the sermon today is I Corinthians, chapter nine, verse twenty-four: "Know ye not that they which run in a race run all, but one receiveth the prize? So run, that ye may obtain." Squire Eagan winds into his theme: The great race, which every one of these poor sinners in Key West must run, is for eternal salvation. Who will win the prize? His hot eyes roam along the rows of faces of those he knows to be strong in ardor and weak in will—lotus eaters, hankerers, those with red noses and lubricious lips, sensualists whom he has reason to suspect as trespassers in the meadows of wedlock. Squire Eagan looks you, too, dear reader, in the eye, and you, too, tremble, thinking of the wrong that you, too, have done. Do you feel the fire ant's bite?

Now, it happens that some twenty minutes into the dominie's harangue, his eyes dart for a moment out the window to his right. And what does he see? He sees a handsome brigantine, tacking into a strong sou'wester, staying well inside the contrary current of the Gulf Stream and therefore close aboard the terrible stretch of the reef known as the Sambos. And look! She is trying to come about—a miscalculation. She loses steerage way—she is in irons!—she drifts! There! *She is fast on the reef!*

The automatic cry "Wreck ashore!" *almost rises in Squire Eagan's throat. But he chokes it back. God has vouchsafed him a timely thought. If he gives the lookout shout from up here in the rostrum, nine tenths of the men in the congregation will be out the door at the other end of the hall and racing for their vessels before he can climb down from this height and chase them.*

His furious gaze swivels back onto the faces of the more or less rueful transgressors. His voice rising to new thumps of thunder, he makes his way down the steps of the judicial bench to the floor level, and ambling as he roars, he eases into the center aisle. What he is doing is most necessary. He has reached the stage in his sermon when he needs must face each parishioner close at hand—lean into the end of each row on either side, stare down both male and female sinners one by one, and drive the message home.

And so he goes down the center aisle, shouting, "Prepare! Prepare for the great race—for salvation!"

Having reached the very last row, three paces from the open door to the town, he roars, "Wreck ashore! *Now we will run a race and see who receiveth the prize.* Run, *that ye may obtain!"*

His church is emptied as fast as if he had smelled smoke and shouted, "Fire! Fire!" Virtually all the men in his flock are in full chase behind him—Methodists are keen wreckers. But he has a goodly lead. Some of the men of his crew have been rendered sufficiently uneasy by his sermon to run extra fast, as if the Devil himself were chasing them, and so they catch up with him at the docks. They scramble aboard Godspeed *on the parson's coattails.*

What a beautiful parade of sails on a Sunday morning! Godspeed *gets the jump on the* Hester Ann, *the* Splendid, *the* Orion, *the* Olive Branch, *the* Fair American, *the* Whale, *the* Brilliant*—and all the many other craft that heel smartly out of the harbor on a tight close reach.*

It goes without saying that the Godspeed *reaches the wrecked brig first. Once again, as has so often happened, Squire Eagan is the Wrecking Master. The prize of* this *race, at any rate, thanks to the merciful hint that God gave him up there on the rostrum, is his.*

Get Up, Sweet Slug-a-bed

Billy's hibiscus blooms every day, summer and winter. That shrub can almost talk. Nothing else in Paul's garden acts the way it does. Paul impartially waters all five of the hybrids in his garden twice a week, feeds them all on the first Sunday of each month with a special hibiscus formula they sell at Strunk's, tosses snail bait equally around under all of them, mulches them all—but only Billy's blooms every single day, the year round. It's a hybrid called Tamara, bearing a six-inch pale-yellow bloom with the most extraordinary deep grayish-lavender mouth at the center, which sends whispers of its color, like mischievous rumors, out onto the petals.

Those were the last colors Billy ever saw. The plant was in a pot in the window nearest his bed. Paul told me that the day after Billy died, the amazing Hospice people came in to "de-hospitalize" the room—arranging to return the crankable bed, the IV tree, the trapeze for Billy to help lift himself onto bedpans, and all the other rented gear back to Cobo's—and Mary Conover, the most equal among the several equal angels of Hospice, said to Paul, "Of course you'll want to plant Billy's hibiscus outdoors." She understood what Paul didn't yet understand.

Paul needed a lot of care from all of us after Billy died. It might have been easier if Paul and Billy had been lovers, for then Paul would have grieved normally. They were best friends. They lived in turbulent amity a couple of blocks from each other, Paul in a guesthouse on Simonton called Swann's Way, and Billy in a small apartment on William Street. Paul told me that one night, a couple of years ago, when they were sitting around, both quite tight, Paul asked Billy whether he thought they might have been lovers if they'd met when they were younger—when Billy, say, was twenty-one and Paul still in his mid-thirties. "Not a chance," Billy said, and then gave out that hoarse laugh of his, which, Paul thought at the time, put a puzzling and maybe not too nice edge on his answer. Paul tends to vibrate when he doesn't understand exactly what you mean.

Paul's rooms are on the ground floor of the guesthouse, and it has its own garden. He planted Billy's hibiscus on the side of his plot nearest Simonton. All five shrubs get plenty of light. Paul told me a few days ago that he'd been struck almost blind, that afternoon, by the sight of Billy's bush, which was prospering as usual, holding up for the pleasure of the sun's rays a dozen big dishes of those wizard colors. They made Paul dizzy, at first, with a perverse happiness, as he thought of Billy's energy, his zest, which came through in weak flickers even in his most vegetative state toward the end. His wit, always with a little price tag on it. His thick and merciless laughter. His anger, tumbling out through his utter helplessness in those last days. Remembering those things filled Paul with an enigmatic joy. "But then," he said to me, "I picked a bloom to take inside, and

I felt a horrible stab of guilt, as if I were killing the whole plant plucking off that one flower."

Paul still lives a life of self-blame. Pain mostly, I guess, about having turned Billy over to Drew. He'd had to hire Drew. He'd really had to. Billy was alone. Billy had booted little Vanya Bronin out a month before he tested positive. He'd waited too long, years too long, to be tested, and on top of that he was destined to have a galloping case. He had full-blown symptoms within weeks, and since Bronin was no longer around, the entire care, when the bad signs set in, and for a long time after that, fell on Paul, who gave up his lunchtimes to fix Billy something to eat (or not eat) and used to sit by the hour, after he came home from work in the evenings, with what the rest of us considered an immaculate purity of friendship, reading to Billy, listening to CDs with him, holding his hands, massaging his feet, giving him back rubs, rolling him around to remake his bed with him in it, settling him for the night. Paul finally began to fall apart, just at a time when he thought he was taking another kind of fall—into love. He decided he had to get away from Key West for a few days, away from caring for and about Billy, to see whether what was happening with his new friend, Stanley, was for real. That was when he asked around and found Drew.

"I've combed the town," he said to Billy, announcing the change with what he later thought might have been a little too much sales talk. "This Drew person is a classic. Wait till you see him, Billy, with his nurse's cap. He's a howl. But everyone says he's the tops, really dedicated. Gourmet cook—you'll start eating again. I checked a hatful of references. They all say he's wonderfully sweet, oozes TLC. But also very strong—he could hoist you out of bed like a baby and put you on the potty. You know what a mess I am, helping you to move."

"You S.O.B.," Billy said. "You're running out on me."

People didn't run out on Billy. It always happened the other way round. Billy didn't know the meaning of the word loyalty. His idea of love was a romp. He was the best fun in the world, and you couldn't help wanting to be with him, but you'd better be careful.

Little Vanichka Bronin dropped in on Paul at the worst possible time, when Billy was beginning to fade fast. Vanya said to Paul that he wanted to warn him. Didn't want Paul to get burned the way he had been. Vanya is a short, butchy street kid—could pass for a featherweight boxer. He has a swaggering cockiness that I'd guess encodes a mess of self-doubt close under a thin skin. His unlikely line of work was as a taxidermist, mostly stuffing big fish for flabby-armed one-day charter-boat anglers—instant Hemingways—to take home as trophies. Occasionally he did up exotic birds, and once he claimed to be really pissed off at having to stuff a Key deer that had been illegally killed by a bow-and-arrow hunter.

Vanya said to Paul that he had done *everything* for Billy: kept house, gone shopping, cooked, done the dishes—and given him any pleasure that his whim might choose at any moment of any hour of the day or night. "The guy used me," Vanichka said, his face splotched with puddles of his outrage. "I was just a servicer. Some kind of, like, fuck machine. He had no more feeling for me than he did for his right hand when he jacked off—less." Toward the end of his tirade, Vanya said, "Son of a bitch tried to accuse me of having infected him." That ugly claim of Vanya's Paul knew wasn't true, because Billy threw Vanya out a full month before he even tested positive, and he never saw or spoke to him again.

"Not to worry," Paul said when Vanya finally ran out of steam. "I'm not in love with the guy."

Vanya couldn't believe that. I do. Because when Billy said, "Not a chance," that time, I think he spoke for both of them, whether Paul knew it or not. They were made to be just friends.

13

. . .

I'll never forget the first time I laid eyes on Drew Patterson. I dropped over one afternoon to see Billy, as I often did. I didn't know Paul had hired a nurse. I was one of half a dozen friends of Billy's—our little support group—to whom Paul had given keys to Billy's apartment, so that we could let ourselves in at hours when Billy was apt to be alone. So in I went, and there, leaning over the bed, gradually and it seemed endlessly straightening up at the sound of my entrance, was this six-foot-three-inch androgyne dressed in a white T-shirt and nothing else, it appeared, besides a white wrap-all-the-way-around apron that looked like a sheath skirt, and God knows what—pistil? stamen?—was hidden under it. His long, slightly curly, and very bleached hair was pulled back in a ponytail that hung nearly to his waist; on top of his head stood a lacy and frilly nurse's cap interwoven with a purple ribbon—the only color, aside from his green eyes, in the whole apparition. For some reason, perhaps the way the long torso sagged, with its weight on one hip, I had a sudden thought of a Saint Sebastian—was it Piero della Francesca's?—for there was something about this drooped figure that suggested multiple wounds.

"You're . . . ?" the nurse asked, in a challenging, officious tone, with a full, deep voice, as if to say, "What do *you* want?"

"He's Phillip," Billy said from his bed. "This is Drew, Phil. She's come to take care of me. She's very sweet."

The gender of the pronoun didn't come from Billy as a slip of the tongue. He knew perfectly well what he was saying. He may have grown weak, but he was still Billy the Kid. Drew didn't flick an eyelash.

The reports after that were that Drew was a wonder of thoughtfulness and solicitude. He wore membrane-thin rubber gloves for direct dealings with Billy, and he'd rub a little Oil of Olay on them, so that whenever he touched Billy, it was with fragrant satin hands. With bare hands he fixed delicacies like *crème brûlée* and raspberry mousse, and on Billy's lunch and dinner tray, surrounding the dishes, he scattered emblems of the outdoor life that Billy had once loved—pastel bracts of bougainvillea, fragrant leaves of rose geranium, feathery ends of fresh dill, awakening buds of dwarf carnation: tiny gardens of distraction from the very thought of food. He sat by Billy's bed and read aloud to him by the hour, books Billy wanted to experience for a second or third or fourth time: Armistead Maupin's tales, David Leavitt's first collection, the George Stambolian anthology, Andrew Holleran's essays, and, most often, Edmund White's pre-danger *Joy*. Straight books aplenty too, of course; above all, the poetry of Billy's beloved Donne and Herrick. And it was true that Drew could lift Billy right out of bed like a baby to sit on what Drew called the "toidy."

Billy seemed to accept all this as a matter of course. "She's okay," he would grudgingly say, in Drew's presence, to Paul or to me. You never saw any sign of resentment from Drew of Billy's belittling offhandedness.

Little Vanya Bronin was right, of course. We had all known it: There was a hard place in Billy Chapman. Paul told me that with all the excruciating compassion which he couldn't help feeling for Billy's waning—Billy's terrifying evaporation—he nevertheless considered himself entitled to remember that Billy had done plenty of mean things in his time. You gave, he took. Paul says that in a way, this made Billy's lot as a helpless, needful sickbed creature even more heartbreaking than it would have been had he been a less selfish person. Someone with that kind of ego needs power; it was terrible to see him without a shred left. You saw that he was driven to hurt with the only weapons left him—words—as if to unload on others some of the excess of his own psychic pain. It was not at all, though, a matter of his suddenly having found a way to exploit his pitiable state; he had always been a predator.

. . .

But I remember the afternoon when Paul came alone to have drinks at our house, and he told Sarah and me about Billy's one tender spot. His only true love. It had gone on for thirty years. This was the one emotion in which Billy had invested, to be kept in trust for the rest of his life, his entire fund of altruism. In this single case he gave and gave—but it was all in his head, it was all a fantasy. He fell in love with a classmate in sixth grade, a boy named Sylvester Franklin. Billy and Sylly. Billy and his idol went off to Peddie together, and then to the University of Virginia. They never roomed together. Billy never declared his love. Paul isn't sure whether Franklin ever even knew about Billy's feelings, to say nothing of reciprocating them. Franklin went on to Johns Hopkins Medical School, became a surgeon, and took up practice in Charlotte—where, as it happened, both of Billy's sisters had also settled. There Sylvester Franklin lived a straight life; he got married and had a son and a daughter. While, all those years, from a distance, Billy still hankered after him with something like the yearnings of an eleven-year-old.

Billy used to go to Charlotte to visit his sisters, one of whom he more or less liked, and one of whom he didn't, just to be in the same town with the doctor. They saw each other rarely, as "old school friends." Franklin's children, and particularly the daughter, Molly, adored Billy. To them, he was jolly "Uncle William," on the few occasions when he dined with the family. He knew how to make a quarter disappear in a person's ear, to the amazement of young Tommy Franklin, and he showed Molly how to weave a cradle fit for the king of the cats with a loop of string. He safely lavished on the children the love that really belonged to their daddy.

Years later, a grown-up Molly came somehow to guess Billy's secret; perhaps she sensed the padlock on Billy's emotions, his rapt caution, when he was around her father. She was open with Billy about it, for which he was grateful beyond words. He had confessed the secret to Paul, long since, and so had had a neutral ear to pour it all out to, but being able to talk openly about the secret with Syl's daughter, Molly, was to creep up to the very edge of the forbidden green glade of his dreams. Once—inflaming him, much too late, with absurd hopes—she said she had often wondered whether her so very conventional father had, as she put it, "a hidden bohemian side."

About four years ago, long before he tested positive, Billy developed a sudden severe back pain, and it turned out that he was going to have to have his gallbladder removed. He called Sylvester Franklin and begged him to do the operation, and on the basis of their long acquaintance, the doctor arranged a bed for him, on astonishingly short order, in the Charlotte hospital. In the days before leaving for the surgery, Billy told Paul that he didn't know whether he'd be able to trust himself on the operating table. "This'll be the first moment of real intimacy," he said, "that he and I have ever shared." It would be the first time his beloved had ever touched him. He was terrified that with the palpations of the first routine exam, and then, God help him, in the operating room, all prepped in a hospital gown—and perhaps even under anesthetic!—his traitorous flesh, at Syl's touch, might be aroused and give him away.

He never told Paul how it turned out, and Paul, with his good manners, never asked. I certainly would have, if I'd been Paul. Because that anxiety of Billy's was such a clue to his vision of love: the be-all and end-all, for him, I always thought, was the joy and confident anticipation that came with tumescence. I suspect that whatever followed the pleasure of a buildup was never quite as good as it should have been. Billy lived for buildups. With Dr. Franklin he'd had one that lasted three decades—and led, at last, to a bizarre consummation of sorts on the operating table. The gallbladder removal was a medical success, in any case, and he soon bounced back, back then, into his usual robust well-being.

That he had to have an operation of that kind at all came as a great surprise, at the time. Having seen him so blighted in his last months, I find it hard now to recall his abounding health in the good years. He had, back then, a most cheerful and kindly rounded face, clean-shaven every day, near-chocolate irises, fine dark-brown hair with a hint of red in it. His frame was sound; clear skin lightly tanned; good proportions; his clothes always neat and clean, though he liked limp, unironed shirts. He was jaunty. He rode his bike all over hill-less Key West, and from a block away you'd hear him shouting greetings in his foghorn voice to his many pals. Late each afternoon he sat like a dignified, if slightly rakish, professor, with heavy horn-rims halfway down his nose, reading the paper and sipping coffee on the porch of Le Bar, on silent lower Duval, far away from Sloppy Joe's noisy juvenility, which he hated.

Of course, he *was* a professor, and it's hard to remember that now too. He'd had it made. His plum of a deal at Chapel Hill was to teach one term each year, the autumn semester, so he was free to spend most of the winter, and the spring and summer, in Key West. The sensible people in the university's administration knew perfectly well that he was gay and weren't inclined to do anything about it, so long as he remained—and he always did—meticulously discreet. He stored up his bulk oats for Key West.

His field was late-sixteenth–early-seventeenth-century poetry, the metaphysical and the Cavalier poets. Shakespeare and Milton he left to the men he called the "heavyweights" on the faculty; his loves were Donne, Herbert, Crashaw, Herrick, Lovelace, and Suckling, especially Donne and Herrick. A ridiculous syllabus, you'd think, for students growing up in a world of leveraged buyouts and genetic engineering and computer modems. They *flocked* to his two courses. He hooked them, to begin with, on the glorious love poems of the period—verse, he once said, that it would have taken a eunuch to try to deconstruct. I can imagine him in class—

These poor half-kisses kill me quite
Was ever man thus servèd?

One night about a month before the end, I walked in on Billy as he was reciting Donne to Drew, "The Relique," in just above a whisper. He remembered every word of every surviving poem. His voice was three-quarters gone; you could see in his eyes the dying embers of his love for the quirky lines. Drew was weeping.

But I'm trying to think back to when he was healthy. I have in mind the years before 1981, which is when the terrible black flag of danger was first raised. He was wild. In his idle semesters, *il dottore professore* was a voluptuary. His goat legs danced every damn day and night. In the late mornings he'd put on a G-string and go for a swim at Higgs Beach—an excuse to parade out on what had come to be known as Dick Dock, where the guys lolled in as close to the altogether as the law would allow. He used to settle down to talk with strangers sometimes, but he never picked anyone up, he used to claim, before sundown. Sunday afternoons he showed up at the tea dances at the Atlantic Shores or at La Te Da. After dinner each night he started a round of the bars. His favorite places were No. 1 Saloon, a rackety and somewhat redneck joint, and Michael's, with its garden of encounters. It was all a game of seven-card high-low, he'd say; you had to keep putting chips in the pot; you never knew—sometimes you came away with a beauty of a haul. Often he'd have a whirl at the Copa. Insatiable, he would take home, and then shed, one or sometimes more than one pick-up—often outlanders who had come a-hunting in Key West, interlopers from the Christopher Street haunts in New York or the Castro in San Francisco, or New Orleans or Cincinnati or Seattle or wherever—and having dumped them, he would then go on, in the small hours, to the Club Baths' shadowy orgy room.

Paul, a monogamist and a homebody already for over a decade back then, used to be put off by Billy's satyrical boasts. Those were totally carefree days for adventurers, and it was inevitable, we now know, that someone like Billy would sooner or later become a nightshade, poisonous at the root and dangerous. It was Paul's fateful good luck, as it has turned out, that with his cautious temperament and his modest needs, he was faithful, year in and year out, quarrels be damned, to his partner, Malcolm—pathetically faithful, Billy teased, though it would eventually mean that Paul would be spared while he would not. Paul and Billy couldn't have been more different one from the other; theirs was a friendship of the magnetic attraction of opposite poles. Malcolm's death of cancer five years ago tore Paul up so badly that he became a kind of hermit for a while, with nothing to fall back on save his spiky relationship with Billy, and it was not until Billy was himself close to death that Paul was able to—for surely he needed to—fall in love again.

Until he grew sick, Billy was fearless. One night three or four years ago, as he was walking up Duval with Vanya Bronin on the way to the night spot called The Monster, he became conscious of the sound of footsteps, quite a few of them, close behind them. You couldn't easily have spotted either Billy or Vanya as gay, judging by looks and bearing, but here they were, two guys—of different sizes, kind of a funny combination—out on the town on a balmy night in swishy Key West. In short, a gang of spring-break gay-bashers thought they might have spotted a pair of fruits, and after tailgating the smaller one for half a block, they began muttering taunts and whistling soft catcalls at him. Very soon Billy turned on them and in his hoarse, strong voice told them to fuck off.

The college kids were startled, and you could see that they wondered whether the little bantam really belonged, as they had thought, with this rooster. Billy used to work out at The Body Shop; his shoulders and arms were impressive. He took a step toward the boys. That may have been a tactical error, because now you could hear a slight rustling of chicken feathers in their own group, and this made the two biggest of the heroes get some sort of adrenaline rush, and they jumped Billy, and then all five piled on. Vanya ran, to try to scare up a cop. Billy walked away a few minutes later with a black eye and a broken rib, but he left one of the shits curled up on the sidewalk, screaming and cupping his balls with his hands.

The cops got to the scene just in time. Billy cut out the report of the arrests on page two of the *Citizen* the next day and stuck it up on the door of his refrigerator with a heart-shaped magnet, and he flaunted his black eye around town, till it turned light purple and then pale mauve, a gradually fading medal of the endless wars.

I remember how bothered Paul was by Billy's foolhardiness in challenging those freaks that night. "Jesus, Billy," he said, "that's how people get disemboweled."

"Those children don't carry knives," Billy said, a bit smugly. "Not when they're playing drop-the-hankie in little old Key West."

Paul is probably the kindest person I know, but there is a passivity about him that I'm sure he himself must hate and that Billy used to lord it over. Paul grew up pampered in Boston; his father was a big-time lawyer and his mother was vaguely a collateral Cabot, or something like that. There was an always highly polished brass knob on the front door of their Louisburg Square house, and they belonged to St. Botolph's and the Myopia Hunt Club. All this meant was that when Paul quit his loathsome job in the advertising business in his early thirties, to move to Key West, he had enough money to live on with a dependent lover; and yes, Malcolm moved down with him at the same time. Just to have something to do, Paul bought a part interest in a nice secondhand-book store on White Street. And that is where he and Billy got acquainted, one day when Billy was browsing. Their temperaments may have been different, but their reading tastes converged, and they began to see a lot of each other—always as mere friends but, as time passed, better and better friends.

So. Malcolm died. Paul grieved. Billy fell ill. Paul nursed him . . . and when, in the course of time, Paul hired Drew and flew off to Barbados with his found friend, Stanley, and then came back to town confirmed in a new love, he saw that the pattern of things had subtly changed. As soon as he arrived home, he hurried over to Billy's. He was surprised to see that Drew had rearranged the furniture in Billy's apartment; everything sparkled; there was a lemony odor of furniture oil in the air. "Eine Kleine Nachtmusik" was going at low volume on the CD player. Paul was touched at how happy Billy was to see him. Drew hovered nearby as Paul and Billy talked—mainly, at first, about Paul's recent trip.

They were chatting along inconsequentially when Billy suddenly broke away and said, in a voice that trembled ever so slightly, "Drew called Mildred in Charlotte."

Paul, made suspicious by that delicate tremor, looked at Drew. Drew calmly nodded.

Paul said to Drew, "Did Billy ask you to call her?"

Billy didn't let Drew answer. "No," he said. "She"—he was pointing at Drew—"did it on her own."

"I thought it was time they should come and see him," Drew said.

Paul didn't like the sound of that—the hint, within Billy's earshot, that time was running out. This was shocking, anyhow. Taking it on himself to put in such a call was bad enough, but to make it worse, Mildred was by all odds the wrong sister to call. Billy always had spoken of one sister, Helen, as his "good sister"—relatively good, that is. Mildred was the awful one.

"This was very presumptuous of you, Drew," Paul said.

"The patient's family has to get involved," Drew said. *His* voice—the voice of experience—had a little jitter in it now.

"Please check with me before you do anything like that again," Paul said.

Drew looked sharply at Billy. It seemed to Paul that Billy wilted a little under the heat of that glare. But rallying almost at once, Billy raised his head and said in his habitual gruff tone, "Listen, Drew. Paul here is the Designated Care Person. Don't ever forget that."

With that, Billy threw Paul one of his old-style roguish smiles. That silly phrase had come up jokingly one night, several months before, when Paul and Billy had been gingerly skating around some household questions that someone was going to have to deal with because Billy was losing ground—the paying of bills, laundry arrangements, a quarrel with City Electric. All of us in the support group had begun calling Paul "Billy's D.C.P."

"Of course," Drew said, suddenly virtuous, seeming to accept the phrase as if it were an everyday usage in his high calling. "I'll bear that in mind."

What made this scene awkward for Paul was that he knew Drew was right. Billy had reached a stage at which he did need some touch with his family. There's a mother-wit truth in that old lore about second childhood coming on before death. Not that Billy was dying yet, by a long shot—but everyone, certainly including Billy, was very much aware of what the outcome was going to be, in not too many months. A little boy had begun to peep out now and then from those disenchanted eyes.

Billy needed, most of all, some touch with his pop, as he called him. His mother, with whom he had had an up-and-down relationship, died eight years ago. His stepmother, Fran, was a delightful kook who had crammed the walls of the house with scores of crazy clocks—one with a clown face that winked its left eye each second and lit up its nose on the hour; another that chimed the hours with Cole Porter songs; and others from which cuckoos, Germans in lederhosen, Little Red Riding Hood chased by the big bad wolf, and an old-woman-in-a-shoe spanking a baby all came zipping out from secret hideouts in the clocks to announce that it was later than anyone thought. To her credit, Fran had accepted Billy's sexual preference, but she accepted it as she did everything else in life, blandly. "It's a free country," she'd say with a shrug about whatever came up that was the least bit controversial. Her ease with Billy's choice should have been a comfort, except that she wasn't a woman you could take seriously. She just had a habit of not caring.

With his father it was another matter. Fran did seem to make Billy's pop happy, but her loose liberality hadn't been enough to cancel out what was worse from Billy's father than open disapproval would have been—a very faint but unmistakable air of disappointment in the way the boy had turned out. The only open thing he had ever said to Billy was, once, "I hate to see the family name die out." There were tatters of real love there, though. Billy told Paul about memories he had of his father when he was small, memories of an awkward but tender reaching out to the male child: trying to teach him to catch a ball, hammering up an awful tree house just for him, which he never used, and, later on, patiently and gently—and proudly—teaching him to drive when he was only eleven and could barely reach the accelerator and still see out the windshield.

His sisters were both older than he; this darling little baby equipped with a dingus had come along after them, and they petted him but left sharp objects in his crib. As they grew up,

Helen, the middle child, made intermittent shifting alliances with older Mildred and younger Billy, to guard her flanks, and at times she and her brother were quite close. Eldest Mildred always hated him; she was an overachiever, with an innate gift for scorn. Both sisters were hyperactive Presbyterians. Billy's jumping the closet was seen as a family-wide catastrophe. The sisters were the worst; it was years before they would even speak to Billy. Mildred passed the word around among all their friends that Billy's announcement had killed their mother. Paul always said he had a hunch that both of them were spooked by fear that their own declared sexuality was iffy; their husbands, he pointed out, were real wimps. Helen had finally begun to soften a bit to Billy, when along came the news that brother Will was HIV positive. At that, communication with both sisters snapped off like flipped light switches—but not until after Mildred had written Billy that God was punishing him for the monstrosity of his acts.

For want of a caring family, Billy had "all of us." Our little support system consisted of Paul, Sarah and me, the composer Sandy Planne and his lover, Champ, Herb and Jane Barlow, Buzz Jones, Frank Sarason, Carl Mallow—and, after Paul's return from the islands, a new recruit, Paul's new love, Stanley. Stanley turned out to be an enormous help, because his parents died two years ago, his mother of cancer and his father, a few months later, of terminal loneliness. Having been practically disinherited by his parents because he was the way he was, Stanley had gone home and lovingly cared for both of them over a very rough eight months, so he was practiced in all the modes of giving comfort while asking nothing in return. It was he, by the way, who got Paul to buy the hibiscus for Billy. Paul, with his endless patience, orchestrated our visits, making sure that three or four of us dropped in on Billy every day, without overlapping.

Drew, in his T-shirt and his white tube of an apron, his dizzy cap bobbing on top of his head, was cordial to all of us. He warmly encouraged visits by "Billy's substitute family," as he called us. I think, though, I was the first to notice—I know I was the first to point out to Paul—that whenever one of us suggested something new for Billy, perhaps some little treat, Drew would give a tiny sniff, as if he had picked up the remotest whiff of something ever so slightly revolting that had wafted into the room. But then he would say with an air of great sincerity, "That's a *lovely* idea—why don't you get him some?" In my case, I remembered one day when Billy was having trouble eating because of painful thrush sores in his mouth, that he'd used to dote on strawberries, and I got some frozen strawberry yogurt for him at the Häagen-Dazs shop on Duval, and I gave it to Drew to feed to him. A week later, fetching a beer for myself from the fridge, I saw the little waxy cup there and took the trouble to check. It had never been opened.

And there was the odd business about the hibiscus. Taking Stanley's suggestion, Paul bought the plant and put it in the sunny window near Billy's bed. Drew oohed and aahed over it and kept saying he'd never ever seen anything so beautiful. But two days later, Paul noticed that the plant's leaves looked a bit limp, and poking a finger into the soil in the pot, he found it dry as dust. And it turned out that it was going to be up to him to care for the plant from then on. Drew wouldn't go near it.

In most ways, though, we all had to agree that Drew was a dream. Billy was beginning to have night sweats, and two or three times a night his bedclothes would be drenched, and Drew would always, with great sweetness, sponge him off with cold water and remake the bed with dry sheets and read to him till he dozed off. Drew almost never napped during the day to make up for lost sleep.

Indeed, he was tireless—almost frighteningly so. Once, he said to Paul that he thought he should no longer take a day off each week. Billy needed him. He was quite angry when Paul insisted that he continue to take his Sundays away; everyone in the support group was free on Sunday, Paul said, so there was never any problem about someone to cover. It was Stanley who made the guess that Drew had begun to feel that Billy was *his*.

"Maybe," Stanley said, "he hates to have anyone else touch the strings of his puppet."

"Stanley!" Paul protested. "What a god-awful thing to say!"

One Sunday, Paul scheduled Herb and Jane Barlow to spend the morning with Billy. Herb was tied up for some reason, and Jane dropped by without him. She brought along a slice of Key lime pie, the gooey part of which she knew Billy liked. She spooned it out to him, to his joy. A few minutes later, Billy got cramps, and apparently not thinking it seemly to ask Jane to help him to the potty, he held on the best he could and then fouled himself.

Without any hesitation, Jane went to work changing the June Allyson diapers that Drew had begun to put on Billy, and she carefully cleaned him up. Billy said, at one point, when she was shaking Johnson's baby powder in his bush, "Hey, Missy Jane, this is kind of embarrassing."

"Oh, honey, forget it," Jane said. "If you've seen one, you've seen 'em all."

Billy thought that was funny, and when Paul came by the next day, he told him about the exchange. Paul says he saw Drew stiffen when he heard what Billy said, and for a long time Drew stayed off in the kitchenette in a ridiculous rage, banging pots and pans, slamming plates into the dishwasher, whanging the top of the garbage pail. When he finally emerged, he was his usual calm and sweet and saintly self, as if nothing at all had happened.

It was about then that Dr. Ballastos talked Billy into trying AZT. The medicine was new at the time; it still had to be acquired on the qt, and the main trouble was the expense, far beyond what a half-time adjunct professor's salary from a public university could manage, especially that of a prof who had always had a habit of blowing what little money he had on the notion that "The best of all ways / To lengthen our days / Is to steal a few hours from the night, my dear." Billy whispered to me, one afternoon, not wanting Drew to hear, that Paul was paying for the medicine. "For chrissake don't tell Paulie I told you," Billy whispered. "He has a thing about his money, you know—afraid the beautiful pelf'll stick to his fingers and turn them green." Billy obviously hated the idea of being subsidized, especially by a dear friend, and this may be medically nutty, but I have a theory that his discomfiture at getting into moral—beyond financial—indebtedness to Paul, of all people, had something to do with how he reacted to the medicine. His proud mind damn well wasn't going to let the stuff work. It didn't, in any case. He soon developed chills and diarrhea, and he began to be dehydrated and dangerously anemic. So he had to stop taking the pills. All of us had had high hopes that AZT might at least make things easier for our Billy for a good long while, and the news that he had had to quit after a very few days brought back the terrible fog of gloom that had, for a short while, been partially lifted from us.

One bit of byplay, which Paul later said he'd hardly noticed at the time, was this: Drew kept trying to talk Billy out of dropping the AZT, even after it had begun to ravage him, and Drew also pushed the rest of us to back him up. As he often did, he played his experience card—we should trust him, he'd seen it all before. Patients often had a rough reaction to medications at first, he said, but they'd pull through to deal with it after a while. Sure, Billy was suffering hellish gut pains for the moment, and his blood count was dicey, but those things would pass. Paul had no way of knowing whether Drew was right, and it was only months later, after Billy died, that he remembered

Billy's having murmured to him, out of Drew's hearing, one evening, "Paulie, Paulie, don't let him make me take it."

Paul didn't take that plea of Billy's seriously, because he couldn't imagine that Drew would actually force Billy to do anything he didn't want to do, so he didn't intervene. The issue turned out to be moot, anyway, because a few days later, Dr. Ballastos decisively ordered the pills stopped.

Billy's spirits flagged after the AZT made him feel worse rather than better. Paul noticed how often, and in what far-fetched contexts, during those down days, Billy suddenly began mentioning Sylvester Franklin. Sometimes he dropped the name almost by accident, as if he meant to speak about somebody else and his tongue slipped. At other times, he retold anecdotes about his friend that Paul had already heard many a time. If Drew was within hearing, it was always "Dr. F." that Billy spoke of.

Drew had a keen ear, and he apparently heard—probably no one else but Paul would have noticed it—an infinitely subtle electric hum in Billy's voice when he told one of his stories with that initial in it, speaking perhaps of something Dr. F. had said ten years earlier, or of his part in a college prank, or of something to do with his kid Molly.

One day, Drew collared Paul in the kitchenette and asked him in a fierce, proprietary whisper who "this creepy Dr. F." was.

Paul was annoyed by Drew's nursy-nanny tone, and he said, "If Billy wanted you to know the name, he'd use it in front of you."

Sniff. "Of course," Drew quickly said. "Forgive me. It's none of my business. I apologize."

So courteous, after the tiny sniff, was this speedy retreat of Drew's that Paul felt ashamed of his sharp response to Drew's curiosity—Drew's intuitive jealousy, if that was what it was. Drew was, after all, the most important person in Billy's life just then, certainly more important than he, Paul, was.

A few days later, Paul confided in me that he'd had what seemed to him a really good idea. While Billy was still strong enough to do it, he should take a trip, say for a month, to Charlotte. This would get him in touch with his family; if they had any humanity at all, his sisters would make their peace with him and take him in, and his pop could easily visit him there. And more important for Billy, he would at least be near his cynosure, the doctor. It may not have occurred consciously to Paul, though it certainly did to me, that Billy's being away from Key West would also make life easier for Paul himself, now serenely in love with Stanley but unable to enjoy the relationship to the full because of the hours he had to devote to being Billy's D.C.P.

Paul's first move was to phone the so-called good sister, Helen. She asked, with what sounded like real caring, how Billy was getting along; Paul was relieved by her warmth.

"The reason I'm calling," Paul said, surprising himself, as he went on, with how easy it was to lie, "is that Billy wants more than anything in the world to see his father. He thought the most natural way, if you and Mildred agreed, would be for him to visit Charlotte for a month or so. He says his father often comes over from Raleigh to have some time with you two, and—"

Paul realized that the motor of his falsehoods was running out of gas. Not that there was any shouting or screaming at the other end. To the contrary, a silence had set in like that of the Atlantic abyss.

At last Helen said, "I think"—but more, then, of that noiseless rapture of the deeps (for the silence seemed weirdly ecstatic), broken eventually by a heartfelt "um"—then still more unplumbable silence, and at last, in a blurt, "I think what you suggest might be a little difficult."

Now Paul chose to remain silent himself. She would have to say why it would be difficult.

But she didn't. "I tell you what," she finally said. "I think I should talk it over with Mildred. Of course, for Billy . . . Give me a day or two." Her voice was under control; she tapered off with kindly words about Paul's concern and about the care they'd all heard he was taking of poor Billy.

Paul thought he heard an encouraging ring to that "poor Billy." Perhaps the good sister . . .

He decided at once to call Sylvester Franklin, hoping that as a medical man and an old friend he would be able to put the sisters' minds at rest about any absurd fears they might have of catching AIDS if Billy visited. It would also alert Franklin to the possibility of Billy's being in town. The only number he had was that of Franklin's office.

"Franklin Associates," a woman's very Southern voice, dripping molasses, said.

"Is Dr. Franklin free to talk on the phone? This is Paul Proctor speaking."

"In reference to . . . ?"

"Dr. Franklin knows me. Remind him that I am a friend of Billy Chapman."

"Did you wish to make an appointment?"

Paul, anxious for "poor Billy," was suddenly angered by the woman's tone of saccharine indifference. "No," he snapped, "that's *not* my wish. I'm calling from Key West. I want to talk with the doctor. About Mr. Chapman."

"I'm sorry. Dr. Franklin is with a patient. Would you like to leave a number?"

Paul did. He stayed home all day, but Billy's old friend, the only person on earth whom Billy loved with an unwithholding heart, didn't seem to be in any hurry to call back. Paul, with Stanley covering for him at the bookstore, had a restless afternoon. He fixed himself a cup of tea and sat sipping it at the little round table in his garden. After a while, nagged by a feeling that he'd forgotten something he'd promised Billy he'd do, he walked around to William Street.

Billy was deeply asleep, and Drew was napping too, to Paul's surprise, on the living room couch. The "Trout" was going very softly on the player. Paul went to the bedroom window to check Billy's hibiscus. Six lurid blooms were open. Billy'd said of one of the flowers, a few days before, "Hey, that looks like me with that black eye I got, remember?" The echo in Paul's mind now of Billy's guffaws when he said that was unsettling. He noticed that the shrub's leaves had a sickish yellowy cast. Had he been neglecting the plant? He knew from experience what he needed to do; he went home and fetched a box of Miracid and a sprinkling can. Back at Billy's, without waking either sleeper, he measured out the fertilizer into some water and poured the liquid around the potted roots and sprinkled it on the leaves.

While he was feeding the plant, he was suddenly hit by a momentary paroxysm of the most dreadful horror. He couldn't clearly describe it to me, when he told me about it later: it was, he guessed, part panic, part fury, part wrenching pity. Thinking about it afterward, he said he wondered if he had been overtaken, there in Billy's bedroom, by a terror that he might somehow have become infected by Billy, no matter how careful he had always been in caring for him; though he swears that this possibility didn't surface in his conscious mind until later. Or maybe, he said, this had been a shock of some sort of violent, premature mourning. If Billy went away to Charlotte, would he seem, in absence, already dead? Might he die in Charlotte? Did he *want* Billy to die there? Something in the jaundiced look of Billy's plant had brought Paul face-to-face with his total emotional and moral exhaustion; he told me that he himself, in that reeling moment, in his spate of emotion over his wasting friend, "leaned toward death."

The feeling passed quickly, but it left him trembling, and he walked home with a racing heart and hot cheeks. As he fiddled with his keys to let himself in, he heard the phone start to clang. He picked it up on the fourth ring.

"Mr. Proctor?" A woman's voice, sharp.

He realized at once who it was: the other sister. "Yes, this is Paul."

"Helen told me"—the voice sounded tight with an effort to maintain the church-pew decorum that Paul had always had from Mildred—"about your call. About Billy." Then, all at once, there came a rale of indrawn breath. "You just *forget* that notion. Put it in your hat, him coming up here."

Paul managed to say, "I was hoping—"

Mildred cut him off with a whining, klaxon rush of words. "Typical of William, I must say—gets somebody else to front for him when he wants to sponge on his folks. What a nerve! I don't think you people have any *conception* what him coming up here, sick with what he's got, would mean for all of us. Helen has kids, I've got kids, we both have some standing in this community. We've—"

Still shaky from what had happened in Billy's bedroom, on the verge of losing his temper and spoiling everything, struggling to keep his voice steady and caring, he now took his turn at breaking in, saying, "Forgive me, Mrs. Train. I think you may have a mistaken idea of the risks. Why don't you talk with Dr. Franklin? He could tell you—"

But no, it now came clear that of the two, Paul or Mildred, it would be she who first exploded. Everything respectable in her makeup seemed suddenly to have curdled. "Listen, Proctor," she shouted, "Dr. Franklin couldn't tell me anything I don't already know about people like you." Her voice shook. "You effing faggots. Stay out of our hair, you hear me?"

What Paul heard next was the clunk of her phone slammed down. He saw that his hand was wobbly as he, in turn, hung up. Effing! He fought to control himself. Why should he waste the energy of flying into a rage? Better just to think: So much for my brilliant idea. Jesus.

Another idea turned up quite by chance a couple of weeks later. Two men who were close faculty friends of Billy's at Chapel Hill—both of them, as it happened, straight—drove down from North Carolina to see him. One, Francis Pinckney, taught Milton and Blake, and the other, James Glover, lectured and wrote on the world of Samuel Johnson. Their taking the trouble to visit Billy—they drove nineteen hours without stopping to get to him—was a touching declaration of friendship by men who relished Billy's lively, mischievous mind. For three days you could hear Billy's throaty laughter again, and he generally perked up, seeming to throw off the depression that had flattened him after the AZT business.

One night, when Drew had tucked Billy in to go to sleep, Glover and Pinckney went around to Swann's Way with Paul for a nightcap. As they talked, Paul told the two men about the fiasco of his proposal to the sisters that their brother visit them.

No sooner had he finished than Pinckney said that he had a house up at Blowing Rock, in the Smokies, where he and his family went in the summer. Billy could visit them there, and his sisters and his father could easily come up the mountain to see him. The cottage was ramshackle, he said, plain and rude, slash-pine shingled, possibly haunted by a blue-nose parson; it had umpteen rooms. It would be wonderful to have Billy there for a while.

"We have two teenage kids, boys," Pinckney said, "and there are always a raft of high-schoolers around raising a racket—loud music, you know—if Billy could stand that. Maybe you and

Mabel could come up for a while, Jim, if Billy makes it," he said to Glover.

Glover obviously liked that idea.

"You too, Paul, of *course.*" ("I'm used to being included as an afterthought," Paul said with a twisted little smile, telling me about this later.)

Blowing Rock was a good-luck place, Pinckney said; maybe its luck would even reach out to Billy. The local legend, he said, was that the squaw of a chief who had been unfaithful to her tried to kill herself by jumping off a boulder at the top of a cliff, but a strong judgmental upsweeping wind blew her back up again, and the chief, frightened by this, took her back, and she lived to be ninety years old.

"Oh, God," Paul said, "if only something magic like that . . . But do you really have room for him? He'd have to have Drew."

The house, Pinckney said, had been built seventy-five years ago by his grandfather, a rich eccentric dominie from Raleigh with seven children and, apparently, a flock of monklike live-in disciples. A lot of the rooms were just cubicles, but there was no end of them. A couple of kids could move into the cubicles while Billy and Drew were there. Pinckney said he'd naturally have to talk this over with his wife, but he knew she was fond of Billy, and furthermore, she'd be able to help in many ways with his care; she was a nurse practitioner, almost a doctor in value, at the university health center.

Paul was moved by Pinckney's spontaneous generosity, and even more by his having no fear at all, for himself or his family, of what Billy would bring into their home. He could hear in the back of his mind Billy's sister's tense, deprecating voice—"him coming up here . . . with what he's got."

One night after dinner, Pinckney, back at Chapel Hill, called Paul to say that his wife was all for having Billy visit them in

Blowing Rock. Next month, July, would be ideal. It would be a lot cooler there than in Key West. How would it be best to invite Billy? Should he write?

Paul said, "Why don't you just call him?" Then, for reasons he later wondered about, he added, "I'd like to be with him when you call. Could you wait, say, ten minutes? I'll go right over."

Drew, who was reading to Billy, seemed surprised to see Paul show up, without phoning ahead, at nine o'clock in the evening. Paul pretended he'd suddenly felt unbearably lonely; he told Drew to please go on reading.

But Billy said, "No, no, let's just talk. God damn it, Drew, up off your butt, get Paulie a Scotch."

Almost imperceptible sniff. Book closed a tiny bit decisively. Then Drew, suddenly a model of dignified servility, went for the drink.

Soon enough, the phone rang. Having delivered the drink, Drew picked up the receiver and handed it to Billy.

Billy answered warmly, and soon a radiance, a flush of joy, spread on his face such as Paul had not seen there for many months. "You bet!" Billy said. "I'll be there with bells on."

As soon as he'd said goodbye and handed the receiver back to Drew, he almost shouted—it came out as a kind of croak—"Drew, baby! We're going on a spree!"

Drew asked what in the world he was talking about, and as Billy went on to explain, Paul was puzzled and somewhat disturbed by Billy's giddy euphoria.

So, obviously, was Drew, who, furthermore, said in a hushed voice, "Oh, honey, I don't know if we're up to a long trip like that."

Paul, annoyed by that nanny's "we," quickly broke in—and, meaning something different, used a "we" of his own. "I think we can manage it," he said—and by the use of the pronoun he allied himself with Billy's happiness and announced that he was going to be a player. "We can charter a plane. We can make it easy for Billy, Drew."

Billy and Drew couldn't help realizing that this was an offer on Paul's part, and this time, Paul noticed, Billy showed no sign of feeling patronized. It was Drew who seemed to have reservations; he kept shaking his head. Billy repeated every word that Pinckney had said, his voice trembling with delight.

A few minutes later, with Drew still trying to persuade Paul, if not Billy himself, that such a trip might be dangerous, Billy suddenly—and very foolishly, as Paul at once saw—spilled out the reason for his joy. "Know something, Paulie?" he said. "Dr. F. has a house up there in Blowing Rock. Just weekends, I guess. But!"

Paul at once deciphered Billy's folly: That single sentence with the initial in it turned Drew right around. Paul could see that Drew was stung (another arrow or two, I would have ventured, in the saint's flank) not just by vague jealousy, this time, but also by a curiosity so sharp and so childish as to cause him new pain. But then you could see dawning on his face a realization that if they took this trip, he'd find out whom that reverberant initial stood for—the initial that had so humiliatingly fenced him off from the other two; that had kept one string to his puppet, if you accepted Stanley's harsh reading of the relationship, in another person's hand. Drew at once began to hedge away from his earlier objections, and before long it was settled that the trip was on.

When Paul returned home the next afternoon from the airport, where he arranged for Billy's charter, there was a message on his answering machine from sister Helen in Charlotte. He phoned her right away.

"Oh, Paul!" she said. "I'm glad you got my message." She inquired after Billy and politely asked how Paul himself was bearing up; then she quickly came to what she had called to say. "I just wanted you to know that Millie told me she felt real rueful, the other day, about—"

"Never mind," Paul quickly said. "I guess I understood what upset her."

"She says she hates herself for the way she . . . Anyways, she said she was right uncharitable. She hasn't quite come around all the way to where she wants Billy to be here—you know, visit us—but if you'd give me a few more days, I might could—"

Paul cut in to tell her about the invitation to Blowing Rock.

"Oh, that's *great!*" Helen said, obviously not realizing how naked and heartless her relief was. "That'll be super for Billy."

"It would be important for you and Mildred to drive up to see him. And the one thing you could really help with," Paul said, "would be making sure Billy's father gets up there."

Of course, of course. Helen said she'd take Pop up the mountain herself.

Paul had arranged for Billy to fly to Winston-Salem and then be driven up in an ambulance. Paul took the tickets and itinerary for the trip to Billy on an afternoon a few days before he was to leave. Billy, in his usual curt manner with Drew, ordered him off to the kitchen to fetch a couple of Cokes.

Looking over his shoulder to make sure Drew had left the room, then pointing with his thumb toward the kitchenette, Billy hastily whispered to Paul, "She's been acting up." At that moment Paul saw in the eyes of his friend Billy, who had always, in the good years, been so feisty and reckless, a disturbing look of raw hesitation and appeal.

Paul whispered, "What do you mean?"

Billy whispered one word: "She's . . ." And then, apparently hearing something that made him think Drew was returning, he just shrugged.

That was all. Drew came back with the Cokes. Paul couldn't make out anything unusual in Drew's manner. In fact, he seemed more agreeable than ever; if there was anything unpleasant about him, it was his seeming to fawn on him, Paul. Telling me about all this, weeks later, when the significance of that too tightly coded message of Billy's had finally become clear, Paul said that back then he dismissed Billy's mysterious, anxious whispering as just one more queer twist of his convoluted illness.

Billy left for Blowing Rock. Paul, considerate in all things, had paid the charter service to have some seats removed from the plane, so Billy could take the trip on a stretcher fitted with a mattress. Word came back that evening that the ambulance had shown up at the Winston-Salem airstrip just as planned and that the driver had taken it right out onto the tarmac beside the plane to pick Billy up.

You had to say for Drew that he phoned Paul from Blowing Rock every evening at about six. The reports seemed to get better and better. The air was like fresh lemonade, Drew said. Most mornings the mountaintop was in the clouds, then the mist burned away and a breeze came up from the piedmont, and the light on the landscape became, Drew said, as soft and painterly as a midday glow he'd once seen, in his wanderlust days, at Fiesole, looking down on Florence. Pinckney's sons were dears. Billy's shingles were a little better. He loved to sit in a window with a blanket over his knees, watching the boys and their friends playing lawn bowls. Pinckney's wife cooked grits and soft okra and a kind of corn mush for Billy, who was getting more food down than he had for weeks. Billy's wild yarns enthralled the kids, who, amazingly tuned to his illness and unafraid of it, sat around bantering with him for half an hour after supper each night and tactfully melted away when they saw that he was tiring. "A fillip for Billy"—Paul said those were Drew's words one evening—was that a doctor from Charlotte, who seemed to be an old college friend, "or something like that," came up the mountain for weekends. Paul said Drew went into this as if there had never been a word spoken about a certain Dr. F. They hadn't seen the doctor yet, Drew said, but Billy had talked with him on the phone, asking him about medication for a stomach upset he'd had. The doctor had been "so thoughtful." Professor Glover and his wife might visit. And Billy had been in touch with his father, who promised to come and see him. All in all, Billy was "looking ten years younger than he did a couple of weeks ago," and the one hardship he was suffering from, Drew reported Billy's having said, was being "deprived of his good old Paulie."

Francis Pinckney called up one afternoon to fill Paul in on things, and he, too, said that Billy was in pretty good spirits and seemed to be gaining some strength. It turned out, though, that Pinckney really wanted to talk about Drew, who, he said, had just gone out shopping. He told about how very kind Drew had been. You noticed a hundred considerations he had for Billy. He anticipated every need or want Billy had, and even, it seemed, every thought in Billy's head.

"I can't find anything like a self in Drew," Pinckney said. "And yet he's so definite! He guards Billy fiercely, like a mother cat. If the kids are too noisy, he shushes them up—and they respect him, they do exactly what he says. I think he's made AIDS seem especially awesome to them—it's anyway a monster fact of life for their generation; I hear these adolescent boys and girls talking about condoms as if they were as everyday as pencils or spoons or postage stamps. But I don't know, Drew almost makes out to them that AIDS is some sort of sacred condition, as if Billy had a special privilege none of them would likely ever have. I hate the idea of my sons' swallowing guff like that. What is it? Do you think Drew may have supervised a few too many deaths for a guy so young as he is? What do you think, Paul?"

Paul was silent for a moment, then he said, "He was the best person I could find."

"I see what you mean," Pinckney said. "One other thing I've noticed, though: Billy seems so cruel to him. He calls him 'her,' says, '*She* did this or that,' never thanks him or has a single good word to say about him or to him. And yet he's so obedient to Drew. Whenever Drew gently asks him to do anything—'Take a sip of this, honey,' 'Try to belch, it'll feel good,' whatever—Billy does it right away, like a little boy. It's as if he'd been hypnotized."

"There's a lot of AIDS down here," Paul said. "It's not easy to find a good male nurse. I guess I have to say I think Billy's lucky to have Drew."

"Hey, Paul," Pinckney said. "Don't get me wrong. You sound like I'm blaming you for something. I'm not. I'm really not. I'm just trying to understand what's happening."

"I know. You've been wonderful," Paul said. "We're all this way because we know there's no hope."

Paul got a letter from Jim Glover, after a week's stay he and his wife had had in Blowing Rock. In general, the letter confirmed that Billy was doing fairly well. Further on, however, Glover wrote:

> I hesitate to go into this, Paul, because I'm not at all sure of my ground, but I have a feeling that there may be something brewing between this remarkable Drew person and Marny Pinckney. She has a professional medical competence, I'm sure you know, and perhaps you don't know that she's also a rather strong-minded woman. I like her a lot, and I know she's wise and kind, but I'm also aware that she can be pretty obdurate. I suspect that her role as a nurse practitioner is not entirely easy—*almost* a

doctor, you know, who surely can't find it pleasant to defer to men at the university health center who *are* M.D.'s and who may very well be less wise and kind, to put it mildly, than she is. In a way, Drew has the same sort of vulnerability, in the present case, only maybe more so. Properly speaking, he's obliged to defer in this situation to Marny, with her degrees and license and so on, but the fact is, he's had a lot more practical experience with AIDS than she has. And he's amazingly kind to Billy. There hasn't been any grand *crise*, but a few minor differences have come along—you know, decisions about diet, what to do about a slight fever or if Billy gets a headache. What's complicated, Paul, is that if there's a discussion, Billy *always* sides with Marny. So far, Drew has accepted all this with total dignity. I'm inclined to think that he's a much better judge of what to do about these little things than Marny is, but of course I'm not a medical person. He had an accident the other day that embarrassed him a great deal. He dropped Billy to the floor when he was carrying him to the toilet—no terrible harm, though Billy's hip was quite badly bruised. Drew said Billy had squirmed or something in his arms. Drew was absolutely crushed with remorse. For her part, Marny was perturbed, I thought, more than she needed to be and argued for just letting the diapers take care of things from then on. She was quite vehement about it. They hadn't resolved that question when we left. I hope I haven't worried you by going into this; it's just something to keep your ear to the ground on. I take it you'll be going up to be with Billy. You can see for yourself.

Paul had indeed been invited by the Pinckneys, but he had put his trip off until after Billy's father's visit, which, he had been told, was to come in the next few days.

Billy's pop apparently reached Blowing Rock late one afternoon, alone, at the wheel of an ancient VW. The "good" sister had not taken him up the Ridge, as she had promised to do. She had, however, made a reservation for him at The Cedars, a small inn out along the Parkway toward Grandfather Mountain, without telling Billy or the Pinckneys anything about the plan. Mr. Chapman spent three whole days there before he got in touch with the Pinckneys, saying he was heading for home late that morning and would like to drop in on his son for a few minutes. Drew, telling Paul about this on the phone, was furious.

"He came in here, white hair, florid, you know, a deerskin jacket—with a fringe yet!—cheerful as a silver dollar, and all he said was, 'Hi, Billy boy,' and then, 'How're you getting along?' I couldn't believe it! As if Billy had a slight cold. Seemed to me he didn't have a *drop* of feeling for his only son, who was, you know, in this kind of shape. Billy was lying there. His eyes filled up; I've never once seen him overcome like that. I could have killed the old man. 'You look first-rate, my boy,' he says, real loud, you know, as if shouting would make it true. How could a person be so dishonest—his own flesh and blood? All I can think is, total denial. Total. Maybe he was scared—you know how outsiders are, think the air in the room can give it to 'em. Kept his distance from the bed, never even shook Billy's hand, say nothing of a hug. Four or five *sentences*, and he's gone. Left. Just like that. My God, I *tell* you. *I* went to hug Billy after the old man cut out, but Billy pushed me away. He was just plain delirious with joy—his father'd come to see him. Couldn't seem to take it in how insulting the whole thing was."

Drew mentioned, in the same phone call, in the same angry tone, that Billy had left several messages on weekends on this Dr. Franklin's box at his Blowing Rock house, but the doctor hadn't had the courtesy to call back. "Some friend!" Drew said.

Pinckney's report to Paul on Mr. Chapman's visit was somewhat different from Drew's. He thought Billy's father had handled it exactly right—a brief call, a cheerful mien, a father's love and concern decently muffled (or possibly, in Billy's ears, stated all the more loudly) by understatement, reserve, and a dash of jocularity. And Paul was fascinated, after what Drew had said, to hear Pinckney report that Drew had agreed with him that those few intense minutes gave Billy just what he had needed from his father.

Pinckney went on to say that Drew was a big hit on the mountain. He had made a number of friends among the rich younger set from Charlotte and Winston-Salem, a few of whom, Pinckney let it be known, were gay. Marny, "who, by the way, thinks worlds of Drew," acted as a Billy-sitter for him sometimes in the evenings, and Drew, shedding his nursing outfit, sported himself in clothes that were, as Pinckney put it, "high-class camouflage of precisely the right tone." Something had happened that had made Drew, Pinckney said, "an instant legend along the Ridge most all the way from Asheville to Roanoke." He showed up at the local Presbyterian church one Sunday morning in a splendidly modish gabardine three-piece suit with a flared waist and side vents in the jacket—but he'd forgotten (or, Paul wondered, *had* he really forgotten?) to take off his nurse's cap.

Paul kept postponing his trip to North Carolina, for reasons that weren't clear to him, he told me. It wasn't simply that the zone of free time in which he and Stanley found themselves, after Billy's departure, seemed to them like a new and beautiful foreign country they'd never seen together. My hunch is that he was deeply shocked by the relief he felt at not being so constantly in the presence of Billy's revolting symptoms—because, heartrending as those symptoms were to watch in their inexorable progress, they *were* disgusting, especially so in that they were being suffered by his dearest friend. I saw Paul struggling hard to find enough courage to rejoin Billy. Perhaps (for he had told me about his moment of panic and despair by the hibiscus plant that day) he did have a hope—though he swore he couldn't believe it of himself—that if he delayed long enough, Billy might die far away from him.

And, indeed, Paul confessed to me that when the phone waked him up one morning at eight o'clock and he heard Francis Pinckney's voice greeting him, so early, with an unusually somber tone, his mind took a disgraceful leap of joy at the thought that it *was* over, yes, yes, thank God, Billy had died.

But what Pinckney had to say was this: "Paul, you'd better get yourself up here. Billy needs you."

Paul asked what he was trying to say.

"Something happened—I can't go into it right now, not on the phone. Just believe me. Come as soon as you can."

Paul couldn't get plane connections from Key West to Miami to Charlotte until late that afternoon; at Charlotte he rented a car and started for Blowing Rock. He spent an anxious, sleepless night in a motel in Lenoir, at the foot of the mountain, and early in the morning, tightly wired on three cups of coffee, he started the climb into the clouds. Before long, he could see no more than twenty feet ahead on the steep, narrow, curving road. There were times, he told me later, when he had to fight off an impulse to close his eyes and grip the wheel and go off the edge. But he managed to hang on, and at the summit, following Pinckney's directions with difficulty in the fog, he finally found the house where Billy lay.

Francis, obviously having been watching for him, came out on the porch to greet him. He said in a hurried low voice that he'd like to take a walk with Paul, but he supposed he'd want to see Billy, for a minute anyway, first. He waved Paul inside. Paul had a fleeting impression of a dark, wainscoted haven of generations of vacations—fat, sagging, slipcovered chairs and sofas, a scattering of faded hooked rugs, a half-finished jigsaw puzzle on a green, wooden-legged card table, a bookcase full of old jacketless books with mildewed spines. Francis led the way up some oaken stairs and into a room where, on a brass bed, Paul saw a huddled figure turned to the wall.

Drew stepped forward to greet Paul, but Paul hurried past him to the bed and, leaning over it, gently put his hands on the thin shoulder and flank. "Billy boy," he said.

Slowly Billy turned onto his back, and Paul saw a ghost. After all the reports of Billy's thriving, Paul was shocked by how wasted and hollow he looked. Oh, God, he *is* dying, Paul thought.

"You," Billy weakly said. "Oh, am I glad."

Francis lied to Billy, saying Paul hadn't had anything to eat, he was going to give him some breakfast, they'd be back soon.

The two men walked out on a curving asphalt road in the foggy air, past dimly seen cottages, gleaming wet cars parked in drives, deep-green conifers standing as discreet pickets on property lines, with tiny shining droplets on all the needle ends. As soon as the two men were well out of earshot of anyone at the house, Francis said, "Why I called you, Paul . . . You saw how set back Billy is. Our friend Drew did something very foolish. Very, very foolish."

It came out, in Francis's hurried telling, that after lunch two days before this, Drew asked Marny to cover for him for an hour or so. He said he had an errand he wanted to go on. He left the house a few minutes later, dressed "like a vacationing professional gent from the Carolinas with a fair amount of money," Francis said, in carefully pressed chinos and an obviously expensive sport shirt, with an upscale logo on the left breast, and gleaming brown loafers—an entirely new version of this protean Drew. He was gone, as it turned out, for less than half an hour. When he returned, Marny noticed that he seemed unusually elated; he had the half-triumphant, half-modest look of someone who has just won a prize and knows his worth. She left him at the door of Billy's room and went to patch away at her jigsaw puzzle. The kids were all out of the house at the time. Francis was reading.

A few minutes later, Francis and Marny heard raised voices. Then, suddenly, there was a faint, hoarse cry. "Help! Someone help me!"

The Pinckneys hurried to Billy's room. Drew, having changed back into his nurse's outfit, cap and all, was calmly leaning against the far wall of the room, his arms crossed. Billy didn't seem to have been harmed. When he saw Marny and Francis, he said in a voice that sounded as if it came from the pit of his stomach, "Get that . . . that Medusa out of here! . . . No, no, tell them, God damn it—tell them, Drew."

Drew said, "I did him a big favor because I care about him." Then he lapsed into silence, looking so pleased with himself that Francis wondered if he had been tippling—though he had never, come to think of it, seen Drew drink anything stronger than a diet Coke.

The couple heard a groan from Billy.

Marny broke the jam. In a strict, motherly voice, she said, "Out with it, Drew!"

Drew moved away from the wall and sat down, completely at ease, in the one overstuffed chair in the room. And with an air of command, sure in the telling, he gave his account.

Did the Pinckneys recall Billy's having had the trots two or three days after he came up the mountain? They did. And Billy called this doctor friend, who happened to be up here on a weekend, for a prescription? They remembered. Drew had taken the trouble to find out which house the doctor lived in; it was about a ten-minute walk from the Pinckneys', not far from the riding ring. That was where he'd gone.

He pushed the buzzer button at the front door, and the doctor himself came to answer. His was a straight, spare figure, soft eyes of a deer, nose too big, dark mossy hair neatly combed, long-doctor's-hours lines cut in his face on either side of his mouth—the total effect, Drew said, that of a gentle and beautiful person with some problems. He was dressed—this was told proudly—almost exactly like Drew, who had had the good luck, as he put it, to guess right on what to wear for this diplomatic mission.

The doctor asked, courteously but with slight impatience, as if he suspected that such a neatly dressed caller at that hour might be a salesman for magazine subscriptions or for the love of Jesus Christ, "Can I help you?"

Drew said he had a message from a friend.

At that, without hesitation, the doctor invited Drew in. The living room was almost exactly like the Pinckneys', even to the mildewed books and the half-done jigsaw puzzle. Drew had a sense of convention, of proper vacation form a little green with mold, in this summer resort, an impression that things here had always been this way; that nobody had ever thought of breaking the back of the past. With a polite gesture, right out of the rules of that past, the doctor urged Drew to sit in the heavy sofa in the middle of the room; he let himself down with a sigh in a wicker chair, which creaked at accepting him.

"I come to you from William Chapman."

A brief pause, then, "Did the diarrhea clear up?"

"Oh, yes, it's not about that."

"Glad he's better."

"He's not better, Dr. Franklin. He has AIDS."

Again the doctor seemed to need a moment to stake out the territory. Then he said, "I'd heard that. His sister, Mildred Train, called me. There was some talk of his coming to Charlotte."

"But he's *here*, doctor, as you know. Why haven't you answered his phone calls?"

This time the silence lasted longer; the doctor's face ran through some fleeting changes, including a distinct wrench of quickly controlled annoyance—not quite anger, Drew was encouraged to see—and after that a sign of some other momentary inner grinding, possibly caused, Drew guessed, by a collision between that annoyance and . . . could it have been curiosity?

This gave Drew hope and made him want to press harder, and he said, "He's left four messages on your box."

"I come here on weekends to rest," Dr. Franklin said, his voice suddenly firm. "I don't do any doctoring up here on the mountain. I just can't take on any new patients at this point."

"He didn't call you for medical reasons," Drew said. The silence then was Drew's, as he waited to see what his announcement would bring.

It brought nothing. The doctor didn't seem to have the slightest intention of asking why his old, old friend had called.

Drew said, "He wanted to see you. He wanted to tell you something. This is the message I bring you: He loves you. He has been in love with you for years and years, and—"

As Drew told this, Billy on his bed gave out a hoarse cry and with unusual energy turned, under the covers, and faced the wall.

Drew urgently and triumphantly said to the Pinckneys, as if Billy were not even there with any possibility of speaking for himself, "I knew it. I *knew* that was what he wanted."

"Are you crazy?" Marny asked, appalled.

"They talked about this doctor all the time; I have ears, I'm not deaf."

" 'They'? Who are 'they'?" Marny sharply asked.

"Billy and that Paul. Paul Proctor. You can ask Billy if it isn't true."

The only sound from the bed was of a sighing of its box springs as Billy moved closer to the wall.

"I know my Billy," Drew said. "Inside and out I *know* him.

I could hear it in the way he talked. He wanted this. It's gone on since he was a little boy—you should have heard! He needed someone to do this. If he'd begged me to go, I couldn't have been more sure of it."

Marny said with sudden fury, "You're an absolute *idiot*, Drew! My God!" Waving a hand toward the bed, she added, "Look what you've done!"

Drew looked over to the bed. He began to cry.

Francis quickly asked, "So what did the doctor say?"

Drew pulled a handkerchief out of a pocket in his apron and blew his nose. Then he unexpectedly broke out laughing—or, more exactly, tittering. "*Say?* What did he *say?* He stood up out of his chair and brushed off the front of his shirt, as if he'd spilled crumbs on it. It was like lunch was over, brushing himself off that way. He didn't say a word. He just stopped brushing and flung his hand out toward the door—you know, 'Get your ass out of here, mister,' only he didn't have the spunk to put his mouth behind it. He shooed me out is what it was, like a mosquito or a yellow jacket that'd got into the room. But I'll tell you something. I told Billy this. Billy didn't listen to me. This was the guy's answer. He blushed. He turned as red as a—I don't know—a what?—a cardinal bird. That was so eloquent! To me, that said everything." Drew turned toward the bed and almost shouted, "*Think* about that, Billy, honey!" And he started to cry again.

Pinckney and Paul, having looped around on the foggy roadways, were almost back at the house. "Ever since," Francis said, "Billy has been lying with his face to the wall, the way you saw him when you first went in. Won't eat. Won't talk. Marny's wild. Why do you think Billy's taking it so hard?"

"Who knows? Maybe 'cause what Drew said is true."

"Billy's in *love* with this doctor?"

"For three decades. Has been. Yes."

"And this was *news* to the doctor?"

"I don't think he ever knew it."

"But it's ridiculous. Man has a wife and family, Paul. I've seen them around the village. What are you saying?"

"Don't ask me to try to explain, Francis. It's a long story . . . We've got to talk about what to do."

"Marny says you have to fire Drew. She says he's dangerous."

Paul thought about that and said, "And then who takes care of Billy?"

"She says Billy should be in a hospital. She says he's willing himself dead."

Paul put through a call to Dr. Ballastos in Key West and described as best he could Billy's state—his seeming to have gone on strike against life. Ballastos recommended bringing him home to Key West as soon as possible; he would examine him and decide whether he needed hospital care.

Two days later, Paul and Drew and Billy rode down the mountain in the Winston-Salem ambulance, and the same charter service as before flew them to Key West. As soon as Billy was back in his own bed, Paul, with a very heavy heart, called Mary Conover from his apartment; he knew from several friends who'd had lovers die that the local Hospice people were superb, and he knew, too, that no matter what Dr. Ballastos might decide, the time had come for Mary and her team to begin, in their manifold merciful ways, preparing Billy—and "all of us" too—for what he and we were going to have to face, quite soon. That very afternoon, Mary and three others "hospitalized" Billy's room, trucking over all the necessary gear from Cobo's. Drew lurked and sulked while Mary's crew bustled around.

It came clear, soon, that Billy hadn't run out of his stock of surprises. As he was lifted into the metal-framed bed, he seemed to start up out of his lethargy, responding to Mary's quiet firmness with a show of spirit that Paul was astonished and happy to see. No! No! He would not *stand* for restraining bars at the sides of the bed. Mary quickly said that he was absolutely right; he didn't need them ("—yet," she later said to Paul). He lay back then, as limp and out of touch as he had been before that outburst.

When Paul went around to Billy's apartment the next morning, he was greeted by Drew, who seemed a new person. Sunlight streamed in the window on the revived hibiscus. Haydn's "Farewell" Symphony was going, pianissimo. Drew said with happy eyes that Billy was much better. "He *adores* the bed. Look at him!"

Billy had had Drew crank up the backrest and knee lift, and he was trifling with a custard Drew had made.

"I see you're glad to be home again," Paul said, trying to mute his surprise at the change.

"Too cold up there," Billy said. His voice was hardly more than a murmur, but Paul recognized Billy's way of sardonically covering up what Paul had so often heard from him when he was himself. "Come *on*, Drew. Coffee for Paul."

Drew, instantly obedient, went off to the kitchenette. And Paul thought he saw—coming, it seemed, out of nowhere—a trace of Billy's bad-boy grin of other times. He wondered what in the world had been going on between these two.

They chatted awhile, then Paul left for the bookstore.

Drew phoned at about noon to say that Ballastos was coming, and Paul went back to Billy's to see what the doctor would have to say. After a thorough going-over, he took Paul and Drew into the kitchenette and said that he couldn't see any reason at this point to put Billy in the hospital; his life signs were all right, everything considered; he had a few puzzling bruiselike discolorations on his torso, possible signs of some kind of blood disorder, which would need to be watched; and the sores on his arms might well be early lesions of Kaposi's sarcoma—he'd keep an eye on them in the next few days. Might need chemo. "The main thing, though," Dr. Ballastos said, "is that his attitude is better than it was before he took this trip. Must have been good for him."

As soon as the doctor left, Paul said to Drew, "What in God's name has happened, Drew?"

Drew waved his hand in front of his face, as if to drive away Paul's question; Paul told me Drew almost miaowed—the canary must have tasted so good. "It's up to Billy to tell you. If he wants to, that is."

So, Paul thought, he's paying me back—F for Franklin.

"I watered the hibiscus," Drew then reproachfully said. "It was awful dry, Paul." He quickly added, "Of course, you couldn't help it; you were called away to Blowing Rock."

One would never have known, from the way Drew said this, Paul told me, that there was anything the slightest bit peculiar about why Paul had been summoned to Blowing Rock.

Francis Pinckney phoned Paul that night and asked how things were going. He said he had put in a call to Billy the day before, ostensibly to see how he was but really, if he was honest about it, because he was bursting with curiosity to hear how Billy would take a piece of news that he wanted to give him.

"And what was that?"

"Dr. Franklin telephoned us."

"He *what?*"

"He wasn't aware that Billy had gone down the mountain. He was very low-key, very professional, you know. If Mr. Chapman had any, well, 'unexpected difficulties,' I think he said, flare-ups or whatnot, that he might be able to give some advice about, he'd be glad. That was all. It was bizarre, Paul. He must have thought Drew wouldn't have dreamed of telling us about his errand. What do you suppose made him make that call?"

"You tell me," Paul said. "Billy's transformed. You should see him."

He was, indeed. He was almost a real Billy. He was a pathetic sight, but he was alert and cheerful. The next afternoon, while he was sitting cranked up in the bed, toying with some raspberry sorbet, and Paul, across the room, was sipping at a Scotch, Billy told Drew to read aloud to them. Drew chose from the shelves a book of Herrick's poems; riffled the pages; started in on "Corinna's Going A-Maying." Paul could hear from the way he read, reaching for the ironic teasing of the first verses of the poem, that he was on top of the world—exultant, forgiven by Billy, put in the right.

But Billy suddenly said, quite angrily, "Don't put so much expression in it. You're trying to dramatize. You kill the stuff. Just give me the *words*."

Drew, instantly appeasing, picked up where he had left off, in a flatter mode.

"That's better," Billy said, after Drew's

Get up, sweet Slug-a-bed, and see
The dew bespangling herb and tree.

Patient and nurse, Paul felt, that afternoon, were back in tune with each other, Billy ascendant, Drew wanting to please. This got Paul guessing about the pride—it *must* have been frustrated and wounded pride—that had laid Billy so low after Drew's intrusive errand up on the mountain. For thirty years, Billy had proudly never breathed to Sylvester Franklin a word of his feelings, and then this brash Drew, believing that he knew best and out of a perverse impulse of tender loving care, had in ten minutes ripped off from Billy's most private place its hard-earned, but obviously very thin, callus. It seemed as if Sylvester Franklin's *knowing* was the unbearable thing for Billy. But here was this sudden recovery now, a recovery really on both their parts, with no more basis than that stiff, enigmatic phone call of the doctor's to the Pinckneys. What mattered in Paul's eyes was that Billy's new joy, perhaps even a wriggling new worm of hope in his head, had revived some habits of his old, well self: his tendencies, at any rate, to skirt all around the truth and to grin—or try to, anyway.

In the next few days and nights, however, Paul, dropping in from time to time, became at first curious, then more and more uneasy, at what seemed to him a subtle, swift, progressive shift in the ways Billy and Drew dealt with each other. He began to hear Drew defending himself, talking back; sometimes he glared at Billy after Billy asked him to do something. Billy seemed to be losing the rough edge of his commands. Once Paul heard him almost beg for a glass of water.

With this change of balances there came a dramatic rapid draining away, Paul could see, of Billy's strength. He was in obvious pain whenever he moved. One afternoon, Paul, worried by Billy's shallow and rapid breathing and his flushed face, put his hand on Billy's forehead.

Alarmed at what he felt, he said to Drew, "Billy has a fever."

"I know," Drew said.

"You know? It feels . . . Have you called Ballastos?"

"There's no need," Drew said. "I'm taking care of it."

Paul heard a whisper from the bed. "Paulie. Paulie."

He leaned down over Billy and said, "What is it, Billy?"

Billy took a deep, sighlike breath and then whispered one word. "Scared."

Without stopping to think what Billy was really trying to say, Paul went to the phone and called the doctor.

. . .

Late that afternoon, an ambulance took Billy to De Poo Hospital. Perhaps because he had AIDS, he was put in a single room. Ballastos said that he thought Billy probably had "the usual" PCP—he spelled it out for Paul, *Pneumocystis carinii* pneumonia—a guess that would be confirmed by tests in the next couple of days.

Drew, who had ridden in the ambulance to the hospital in street clothes, announced that he was going to stand by in the room with Billy around the clock, but Paul heard a tiny, tyrannical floor nurse say that wouldn't be allowed. Drew asserted that he was the patient's private nurse. So much the worse, she said. The patient has AIDS, she said. Strict hospital rule. He would only be allowed to come, like anyone else, during visiting hours. Drew threw a scene that echoed through the halls and wound up in the hospital director's office, but no matter how loudly he shouted that he was the only person who knew what the patient needed every minute of every hour of the day, he was not only turned down, he was threatened with arrest if he didn't subside. With set lips, he strode out of the hospital. He didn't even say goodbye to Billy.

When Paul got home from the hospital, he called sister Helen in Charlotte to tell her how sick Billy was. She and Mildred hadn't made it to Blowing Rock; they really must come to see him now. Helen said she was sorry to hear the news, but she didn't see how she could possibly get away from her volunteer work on behalf of autistic children just then for the two days it would take to drive down—she never flew—and a day to see Billy and two days to drive back again. Within an hour, Mildred called back to say they would both start down on Thursday, in two days. It was mischievous Stanley who, hearing this, asked: Was this something from a fairy tale? Had the good sister turned into a wicked witch; the bad, into Tinker Bell?

Assuming that Drew must have walked all the way home from De Poo, Paul went around to Billy's apartment to see whether he had recovered from his snit. He tried to let himself in with his key, but Drew must have thrown the burglarproof dead-bolt lock inside. Paul then went home and tried to phone, but there was no answer, and for that entire day—and all through the days that followed, for the whole time Billy was at De Poo—Drew would answer neither knocking nor the phone. He must have sneaked out to Fausto's sometimes for food, but Paul never happened to see him doing that. Not once did he show up at the hospital.

Friday morning, Mildred called to say that she and Helen would be arriving in Key West late that evening; they'd arranged to put up at the Pier House. They'd like to see William fairly early on Saturday, so they could get on the road as soon as possible for their return. Saturday-morning visiting hours at De Poo, Paul said, were from ten to twelve; he'd look for them there at ten, or after.

They arrived on the tick of the hour. Paul had first met them nearly twenty years back and hadn't seen them since. Mildred had grown tubby; Helen was lean and stringy. Somehow he'd guessed, from the sounds of their voices on the phone, that the opposite would be the case: Helen fleshy, Mildred wiry. Paul's impression now of their beings was just what it had been two decades before, that these were two women who made a masquerade of being proud of their lot in life—but, overacting their parts, they gave you glimpses of two separate chambers in a hell of conformity, of struggling, above all, to be "nice." They both now had almost identical tight little blips at the corners of their mouths, which suggested that ardent disapproval of many things had become a habit with them—the habit itself a painful object of their disapproval. Both were wearing flowered dresses and smart straw hats with dipping brims and white cotton gloves—gloves for *safety*, he wondered, in case they were obliged to *touch* Billy?

Billy coughed twice and feebly said, "Look who's here."

The sisters stood in the doorway. Helen looked really frightened. Mildred spoke first. "How're you doing, Will?" she said. Before Billy could answer, both sisters broke into a torrent of chatter. Pop was having a lot of trouble with his arthritis; still played golf, though. Twice a week or so. Melissa, Helen's older daughter, was engaged; the nicest boy, civil engineer, office buildings, good big jobs. Millie won the club bridge championship. Munson, Mildred's second son, broke his arm, took a spill ice skating. Yes, they skate on ice in summertime, indoor rink, isn't it silly? . . . The two women relentlessly poured out their tepid air. Billy sat blinking. Paul couldn't tell how he was taking it all. Helen kept one hand on the doorjamb, as if to be able to shove off quickly in case she had to run for her life. This much was true: Awful Mildred, putting a decent measure of warmth into her prattling, had somehow turned the plot upside down in the children's tale of their lives and had transmogrified herself into the lighter-winged sister of the two. Stanley was right.

Almost lost in the haste of the sisters' embarrassed run of blather came these two sentences (Paul, in his befuddlement, wasn't sure later which mouth they'd come from): "Syl Franklin called. When I told him you were so bad, you know, like this, he said give you his best, anything he could do he'd be glad."

At once, on top of that, Helen cut in with apologies that they hadn't made it to Blowing Rock; Pop had *so* enjoyed seeing Billy, "thought you'd be on your feet before you knew it." Then Mildred again, with something about their father's VW overheating on the way down from Blowing Rock. On and on they skidded.

Five minutes more babbling, and suddenly they were gone.

The first thing Billy said, with an effort, was: "Did you see that? They didn't even touch my feet."

"Safety first," Paul said with a smile.

Then, with a much stronger voice: "You hear what she said? Paulie, call him for me. Would you?"

It was hard for Paul to tell the effect on Billy of his sisters' visit. Feverish and restless, he said not a word more about them. It was clear to Paul, at any rate, that there was no use hoping for anything further in the way of support from Billy's family, and this made him resume constantly calling "all of us" to make sure we'd show up, one or two at a time, at Billy's bedside. I myself, when I dropped in, was astonished by the dogged spark in Billy's eyes, though he seemed to find it a great effort to speak.

When the diagnosis of pneumonia was clear, two days after the sisters came and went, Paul did put a call through to Dr. Franklin's office, and he left his name and number. It took the doctor a day to do so, but this time he returned the call.

Paul thanked him for calling back.

Was Paul's call—the doctor's voice was cool and business-like—a request for a consultation? He would be glad to talk with Mr. Chapman's physician.

"Tell the truth, I had something else in mind," Paul said. "Like a visit. Could you? It would mean the world to Billy to see his oldest friend."

A long wait, which gave Paul some hope. But the doctor said he was really sorry, but he was afraid that was out of the question. "Appointments. Patients," he said. "I'm booked solid." Then he pushed the excuse, Paul thought, over the border into the open country of fibbery. "Next five weeks," he said, making it sound like a boast.

"What about coming here on a weekend," Paul, furious, asked, "instead of going to Blowing Rock?"

For a few seconds Paul thought he could hear the doctor breathing. Then there was a click. And silence.

When Paul told me about all this, I asked him, "Did it ever occur to you that Franklin may have figured out that when he did Billy's gallbladder operation—what was that, four years ago?—Billy must have been HIV positive? Test or no test, whether Billy knew it at the time or not, it figures, doesn't it?"

"What's that supposed to mean? How was *that* supposed to affect an old friendship?"

"I don't know what it does to the picture, Paul. I just wonder."

"A surgeon wears rubber gloves, doesn't he? Condoms on his fingers?"

"Paulie!"

"Oh, Christ, I know. . . . Thing is, I let Billy down. I should have been able to talk that bastard into coming down here."

I said, "Did you think of trying the doctor's daughter—isn't it Molly? Billy was always so fond of her. She might be able—"

"She's in Europe, Billy told me. He said he'd hoped like everything she'd be at Blowing Rock. Yeah, she might have made all the difference." Then Paul added, "I've screwed things up again, haven't I?"

At that moment I didn't think: Poor Billy. I thought: Poor Paul. He'll always manage to find some shortcut to remorse.

At first he didn't dare tell Billy about the phone call, and Billy—God, there was still some pride in him!—didn't ask whether Paul had honored his request to call. After a few days, the Bactrim that Billy was getting intravenously began to take hold and the fever went down—though tests, Ballastos said, had turned up some new bad news: some nasty intestinal parasites.

Paul decided he'd better go ahead and take his chances and lie a bit if necessary. He told Billy he'd invited Sylvester Franklin to come down to see him.

"*Invited?*" Billy said, his voice flaring up. "I didn't want you to do *that*."

"You didn't?"

"Hell, no, you silly shit," Billy said. Paul was taken aback by how angry he was. "You were just supposed to thank him for that offer, you know—willing to help. Christ!"

"I'm sorry. I misunderstood, Billy."

"You had no *right* to do that."

"But wait, Billy. He was real nice. He said he couldn't get away at the moment, but maybe he'd try to get down for a weekend, skip Blowing Rock for a weekend, sometime next month. He said that, Billy."

"Like hell he did, Paul." Billy panted between sentences. "You're lying in your teeth. . . . You forget I've known that guy thirty years. . . . He doesn't have the guts . . . to come down here and see me."

Anger seemed to be as good for Billy as joy had sometimes been. His eyes were clearer, his voice stronger. The lift lasted only a few hours, however; he was quickly let down onto the surface of a profound torpor, as if he were just barely floating on a sea of dreams. Sometimes his mind wandered. It was being tugged off somewhere by a force that he seemed to welcome.

Ten days later, though, Dr. Ballastos said the pneumonia was pretty much remitted; he was well enough to go home. In view of the patient's general condition, Ballastos advised Paul to have Hospice now take over full-time care. Paul understood all too well what that meant.

On the morning Billy was to be checked out, he groped with his right hand to take one of Paul's, and just managing to make himself heard, he whispered, "Get rid of him, Paulie. Please?"

Paul thought at first that this was some queer message having to do with Dr. Franklin, but then quickly he knew—despite the masculine pronoun, used for the first time ever—that Billy was speaking of Drew.

With that realization came another. Drew was bolted in. He was still there in Billy's apartment. That very morning, Paul had tried three times to call him. How were they going to get Billy in, if Drew wouldn't answer the doorbell?

"*Please?*" Billy said.

Paul, frantically wondering whether they'd have to break down the door, hardly heard him.

When the ambulance pulled up at the entrance to Billy's apartment, Drew was standing on the sidewalk in his nurse's togs, calmly waiting for its arrival.

As the attendants lifted Billy out, Paul asked Drew, "How'd you know he was coming home?"

"I've called that shit-hole hospital five times every day to keep tabs on him." Tears brimmed in Drew's eyes. "Thank God he's home for me to help him. Thank *God!*"

Paul said, "Mary Conover's in charge now, Drew."

Without a word, Drew turned away from Paul. He walked beside the bearers as they started in, with one hand lightly on the rail of the stretcher.

Mary Conover did now take full command of Billy's slow glide down the final slope. Yes, he was dying. We all knew it. You could see in the shape of his helplessness that he had made his decision. There were short periods when he seemed to drift away from knowing who he was and who we were. Dr. Ballastos, in his flat, demystifying way, said the Kaposi's had made skirmishes under the skin and found a path to his brain. Mary set up a round-the-clock care structure, which, to Paul's amazement, Drew accepted cheerfully. Mary assigned nine nighttime hours to Drew and scheduled three women in turns during the rest of the day and night. She said Drew could be around as much as he wanted, in his off hours, but he must understand that the others would do whatever needed to be done for the patient. Mary cleared every move with Paul and with Dr. Ballastos. Cobo's provided medicines. Trained Hospice people came in to give Billy morphine shots—and even that, Paul noticed, Drew acquiesced in without a whimper.

The three volunteer women Mary brought in—all of them, Paul guessed, in their fifties, all with grown children—seemed quite interchangeably plump, graying, quiet, gentle, and, in every stroke of the hands and look of the eyes, therapeutic. They weren't at all like hospital nurses; they weren't in uniform, and they never looked at their watches. Each of them treated Billy with an amazingly unforced and brave tenderness, almost as if he were a beloved ailing child of her own. One of them, a Mrs. Wren, was not very bright, but she made up for her occasional forgettings and misjudgments with a very special gentleness; Billy's racked body seemed to grow lighter, as if he might be about to levitate, when caressed by the slightly pudgy palms of her magical hands. Watching her one evening, as she tried to get a few sips of the liquid nutriments called Ensure—the nectar of survival Billy was supposed to ingest—into him, Paul was so moved by her devotion and patience, and by the resistant strength of Billy's unwilling lips, that he had to flee to his own apartment, able to cry for the first time since Billy's very first symptoms appeared.

The phone jangled. Paul jerked his head up, confused, thinking his clock alarm had gone off, though he couldn't remember having set it; he saw that it was just past six-twenty in the morning. He heard Stanley groan. When the phone rang a second time, Paul realized what it was, and leaning on one elbow and reaching across Stanley, he picked up.

"Mary Conover here. We need you. In Billy's."

It took Paul, still floundering in the underbrush of his sleepiness, a few seconds to take in what Mary had said. Then he did, and he was wide awake. "Be right over."

So Billy had finally found his refuge in the dark place he had shown so many signs, in the last few days, of wanting to reach. As Paul hastily pulled on jeans and a sweatshirt, he felt that he was on the defensive. He must brace himself; grief was going to strike him an ugly blow. But no, nothing came—was it too soon?—nothing at all. Wrong—there *was* something. He was aware of a faint push of pleasurable curiosity about Mary's word "need." We need you. He hurried into his Birkenstocks, already walking toward Billy's dead body in the act of wriggling his toes under the straps of one sandal and then the other.

There was a policeman at the door of Billy's apartment.

The first thing Paul noticed, hurrying into Billy's bedroom and looking toward the metal bed, was Billy's right hand waving off something or someone. It was an active hand, very much alive—more vigorous in its movement than Paul had seen it be for several days. The room seemed crowded. Mary, Mrs. Wren, Drew in street clothes, Dr. Ballastos, two cops, a man in a gray suit. And Billy. Billy on his non-deathbed.

Then Paul saw why he was needed. He leaned over the bed, his hands gripping the restraining bars, which were raised, and he saw Billy's face. He gasped.

He was aware of Dr. Ballastos beside him. The doctor pulled the sheet down over Billy's bare torso, and Paul, not wanting to see what he saw, drew it back up into place.

Drew was scrabbling at his elbow, and Paul looked up and saw that he was weeping. *Again*, Paul thought.

"He wouldn't cooperate," Drew said in a rush of something between fury and entreaty. "He wouldn't do what I said. His own good. I told him, but he wouldn't cooperate. I—"

"Shut *up*," Paul said. "Mary? Tell me."

Maude Wren had let herself in at ten minutes to six. She was always a few minutes early. Drew had been in the kitchenette. The patient seemed to be asleep. Maude leaned down to pick up a Kleenex on the floor. She had it in her hand, looking around for the wastebasket, when she heard a trace of a groan from the bed.

She hurried over, and she saw Mr. Chapman's face. She saw a bruise the color of a plum on the left cheek; blood had run from his nose; the flesh around the left eye was puffed and darkening; there were lacerations on the chin.

"Drew! Drew! Come here!"

Drew appeared, smiling, dressed in jeans and a T-shirt he'd made himself, with THE EXSTASIE printed on it in block letters.

"Whatever happened?" Mrs. Wren asked.

"That's the way their faces get at the end," Drew said.

"What do you mean? I've seen—I never—"

"They get that way," Drew said.

Maude Wren grew frightened. With her heart beating wildly, she went to the telephone and dialed for Mary Conover. She kept her back to Drew, afraid of what she would see if he was coming toward her. She tried to think what she would do if he wrenched the phone out of her hands.

She heard no footsteps. She heard another faint groan. As the phone buzzed three rings on the other end, she heard Drew say, "It's quite usual. Don't be upset."

"Mary? Can you come over to Mr. Chapman's? Right away? I think you'd better call nine one one."

"You need an ambulance?"

"No. Something else."

Mary understood at once. "I'll call them," she said. "Are you all right? Do you think you could phone Dr. Ballastos? It would save time."

Mrs. Wren made herself look around at Drew. He was standing by the bed, with one hand gently patting one of Mr. Chapman's feet. "Yes," she said. "I'll do that."

"I'll be right over," Mary said, and hung up.

Mrs. Wren had memorized Dr. Ballastos's number at home; it was part of the drill.

Bless him, he answered.

"Maude Wren. Hospice? Remember me?"

"Of course, Mrs. Wren. Good morning." Cheerfully, as if the Mrs. Wrens in his life always called up at six in the morning. "What can I do for you?"

"Could you come to Mr. Chapman's? We have, uh, an unexpected situation."

"Can you tell me . . . Never mind. I'm on my way."

The immediate problem, Mary Conover said—in Drew's hearing, of course—was that Officer Johns maintained he couldn't make an arrest because no one was bringing any charges, not that he could hear. Mr. Chapman was barely able to speak; Mary had tried without success to get him to say what had happened. What had happened seemed obvious, but Officer Johns said that seeming isn't good enough in court.

Having told that much, Mary left what she wanted from Paul—why he was needed—hanging in midair.

Paul hesitated. Out of nowhere came a flash of memory of playing backgammon late one night in Billy's apartment. He couldn't remember the layout of the board; maybe he'd had a block going and Billy was playing a dangerous back game—something he loved to do—and suddenly Paul's defenses must have fallen apart, and Billy with his luck probably threw two or three big doubles in a row and broke all his counters out and skunked Paul. As he lifted his last man off the home board, he said, "Know something, Paul? Trouble with the way you play? Too goddam considerate." The queer thing was, Paul knew—knew then and, remembering, knew now—exactly what Billy meant. Not just backgammon. The thing that always made him yield. Billy always knew what button to push. Paul felt a pinch of rage at Billy—and was immediately deeply ashamed of it. Look at him!

But then the shame seemed to be pushed aside by more—and more—anger. Billy, damn him, had asked for this. He *deserved* what had happened to him—this new pain on top of all his other unbearable pain. Paul knew from the references he'd gotten from Drew's former employers when he hired him that nothing like this could ever have happened before. They all said Drew was a lamb; he was odd—even a bit spooky, maybe, in some of his ideas—but underneath, they said, purely kind and selfless. Paul would never have hired him if he hadn't been convinced of the sweetness within all that oddity. But Billy, damn him, damn his perversity, had known how to probe right to the aching heart of Drew's strangeness; he'd known exactly where to dig to get at the tenderest flakes in Drew. So now this. No wonder. Billy didn't play fair. He never had.

Paul said to the room at large, "I want to talk to Billy. Would you all mind going into the living room for a few minutes?"

Everyone—except Drew—started moving toward the door.

"Him too," Paul said.

Officer Johns waved to Drew to get going.

"He'll stand up for me, you wait and see," Drew said to Paul, and then went along.

Paul shut the door. He stepped to the bed and took Billy's right hand in his, and with that touch he felt all his appalling, selfish anger washed away by a torrent of affection and pity and remorse. He hated himself for what he'd been thinking. Gently he said, "Are you okay?"

Not looking at Paul, Billy slowly shook his head back and forth barely an inch, and he whispered, "No." He was not okay. Paul was startled to see a ghost of one of Billy's naughty grins on his swollen lips, as he murmured, "Death's door."

That mind wasn't wandering now. Whatever had happened had shaken Billy out into absolute clarity.

His breathing labored, he whispered, "Said I was the one told the nurse don't let him stay at De Poo." Then, "I was the one ordered what-you-call-it . . . Hospice, the women, take over from him. Said that too."

"Oh, my friend," Paul said, "this has been going on a long time, hasn't it?" Paul remembered, from way back before Blowing Rock—"acting up," Billy'd said.

This time Billy nodded his head.

"Why didn't you keep after me about him?"

Billy was quiet awhile. Then he breathed deeply and whispered—echoing yet another word that was painfully stored in Paul's memory bank—"I was scared." After a pause, "That there wouldn't be anyone . . . take care of me."

"Oh, Billy—Billy! I would have been there."

Billy looked at Paul for the first time. "Bullshit," he whispered.

This man couldn't be dying, Paul thought. He dropped Billy's hand. The terrible thing was that Billy was Billy, and he, Paul, was—oh, God—considerate! But he didn't care what Billy said; he himself had meant what he'd said. He *would* have been there. And Billy knew that too. He just still had to be someone you had to forgive. He had to be Billy.

Then Paul thought: I was the one who hired Drew. That's it. That's what it is, no matter what. That's why he won't bend.

"Look, Billy. Do something for me, will you? Just say in a

few words what happened—but wait awhile, so I can write down what you dictate in front of a cop. Okay?"

Once again Billy shook his head ever so slightly and very slowly. No. A definite no, expressed this time with an economy that made it seem absolutely final.

"Why not? Twenty words? Jesus, that guy has to be put away."

Billy breathed—or sighed—several times. Then he whispered, "Too . . . much trouble."

At first Paul thought he meant it would be too much trouble to dictate what had happened. Too much effort. Perhaps too painful. Then he realized how often Billy talked aslant, and that he may now have intended something much more copious than just the moment's trouble, may have meant something to do with some of what he'd been through, maybe all of it, the months of it all, the years, even the times with his parents and his sisters and his lovers and his friends, the teaching, the tomcatting, Vanya's trigger temper, the humming of bicycle tires on the hot Key West tar . . . And Paul, what about old Paulie? The Designated Care Person! . . . And—guessing now—long ago, beautiful Syl walking along a path at Peddie, the grace of Syl's movements climbing the many steps on Jefferson's serene campus . . . Headaches, nausea, horrible AZT . . . Facing the wall in a brass bed, on that "spree" with "Drew, baby"—Drew, Drew! . . . Follies, back when, of anticipation and repletion: Dick Dock, Michael's garden of the joy of gay sex, bathhouse frenzies—the earned sickness, sores, diarrhea—denial of fear, fear itself . . . And Fran's clock that on the dot of the wasted hours played "What Is This Thing Called Love" and "In the Still of the Night" and "Love for Sale." God, all the throwaway hours—talk about "time's winged chariot" . . . And oh, the effort to understand—he'd talked about this one night—to understand every glinting meaning, and every dark one, in "A Nocturnall upon St. Lucie's Day, Being the Shortest Day."

He'd recited the poem and taken it carefully apart for Paul—"so deathly winter begets sexy spring, and in short, Paulie, the time comes around again for lust; death and lust are reconciled!"—and then, Paul remembered, he'd been watering the hibiscus on the night, a little later, when Billy suddenly blurted out two lines from a different poem:

I runne to death, and death meets me as fast,
And all my pleasures are like yesterday . . .

The words had shaken Paul and had posted themselves, unforgettably, in his mind. How defiant, how *casual*, Billy had been, at the height of his unimaginable suffering.

Paul put his hand on Billy's thin arm and pressed.

Billy looked at Paul again. This time he said, "Sure."

Paul understood at once that this didn't mean Billy was saying yes, he would accede, he'd changed his mind about dictating what had happened. No. He looked me in the eye, Paul thought; that one word was for me, and it's all I'll ever get.

Paul went over and knocked hard on the bedroom door.

When everyone was back in the room, Paul said, "He doesn't want to press charges."

"I told you," Drew said. "I don't know why you bothered."

What was new, in the next few days, with Drew gone, was a sense of stillness, a deep quiet in the rooms. It was like being in a grove of trees with not a leaf stirring. Not that Drew had ever been especially noisy. It was more—for Paul, anyway—a hush of surcease, of equilibrium. Paul was spending most of his waking hours in Billy's apartment now; for the first three nights, in fact, he slept there, on the sofa. He wanted to be on hand in case Drew, who still had a key—no one had thought to ask him for it—took it into his head to come back; he didn't, as it turned out. Apart from that, though, and more to the point, a muted wait had begun, a silent vigil. There had been a steep falloff. Billy was out of it most of the time. After checking him on one of his visits, Dr. Ballastos said nothing but shook his head. Paul had a feeling that the Hospice women, ghosting around on soft-soled shoes and talking under their breath, had now begun to nurse him, Paul, as much as they did Billy. When Sandy Planne and Buzz Jones and the Barlows and others of the support group stopped by, everyone whispered. I certainly felt the quiet. It seemed as if there were some huge secret that we all had to keep from each other.

Late one morning, Paul saw Billy stir. He went to the bedside. Billy's eyes were open; one was still puffy, but he looked, as he hadn't for days, wide awake. He was staring at the sun-splashed hibiscus blooms. Some inner excitement seemed to be stirring. He was breathing very fast, short, shallow gulps of air. Paul heard him making a sound: "M-m-m-m," that was all.

Billy slowly moved his head and his eyes toward Paul.

He made the sound again.

Paul wondered if he was trying to say something. He leaned down to listen more closely.

Yes, there *was* something. Billy was making another try. "M-m-m-m . . ." Paul thought he heard a faint hum of meaning in that mumbling in the gale of the breaths in Billy's throat. He may have imagined it, but soon he thought he heard Billy say, "M-m-m-m . . . M-m-m-m-u-sic."

Paul hurried at once to the side of the room across from the hibiscus, picked out a CD of Strauss waltzes, and switched on the amplifier and started the player. He turned up the volume until the silence of all those days was routed and the whole room throbbed.

He went back to the bed. There was no doubt in Paul's mind that Billy was trying to smile.

Paul said, "Shall we dance?" And he took Billy's two chilly hands up in his and moved them, gently whirled them, *swoop*

swoop swoop, *swoop* swoop swoop, in wider and wider circles, in time with the exultant beat of the music of a lighthearted once-upon-a-time.

And now it looked to Paul as if Billy was ever so slightly nodding, again and again. Trying to say yes, Paul thought. Yes, he seemed to be saying. Yes.

Did You Ever Have Such Sport?

It was in the salmon-pink light of one of Key West's fabled sunsets, on an evening early in May, that Dr. Benjamin Strobel—surgeon for the army post, physician at large for the community, member of the town council, and editor and publisher of the Key West Gazette*—strolled to the docks with a number of friends to welcome the sixty-foot United States revenue cutter* Marion*, which was under the command of an acquaintance of his, one Lieutenant Robert Day. Dr. Strobel had recently received a letter from a Lutheran minister in Charleston, Reverend John Bachman, a fanatical amateur ornithologist and botanist, who for some time had kept begging Strobel for exotic plants, unusual shells, and pretty bird skins, to add to what must have been a bizarre collection of nature's oddities; the letter urged Dr. Strobel to keep a lookout for the* Marion*, because aboard her would be a good fellow named John James* Audubon*, a hunter of birds for the purpose of making paint-*

ings of them, who intended to spend some time in the lower Keys.

When the Marion was warped in, made fast to bollards, and secured for the night, Lieutenant Day and his crew and passengers disembarked in order to pacify their sea legs. Lieutenant Day, who knew Strobel as one of Key West's leading citizens, introduced him to Audubon, a stocky, vigorous-looking man with a broad face, long wavy hair, arrogant eyes, and a chin thrust forward like a dare. On hearing Strobel's name, Audubon took him aside and with considerable urgency whipped out a letter of introduction from Reverend Bachman and said he required an immediate conversation with the doctor.

Strobel took him to his house, where Audubon asked for advice about where to hunt for birds. The two men hit it off at once. Through the remainder of Audubon's stay, during the few hours each day when he was not at his visitor's side, Dr. Strobel made entries in a diary he was in the habit of keeping. In them he recorded, along with his amazement at the beauty and eloquence of the drawings and paintings that Audubon dashed off with breathtaking speed, his equally great surprise at something else he observed. Here are some excerpts from the diary:

> MAY 6. We had provided Audubon with a smart pair of shallow-draft cutters, manned by half a dozen of the Marion's sailors at the oars of each. Preston, our guide, a grizzled old manatee hunter and conch diver who used to sail to Havana to sell the meat and hides he'd harvested, has marked with his eye, I believe, every nest of every bird on every tangle of mangrove here in the lower Keys. He is better acquainted with what is on these many islets than most learned square-toes are with the contents of their desk drawers. This morning he pointed us in under a Key where an entire congress of Magnificent Frigatebirds had started to build their nests. Audubon, Preston, each man Jack of our

crew, and I—all were armed with artillery, and at a nod from Preston we uttered a bombardment which brought down a heavy downpour of those splendid creatures. Audubon cheered. A few of those "men-o'-war birds" had survived and had taken to wing, and the sharp-eyed Preston raised his weapon, named "Long John," fully charged with "groceries," as he called his shot and powder, and brought several more birds down which, thinking themselves safe, had begun soaring about, trailing their streaming forked tails after them, at a height of at least one hundred feet.

Audubon soon had all of us, even including the Navy men, skinning the carcasses. When we were done, he heaped the entire take of skins in the bilge of a cutter. At home, that afternoon, he stuffed one skin—one skin out of the many—why had he needed so many?—and in short order made a dazzling drawing of Fregata magnificens.

MAY 7. *Rowing round the brow of an island thick with a wild hair of mangroves, we suddenly came, at the leeward side, on a vast number of our most familiar creatures—ungainly Brown Pelicans—perched all together in a harmony of satiation, looking like a retreat of complaisant, elderly preachers. How peaceful their ruminations were!—until our heathen infantry suddenly fired its repeated salvos. At once the water around us was crowded with fleets of the dead, the dying, and the maimed, while others flocked away screaming over the sea.*

"Did you ever have such sport?" says Preston.

"It's a joy," says Audubon. "Out with your knives, boys!"

We bagged twenty-eight skins.

MAY 8. *Our men rowed fourteen miles this morning, till we came to an island with a wide bay rimmed with a white shelly beach and with long pale sandbars reaching out into the shallows. The flocks of birds there, running on the beach, whirring up in sudden wheeling flights, wading, floating, sleepily perching, were so various and so numerous that we wondered if we were dreaming. Sooty Terns and Noddy Terns and Roseate Terns and Cayenne Terns dived for their breakfasts; Great Marbled Godwits strutted by the score under the mangroves; Great White Herons paraded primly on their stilts; here were Wood Storks, Mangrove Cuckoos, Reddish Egrets; I heard Audubon exclaiming in ecstasy at the sight of a flock of Zenaida Doves. We were not so ravished by wonder, however, as to forget to raise and aim our guns. The very first volley was amongst a mob of Godwits. We went ashore and counted sixty-five corpses on the sand. The cargo of the many kinds of skins at the end of the morning were like to sink one of our dories.*

MAY 9 AND 10. *On successive days Audubon had what he called "two frolics" of hunting for ospreys as they soared and dived for prey near their great nests of sticks scattered on old dead trees along the islands on the ocean side. He killed seven of those elusive eagle-like marvels in forty-eight hours. With flashing eyes he said to me, at the end of the second day, "I never saw a sportsman who could do better than that. Did you ever?"*

MAY 13. *We sailed out to the Tortugas, where, at anchor, we made the acquaintance of some hearty wreckers. The next morning these men rowed us in three longboats, with full strokes and a good run of the hull between pulls, as whaling oarsmen are wont to ply, heading for "Booby Island," some ten miles from the lighthouse, where the wreckers said we'd have capital shooting.*

It was early, and we were hungry, and we stopped off en route *at a small island that might well have been named*

"Ibis Island," for every bush on it held several nests of that graceful bird. The men took up from the boat lockers their tin and wooden plates that they used for mess kits. Each nest held a clutch of three handsome eggs, and fanning out, we raided all the nests—the birds flying off in sullen deference to us—and soon we had built fires and cooked ourselves a wondrously hearty and delicious breakfast.

As our little flotilla rowed on with renewed energy, the captain sang rhythmic chanteys to pace the men's strokes, and now and then the three boats would race short sprints against each other. It was all most cheery. All the men, and Audubon *with them, grew even cheerier at the sport that ensued when we reached "Booby Island." Like* Audubon, *the wreckers were all first-rate marksmen, and they were armed with the best of guns. In a very few minutes very nearly the entire flock of boobies which had colonized the island met its* Armageddon.

MAY 17. *By way of relaxation, today, taking a recess from drawing in the sun-room of my house, he sortied out into the town with his gun and right amongst the startled citizens shot a dozen* Key West Quail-Doves. *They were, he said, "easy pickings," on account of their habit of "bathing themselves," as he put it, "with fluttering wings, in the dust of the roadways."*

MAY 19. *"Gentlemen," says* Preston, *"get ready to have some fun. The tide is making up to flood."* We *were out in what has come to be known as "the backcountry"—the vast area of shallows to the west'ard of the* Keys. At *dead low tide, the multitude of birds on the exposed flats and in the merest shallows is uncountable.* With *the wash of the new tide, building a foot or two of depth, however, all, even those with legs like tall reeds, are driven toward roosts in the*

Keys, and behold!—here they came! Each of us was ambushed, in what seems to me the true sense of the word—hidden in a bush—and soon the thronged wings beat their way into the hail of lead Audubon's army threw at them. After our work of flaying the corpses, we gathered the feathery skins all together, and they made a sight not unlike that of a summer haycock.

MAY 21. *Carefully packing a foot-locker and some wooden boxes—for tomorrow the* Marion *sails away—this fiery, affable man, who has quite worn me out with his habit of rising at three o'clock every morning to prepare for a day of hunting and drawing, nourished by nothing but birds' eggs and biscuits and molasses and never a drop of ardent spirits; packing, as I say, he turned to me with a beaming face and exclaimed, "I've made a tally. I've bagged four hundred and seventy-two skins in fifteen days!"*

The Two Lives of Consuela Castanon

There must have been a cruel trigger hidden away somewhere in Consuela Castanon's genes. Slim and airy as a small child, she began when she was twelve to put on weight, a very large part of it below her waist. During her years in grade school, she had many friends of both sexes, thanks to her sweet, appeasing ways and her ready smile. When she grew fat, no one baited her. She played at friends' houses after school, often tumbling around in bodily play with boys and girls alike, as if they were all puppies. She did well in her studies. Everyone spoke of what a happy child she seemed to be. At home she was a good girl.

By the time she went to high school, she was huge. There were always four or five boys who vied for what seemed to them the privilege of turning up, one at a time, at her house, to hit the schoolbooks with her, or to play some board or TV game that was in vogue at the time, or, best of all, to sprawl on the Castanons' living room sofa beside her, listening to the cool (because so hot) broadcasts of dance music from Havana. Her mother never left Consuela alone in the house with any of these boys. She would let the kids be off together without her for short times, as they whispered over textbooks in Consuela's room or bobbed their heads and shoulders to the rhythms of salsas and comparsas and sambas and old-time cha-cha-chas pounding in the living room, but she made it a practice to stick her head in a doorway every fifteen minutes or so, making sure that no funny business was going on. The boys never seemed to mind. For her part, Consuela didn't appear to care that not one of these boys ever asked her to go out on dates—to go to the movies, or to go dancing, or even just to hang out with others after school. Not one of them ever touched her. But they kept trooping to the house, one by one.

By the time she got out of high school, Consuela had stupendous legs and astonishing buttocks. Her whole body was outsized, but the main mass was in her hips and thighs. She was by no means alone in her enormity. Quite often in Key West you could see shapes like hers—whale thighs, elephantine seats. Mostly women, but a few men as well. Blacks, Hispanics, and white North Americans were indiscriminately chosen for this quirk of fate in the Southernmost City. One middle-aged woman could be seen trudging around town, bent forward and leaning her crossed arms and much of the weight of the upper part of her body onto an empty shopping cart with a Winn Dixie label on it, so that her huge legs, swinging in wide half-circles to make their way past each other, could propel at least part of her on wheels to whatever might be her goal. Was something like this to be in Consuela's future?

Consuela had one redeeming blessing. Her pudgy face was pert and pretty—a soft mouth and a tipped nose and dewy eyes set in a comely dumpling of complexion that seemed to have been thinly glazed with honey. She had dear manners, and she still appeared to be deeply cheerful.

She came from a family of Key West old-timers, and some of her classmates, especially some of the Anglos, thought she was a little snooty about it. Her great-grandfather, Julio Castanon, had been brought to the town from Cuba in 1869 at the age of five, when his father, fleeing with many others from the atrocities of the Spanish volunteers at the time of the Bayamo uprising, moved to the small island town and took work with the newly founded cigar factory known as El Principe de Gales, owned by Vincente Martínez Ybor. Julio later also worked there, but when the factory moved to Tampa after the great fire of 1886, he chose to stay on in Key West, taking work eventually in the turtle soup cannery owned by the esteemed French chef Monsieur A. Granday.

The Castanon family, poor at that time, were stubbornly proud of their culture. Consuela's grandfather, Julio's son Limbano, used to tell her about having gone as a boy to the all-Cuban school in the upstairs rooms of the ornate San Carlos Cuban Institute on Duval Street by day and being taken to Cuban musicals downstairs in the evenings. This Limbano Castanon grew into a hulk with unforgiving barracuda eyes and a mismatched bite that gave him the chin of a bully, and he was, besides, shrewd and greedy, and the small bakery he set up soon brought in such good money that he was suspected of running some dubious secondary enterprise under the counter.

A result of his prosperity, in any case, was that his son, Jacinto Castanon, Consuela's father, inherited the bakery and came to own a big house on Von Phister, which had a bright Florida room rimmed with crinkled-glass jalousies. In the yard, a huge satellite dish. Under a carport's aqua-colored metal roof, a black Lincoln Continental, with no-see-in windows. Jacinto Castanon was a wiry Cuban-American Jack Sprat, and his wife could eat no beans—but she did very well, thank you, on surfeits of *lechón asado* and *boliche* and *picadillo*, and hills of yellow rice, and bounties of fried plantain, and parades of long loaves of soft Cuban bread fresh from her husband's bakery. Juliana Castanon was a very large woman, though not nearly so monstrous as her daughter became. No one could say what had happened in Key West in recent decades to cause such a difference. Could something have modified the fundamental code of the DNA of certain Key West mothers over the years? A sinister change, perhaps, in the chemistry of the water table, lying so close under the ground, or a mutated microbe carried by mosquitoes, or reckless new food additives on the shelves at the White Street Fausto's, or even (Santa María del Mar forbid!) a voodoo spell—what *was* it that caused certain sons and daughters who were predisposed to heavy weight to have so much vaster underpinnings than their fat mothers? No one knew.

Since Consuela was the Castanons' only child, Jacinto wanted her, after she graduated from high school, to join him at the bakery. She declined. Quite likely she had become self-conscious about her figure and felt that it would be unseemly for her to be associated professionally with so many complex carbohydrates. She studied shorthand and typing, and she got a job as receptionist and stenographer for Torres & Figueredo, attorneys, with an office on Whitehead. After three years of this she still lived at home, but she had kept many casual girlfriends, and she came and went, day and night, without undue governance by her parents. She had no close men friends, but in the bright front room at Torres & Figueredo, clearly visible from the street through a large picture window, with the surprising parts of her anatomy tucked discreetly out of view behind the reception desk's splendid expanse of Philippine mahogany, and actively bringing into play her dimpled face and her sweetheart manner, she was soon, the law partners felt, attracting new male walk-in clients of sorts they had not previously had.

One day, one of them, an Anglo, a young man with caramel eyes like a spaniel's, a nose worth calling a nose, and healthy tanned cheeks, dressed in a clean plain blue shirt and neatly ironed chinos, looking to Consuela as fresh as a newly baked croissant from The Patisserie, came swaying up to the reception desk and said in a deep, sonorous voice, "My name is Tommy Vance." Then, instead of saying, as most clients did, "I have an appointment" or "I would like an appointment" with Mr. Torres or Mr. Figueredo, he cleared his throat and, blinking slightly as if looking into bright sunlight, said, "Will you marry me?"

Consuela said, sweetly, "Did you want to see Mr. Torres or Mr. Figueredo, or would you prefer it if I called the police?"

Mr. Vance laughed a charming laugh. "Forgive me," he said. "It just popped out. I meant to say—well, I meant what I said, but yes, I would like to see one of the gentlemen. I had to have an excuse to come in, you know."

Consuela ran her flat left hand over the appointment pad on the desk, as if to wipe out all possibility of there being an open hour for such an impertinent person as this, but finally she poised the tip of the index finger of that hand on one of the ruled lines on the right-hand page. "Mr. Torres could see you on Thursday morning at eleven o'clock."

"You have the most beautiful hands," Mr. Vance said.

Consuela tucked both her hands on her lap, under the mahogany desktop. "Do you want me to dial nine one one?" she asked. "They'd be here in two minutes."

"Yes, I'd like the appointment," Mr. Vance said. "Definitely. And no, you needn't call for help. I'm on your side."

Consuela had to bring her right hand up to write in the name.

"Ah, Consuela!" Mr. Vance said, his eyes drinking in the fluid movements of her hand. He must have picked up her name from the brass nameplate beside the appointment book on the desk.

"Thursday. Eleven o'clock," Consuela said, as severely as she could. But she was so used to being polite that she couldn't help smiling as she said this.

"*Sí, hasta jueves, las once,*" Mr. Vance said. "I've started studying Spanish because of you. Oh, I've been walking past this window"—he pointed a thumb at it over his shoulder—"for over a month now. Haven't you ever noticed me?"

"We don't speak Spanish all that much at my house," Consuela said. "We've been in Key West for five generations."

"Ah, well. I wasn't doing very well in my lessons," Mr. Vance said.

"Thursday. Eleven," Consuela said.

"Don't worry. I'll remember," Mr. Vance said.

At home that evening, at supper, Consuela was unusually quiet. She ate hungrily, with a bowed head. Dark shadows, pools of her mood, had gathered under her eyes. Her mother chattered as always, this time about the developer who planned to put in two hundred units up by the airport, he was going to fill the wetlands with a bunch of marl, the crooks on the Commission were going to let him, and the worst crook of all, sad to say, was Agustín Barranco, "*your* friend, Jacinto"—but then suddenly she broke off and asked Consuela whether something was the matter.

"No, Mom," Consuela said. "I'm fine."

"You look like you were run over by a ten-ton truck."

"Leave her alone," Consuela's father said.

"I was thinking," Consuela said, "about a man who came in the office today. He was so funny."

"So funny you look like you're going to cry," Consuela's mother said. "He must have been a howl."

"Come on, Jula," Consuela's father said. "Lay off her."

"Who's this man, anyway?" Mrs. Castanon said. "Tell us about him."

"He just came in for an appointment," Consuela said. "What's to tell?"

"So you started laughing when he asked for an appointment, he was so funny?"

Consuela threw her napkin down on the table. "Why do you always do this to me?" she said, and she got up and left the dining room.

"I suppose you're happy now," Jacinto Castanon said to his wife.

"I think she's getting her period," Juliana said.

The next day, Tuesday, twice, once in the morning and once in the afternoon, Consuela thought she might have seen Mr. Vance walking past the picture window, looking in. She couldn't be sure. Both times she was dealing with a client, and she got only a glimpse of the person, whoever it was. It could have been he. She didn't like the feeling that she might have just imagined seeing him.

Then on Wednesday, in midafternoon, here he was in the flesh. This time she did see him pause at the window, looking in, and then he walked in the door. "*Buenos días*," he said. "Oh, *excuse* me. *Aquí se habla inglés*. Good day."

"Good afternoon, Mr. Vance," she said.

"You remembered my name," he said.

"I'm good at names," she said. "I remember them all."

"I have to bother you with two questions," he said.

"I'm here to answer questions—sensible ones."

"First question. Is my appointment still on?"

Consuela studied the appointment book for quite a while, running her eyes up and down several pages, seeming to have no recollection whatsoever of an appointment for Mr. Vance. "Oh, yes, here we are," she finally said. "Eleven o'clock tomorrow. Did you want to cancel?"

"The second question," he said, not answering hers, "is the same as the other day. I want to ask for your beautiful hand. Really for both of your hands. I'd like to marry them both."

Consuela, apparently thinking it was time for decisive action, stood up, and turning her back to go—for no particular reason—to the file cabinets against the inner wall of the waiting room, she exposed to Mr. Vance's gaze the entirety of her bad news. This would surely shut him up.

"My God!" she heard him say. Then, after a pause, softly, "Please say you'll marry me."

She turned toward him with hot cheeks.

He spoke before she could. "You thought I was teasing," he gently said. "I'm very clumsy. I'm sorry."

Consuela collapsed into her desk chair.

"I meant it, I mean it. I truly do. I'm sorry if I gave the wrong impression. Please just think about it. I'll be in in the morning."

"I don't know you from Adam," Consuela said. "Would you kindly get out of my hair?"

"Eleven o'clock," Mr. Vance said. And slipped out.

A little later, Mr. Figueredo poked his head out from his office door and asked Consuela to come in to take a couple of letters. She picked up her steno pad and went into his room, the walls of which were lined with framed photos of Mr. Figueredo standing in front of various charter-boat racks on the dock at Garrison Bight, on the display hooks of which were hung arrays—unimpressive, on the whole—of amberjack and grouper and dolphin and king mackerel. It seemed he always had his picture taken with his catch, no matter how meager. In his early forties, Mr. Figueredo already had some gray hair, frosty in the sideburns on his sallow cheeks. He suffered from piles. He had a thin wife and was respectful of Consuela. (Mr. Torres, on the other hand, had a fat wife and was inclined to pat or even massage Consuela in a more or less fatherly way now and again on her shoulder, or bare arm, or in the small, if it could be called that, of her back.)

"You've been crying," Mr. Figueredo said.

She shook her head to deny it, just as new tears brimmed. Mr. Figueredo reached in a drawer and pulled out a Kleenex and handed it to her. She blew her nose.

"Trouble at home?" Mr. Figueredo asked.

"No. It's right here," Consuela said. She needed another Kleenex. Mr. Figueredo handed her the box.

"We loading too much on you?"

"No. It's my fault. It's nothing."

"Nothing doesn't make a person cry."

"It's not important," Consuela said. "It's just that my files are such a *mess*. It takes me hours to find *any*thing. It's all my *fault*. Please. Let's not talk about it. Let's do the letters."

Mr. Figueredo began, in a kindly voice, to dictate.

With her steno pad open on her lap, her pencil idle, Consuela suddenly cried out, "I hate myself."

"Come on," Mr. Figueredo said. "You've got no reason."

"Look at me!" Consuela shouted. "Just look at me for once."

Mr. Figueredo was obviously embarrassed. "Come on, now. That's enough. Take this down, please."

"You're like everybody else," she said. "You don't realize."

In a quiet voice, insistent, he resumed sounding out a letter to a client. Consuela picked up her pencil.

When Juliana Castanon woke her daughter at six-thirty the next morning, Thursday, Consuela moaned, sat up in bed, and said, "I don't feel good. I'm not going in today."

"I thought this was coming on," Mrs. Castanon said.

"What are you talking about, this was coming on?"

"Honey, I'm your mother. Remember? I know some things."

Consuela, not finding an answer, sagged back down on the bed.

Her mother said, "You want me to call in to the office for you?"

"Okay," Consuela groaned, turning her face to the wall. "You could call Mr. Figueredo at home. About seven-thirty."

But twenty minutes later, before that time, Consuela appeared in the kitchen in a new yellow jumpsuit she'd bought the previous Saturday at J. Byron. "Changed my mind," she said cheerfully to her mother. "They get confused when I'm not there."

"You look like a four-alarm fire," Mrs. Castanon said.

"So call the fire company," Consuela said.

In two hours, between eight-thirty, when Consuela showed up at the office, and ten-thirty, she made at least a dozen bad mistakes. She dropped two clients from the wire, instead of putting them on hold; she broke Mr. Torres's favorite ashtray; she couldn't for the life of her find the message about a discovery hearing that Judge Blanford had given her on the phone for Mr. Figueredo the previous afternoon; she put a call for Mr. Torres on Mr. Figueredo's line; she loaded the wrong paper in the copying machine and jammed the feeder. . . .

At ten-thirty, she suddenly became efficient. That was when Mr. Vance walked in.

"Your appointment isn't until eleven," she said.

"I am aware," he said. "Yesterday you told me you didn't know me from Adam. I thought we should get acquainted. Do you mind if I tell you a little about myself?"

A little? He talked for over half an hour. He had a pleasing voice, deep and orotund. His puppy eyes flashed with the kind of deferential merriment that goes with a wagging tail. This was a person who was used to being pleasing. Somewhere in the torrent of his words he gave notice that he was twenty-six years old, and he asked Consuela how old she was. She wondered out loud if that was any concern of his, and he said he supposed he would have to guess. Twenty-one? Consuela was so used to being sweet to clients that she automatically smiled. Mr. Vance, apparently not bothering to parse the smile, went right on talking.

He presented himself as the hero of a picaresque tale. The end of the story came first: he had been in Key West three months. He seemed to have a bank account somewhere. There had been a past on a sailboat; he told about a fierce storm. In Boston, he had sat in a box at Fenway Park and seen Wade Boggs go five for five. He had watched bears fish for salmon in a river in Alaska. At college—he did not name the institution—he majored in political science; he had dreamed back then of running for the Senate someday. But since then, candidates' negative commercials on TV had soured that dream. He liked to read books by Tony Hillerman, Joseph Conrad, Robert Stone, Robert B. Parker, and George Eliot. The closest he had come to a religious experience was among the sequoias in Muir Woods, in California. His favorite exercise was riding a bike with the ancient big bands—Benny Goodman, Casa Loma, Paul Whiteman—giving him energy on a Walkman. He loved heights, and for the kicks of it he had taken a job for a couple of weeks as a riveters' helper up in the sky, on the beams of a skyscraper a-building in Dallas, along with some Native Americans who had the gift of perfect balance; they tossed hot rivets around as if playing catch on a diamond on terra firma. He liked cross-country skiing, hated downhill. Once, he won eleven hundred dollars in a poker game.

He said he didn't want Consuela to get the wrong idea. He was a serious person. He cared about clean air. He had been shocked to hear about the mysteriously high incidence of multiple sclerosis among the nurses at the Key West hospital. He had volunteered to work with the homeless in Denver. He had . . .

Consuela wondered, as he babbled on: Was fibbing his game? Was he inventing a jumpy, harum-scarum life just for the fun of it? Why didn't he talk about people? Didn't he have any friends?

What he said next was startling, for he seemed to have read her mind. "I've been in love three times," he said. "Once was when I was sixteen. Once in college; that lasted three years. And then there was a gal I really loved in Cleveland. Oh, Lord! Did I say three times? Because I'm in love again now, you know. You must have realized that, Consuela."

He tried to cover what he'd just blurted out by telling a little about each of those other three, but Consuela was suddenly distracted by a dizzying conviction, and she hardly heard what he was saying. Her heart had begun to pound. She had seen those three all too clearly in the eye of her imagination. Beaming round faces, firmly packed limbs, full bosoms, prosperous waists, swooping hips. Dimples in all sorts of odd places—elbows, cheeks, chins, knuckles. Those three were huge. She was sure of it. And she was very angry.

She was not angry at Mr. Vance. She was angry at herself, for imagining such things. This entire loop about fat women—had her mind played her a nasty trick? Here was where she realized how sensitive Mr. Vance was, because, apparently having picked up vibrations of this anger of hers, which she had tried hard to hide, he immediately backed away and changed the subject. He began to tell about a canoe trip on the Penobscot River in Maine. How bad the mosquitoes were.

Just then Consuela looked at the little clock on her desk and saw that it was ten minutes past eleven. She had been supposed to call Mr. Torres to announce Mr. Vance as soon as he arrived, or at five minutes before the hour if he came in early, in order that Mr. Torres could wind up his business with the previous client and keep things going on time. Hastily, feeling guilty, she buzzed him and said, "Mr. Vance has just come in."

Soon Mr. Torres stepped out of his office with the woman he'd been seeing—a messy divorce case—and after ardently shaking her hand with both of his, he greeted Mr. Vance.

As Mr. Vance went by Consuela's desk, he said, "Thank you for your patience, Miss Castanon."

"My pleasure," Consuela said, but this time she didn't smile.

Less than ten minutes later, Mr. Torres came out again with Mr. Vance. Mr. Torres said, "The gentleman wants to pay cash. The usual, Consuela."

"That will be twenty-five dollars, Mr. Vance," Consuela said, as Mr. Torres went back into his office.

Mr. Vance cheerfully took out his wallet and handed the money to Consuela. "I'll be by again," he said.

"Did you want another appointment?"

"Yes, with you," he said, and before she could think what to say, he had turned and left.

That afternoon, taking some letters in to Mr. Torres, she stood by his desk and asked him what kind of day it had been. Anything interesting? He started talking about Mrs. Carrero's divorce case. Consuela picked up some papers from Mr. Torres's out basket. She asked, offhand, what the young man who came in after Mrs. Carrero—was his name Mr. Vance?—had wanted.

"Oh, that was ridiculous," Mr. Torres said. "He wanted to know what you had to do in Key West if you wanted to get married—you know, did you have to get a Wassermann test, where should you go for a license. So on. I told him he didn't need a lawyer, he could have just called up the city."

"That was dumb of him," Consuela said.

"I liked the guy," Mr. Torres said. "He was, you know, kind of wet behind the ears, but—I don't know—sincere."

"He seemed polite enough," Consuela said. "But still, twenty-five bucks. That was kind of dumb, wasn't it?"

"As a matter of fact," Mr. Torres said, with a teasing look in his eyes, "he complimented me on our receptionist. How's that for dumb?"

"That really was," Consuela said. Feeling a blush rise in her cheeks, she wheeled abruptly to leave, caught the sole of her new yellow wedgies in the shag carpet, lost her footing for a second, and dropped Mr. Torres's papers all over the place. "Oh, man," she said, going down on her hands and knees to gather them up. "Who's dumb is me."

Life speeded up for Consuela Castanon in the next few days. At dinner at home, on the following Friday evening, just over a week later, she suddenly said, looking radiant, "Guess what."

"You got a raise," her father said in a reflexive response to her happy look.

"From those two tightwads?" Mrs. Castanon said.

"It's not that," Consuela said.

"So?" her mother said.

Consuela looked first at her father and then at her mother, and softly she said, dropping her eyes to the plate in front of her, "I'm engaged to be married."

This announcement was greeted by a long, long, long silence from both parents.

At last Consuela's mother said, "You said yes and you never brought this person around to the house? I can't believe what I just heard."

Her father said, "Isn't this a bit sudden?"

"First of all," Consuela said, "I am twenty-one years old. I'm an adult, right?"

"Who *is* this person?" her mother asked.

She told her mother and father all about her Tommy. Everything. Even about being way up there on a bare girder in the Dallas skyscraper on a windy day with the American Indian workmen firing white-hot rivets at each other as fast as arrows. The more she said, the more appalled her mother became. Consuela could see that her father was gradually easing around to her side, but her mother began to break in on her with wild shouts.

"Only been in Key West three months, this drifter?" . . . "No job?" . . . "You never laid eyes on an ID, credit card, nothing like that—how could you know his *name* is even real?" . . . "He's so sweet and sensitive, how come he don't mention the name of his bank?" . . . "Is he some kind of Unitarian or Holy Roller, or you don't know if he even believes in God?" . . . "He says college, but you have no idea which one?" . . . "What can this no-job know about the way we live?"

Finally a question that Consuela's mother asked broke it for her. "Has this creep been in your great big pants? Is that what this is all about?"

Consuela slammed her fist down on the tablecloth, making all the plates jump, and she rose to leave, knocking her chair over backward.

"Jesus, Juliana!" Consuela's father said.

Consuela was out the door when her mother shouted, twice, "I forbid it! I forbid it!"

Consuela's face appeared in the doorway. "Just try," she said.

The sensitive point was this: Tommy had. Been in her pants. Or at least, one of his hands had.

The week had gone by in a torrent of breathtaking surprises. On the Friday, the day after his appointment with Mr. Torres, Tommy had come in the office "just to talk—to correct some impressions I maybe gave you yesterday." Consuela felt confused and irritable while he was there—what would Mr. Torres or Mr. Figueredo think if one of them saw him hanging around?—but after he left she thought about the nice round tones of his voice and about a zany impulse she had had, and had stifled, thank God, to say something kind, something comforting. His eyes were so sad. For a few moments she got the shivers.

All day on that Saturday Consuela mooned away the hours, lying on her bed reading trash and listening to radio music from Havana, the way she used to do when she was in high school. By suppertime she was in a foul mood. Her father seemed especially annoying at the table, making eating noises and talking too loud with her mother. She was about to get up and call her girlfriend Jennifer, to see if she wanted to go to a movie, when the phone rang. She ran to answer it. "Tommy here," the voice said. He asked her to come over awhile. He was staying at The Samoa, he said, a little guesthouse at 1203 Southard, room 4-A, just walk right up, wouldn't it be nice to sit around and chew the rag awhile? Consuela hung up and told her mother it had been her friend Jennifer, she was going over to see her, maybe they'd take in a movie, she wouldn't be late, could she have the car?

Tommy's small room was tidy; all his belongings that showed were lined up as neat as the keys of a piano. He sat on his bed, she on the one chair in the room. They just talked. Tommy ate her up with his eyes. At about eleven she said she thought she'd better be going. He didn't offer to take her to the car.

That got to be the routine in the evenings. He made it clear that she should come over after dark. When she reached his room on Monday evening, he was already sitting on the bed, and he patted the mattress beside him, and quite naturally she sat down there. He held her hand and made love to her with words. She had never had such nice things said to her by anyone. He said she seemed to him an angel of curving lines. She was like the pink full moon at first rising—big coming up over the horizon. Her hand was as soft as silk from Siam. Her legs were made of whipped cream.

On Tuesday evening, at about ten o'clock, he kissed her. It was the first time she had ever been kissed in earnest by a man. He was very gentle. Both his hands were moving around on her, more or less measuring her. Yes, yes, she said, she would marry him. This was when his left hand wriggled under the belt of her slacks and caressed her lower abdomen. She put a hand on top of his. Was this to stop him or encourage him? She had no way of knowing.

He withdrew his hand and said he would get a license the next morning. She asked, shouldn't she go with him? No, no, it wouldn't be necessary. Mr. Torres had explained it all. Key West, he'd said, likes to make everything real easy for people. One member of the couple had to fill out the form and give them a check for fifty-two fifty. And that would be it. "And then, Consuela, they'll give me my ticket to heaven."

And the very next evening, Wednesday, there he was, sitting

on his bed, waving a piece of paper at her when she came in the door. The license!

In her excitement she wanted to make all sorts of plans. She said, "Shouldn't we go out someplace and celebrate? I've never even tasted champagne. Let's go out and have some champagne!"

And she asked, "Will you come and meet my mom and pop? I've told them about you, and they're dying to meet you."

She also suggested, "We've got to look for a place to live. I have a friend who just got a job at Knight Realty; she could help us find something."

She said, "I think we should have a two-ring ceremony. Wouldn't you like to wear a ring too, Tommy?"

His answers seemed agreeable. He said, "Champagne gives me a headache, but sure thing, we should have some fun" and "I'd love to know your parents" and "I can afford the rent, no problem" and "Hey, two rings would be great" and . . .

But something was missing. He never said, When? When would you like to do this or that? When would be convenient?

She noticed this, but she didn't press him, because she was drunk. She was drunk on his sweetness to her, with the joy and abandon and failure of doubt of someone who'd never had an intoxicating drink before. And then he said, "The nicest way to celebrate I could think of would be just to lie down here beside you. Just for a minute. I wouldn't take any liberties. Just to be beside my fiancée."

He stood up to put the license on top of the bureau, and she stretched out on the bed to please him. He lay beside her. He kissed her, and his hands moved around on her, very tenderly, indeed taking no liberties, not reaching under her slacks this time. Again it was as if his hands were taking measurements of various parts of her. He groaned in delight when they calipered her right thigh. Again he groaned as his gentle fingertips took the dimensions of her left breast. "You're from a painting by

Rubens!" he exclaimed. "I would love to see you in the altogether." Then he kissed her some more. He stopped just as she felt she was reaching the moment of abandon. She was dizzy when she got up. Later, she couldn't remember how she got home.

The next day she was bad-tempered. She sat at her desk thinking about things. About how she had started living two lives. One was her life at large. In it, she moved around freely, walked to the office in the mornings, over Von Phister to Reynolds, up to United, across to Whitehead, and five blocks up to the office, a good stroll, a bonfire of calories. Then the office. Tommy always called once a day, at precisely eleven-fifteen—between office appointments. Lunch wherever she wanted, sometimes with Jennifer, or Alejandra, or Polly. A little sleepy at her desk in the afternoon. Home on foot by suppertime. A quarrel with her mother: "Where *is* this Adonis?" . . . "I think this lover is in your head; you made the whole thing up, right?" . . . "Don't you think you better have a talk with Father Valdéz?" And then, in the evening . . .

Then, in the evening, the other life. In a box. The room was like a box. She was like a pet rabbit in a box. Perhaps she shouldn't think rabbit. A pet something. The box was nice enough. On two walls, old engravings of the Custom House and the ruins of the East Martello Tower. Silly lace curtains at a window that looked out on a kind of wall of thick foliage; no one could peep in. A teakwood chiffonier. And—well, she wasn't sure she wanted to think about the bed. Anyway, a chenille spread. Good springs, oh . . . Always arrive after dark. Why? Enter the box. Be admired in the box, be praised, kissed, touched by trembling hands. Leave the box, finally, and go back in a thick fog of a baffling mood to the other life, the life at large.

Thinking these thoughts, she got a sliding feeling in her stomach, a feeling of fear mixed with pleasure. She suddenly realized how much she loved being loved by her mother, all the hullaballoo and hollering was really love, after all—and this, too, frightened her. She wanted to tell Jennifer she was going to get married. She wanted to announce her engagement in the *Citizen*. She wanted to taste champagne, somewhere outside the box. She wanted a wedding at the church, Father Valdéz, organ music. She wanted to live one life, not two.

That night she lost her virginity. Lost? She gave it away. To begin with, soon after she arrived in the box of wild desire, she freely offered to let Tommy see her as a figure in a Rubens painting, in the altogether. She took her clothes off. She stood there. He asked her to turn around, and she revolved. He groaned and said, "You are the Goddess of Plenty, and I'll worship you for the rest of my life." After that, he invited her to recline. He used that word. She got on the bed, naked. He sat on the mattress beside her, fully clothed. "Imagine that we're in a painting. We're on the bank of a stream, near some woods, and we're having a *fête champêtre*." She didn't know exactly what that meant; it frightened her a little, but the last word sounded a bit like champagne, so she thought it was probably all right. He gazed at her awhile; she felt as if his glances were considering her—delightedly weighing every cubic inch of her. Then he, too, removed his clothes and reclined beside her. There seemed to be a good deal of kissing of new sorts to be got through, and of sweet measuring of everything with loving hands, until she was almost out of her mind, and then, quickly, it was done. She had given him her gift. He was very dear, and she wept for joy.

Her happiness the next morning was on the edge of being unbearable. She sat at her desk. She felt as if she were listening to Radio Havana; she wanted to cha-cha-cha on top of her desk. Now she had the confidence to tell Tommy that they were going to have to have a life at large. They were going to live one life. They were going to leave the box and go out into the world together. Her family couldn't help liking him; he would look at her mother with his petitioning eyes, and she'd fall for him, she'd stop complaining. They'd find a place to live. Maybe she could persuade Tommy to go and have a talk with Father Valdéz. First of all, of course, they would set a date.

For a while she thought she would announce these and other upcoming changes in their lives right that morning, when he made his eleven-fifteen call; then she decided to wait and break it to him that evening. She wanted to look him in the eye. She had absolutely no doubt of her power. He would helplessly agree.

When she entered the box that night, Tommy was sitting on the bed. She sat down in the chair against the wall, facing him.

"Hey, sweetheart," Tommy said, patting the mattress. "Over here."

"Just a minute. I want to talk a minute."

All afternoon she had rehearsed what she would say. She had been sure of her words, which were full of love and persuasion and consequence. But now she brought herself up sharp. She was amazed at what she heard herself say.

"I have a present for you."

"All right!" he said.

"Want to know what it is?"

"Do I have to unwrap it? I'd like to unwrap you!"

She felt as if she hadn't heard him. "My present is . . ." She had to breathe. "I'm going to reduce."

"You're . . . ?"

"I know I can. I know it's just eating, that's all it is. You'll see. I'll get completely down to normal. Tommy, Tommy, I'll do it for you."

Something peculiar was happening to Tommy's face.

"I've wanted to do this for years. Years and years. You've given me what I've needed all along, in order to know I can do it."

Then, looking at him, she understood that she was angry. This was something like the anger she'd felt the other day in the office, when he talked about his three loves. His other three loves. But now she was angry not at herself but at him.

"Usually when a person gets a present he says, 'Thank you.' "

"Hey, come on over here." He was patting the bed again.

It took a while for her to realize she couldn't help herself. She got up and sat on the bed beside him. She felt her anger swerve heavily toward herself.

This time he helped her undress. The same things happened as before, yet they were not the same. His spanning fingers had no tremor. His kisses didn't reach into her being. She felt, in what seemed to be love's labor, the force of some awful mistake she couldn't name. . . .

At her desk, the next morning, a jumble of thoughts raced through her mind. She was still excited by what she had offered to Tommy. She wanted to talk with him about it some more. There was a puzzle wrapped up in this desire; she would unravel that later. There had been a hush, a silence, when they got dressed afterward last night, a feeling of waiting for suitable words. She'd had none. She hovered, on this account, now, on the edge of some kind of shame; the embers of her exhilarating anger had gone to ash. She thought a little about how happy she'd been yesterday, polishing the speech she planned to make. Her feeling, all day, of so much strength.

This morning was a hectic one. There seemed to be more phone calls than usual. Numerous appointments. Both partners called on her to take letters. She did her work passably well. She felt hurried, though, typing the letters, with so much on her mind.

A client walked in for an appointment with Mr. Figueredo. She glanced at the digital clock on her desk. Shocked by it, she quickly checked her wristwatch. Yes, it was eleven twenty-seven.

He hadn't called. He must have been delayed somehow. There was no phone in his room; he called from a pay booth; maybe someone had been making a long call in the booth.

She tried to go back to typing. She made a slew of typos. Two more clients came in at noon. She didn't dare go out to lunch, in case he should call.

She survived the longest afternoon of her life. Mr. Figueredo and Mr. Torres left together at a few minutes past five. She locked up, and instead of going home, she walked all the way across Fleming to The Samoa. In broad daylight. She made her way up the stairs to 4-A. The door was locked. She went down to the entrance hall and pressed the button with the little sign below it: RING FOR MANAGER.

After a few minutes a woman in a baggy cotton dress and bedroom slippers came down from the second floor. "Can I help you?" she said.

"Do you know when Mr. Vance will be back? Did he say when he'd be back?"

The woman tugged at her messy hair. "Oh, honey," she said, "he checked out. Early this morning."

Consuela's heart jumped. How wonderful! Her gift, her promise, had brought him around. He had known, without her even telling him, that it was time to leave the box. To have a single life with her out in the world. "You see," she said to the lady manager, "we're engaged. He knew we couldn't both live in 4-A. It's very nice, but two of us . . . Myself, I was thinking of, you know, one of those low-cost apartments in the Truman Annex? Did you get to know him at all?"

The woman shrugged in her ill-fitting dress.

Consuela felt a moment's hesitation. "He's a very unusual person," she said.

"I guess you could say that again," the woman said.

There was something not quite right in the sound of these words as they came out of the lady manager's mouth, and

Consuela wasn't sure she liked the way the woman was looking at her, with her head canted to one side. She heard herself asking, a little too loud, "Just what did you mean by that?"

The woman shrugged again and looked at the wall. "Didn't mean anything special, dear," she said. Then she looked at Consuela and said in a rather quarrelsome way, "Your boyfriend checked out. He paid his bill and went, you know. I didn't mean to offend you."

They're Signaling!

Mr. William Adee Whitehead is roused in the middle of the night by an urgent rapping on the front door of his house. He has been having a restless night. All Key West is on the qui vive. Nerves are raw. Every scrap of the news from Indian Key is scarifying. Many of the people who were killed in the recent massacre there had kinfolk in Key West, and anecdotes of the terrors suffered during the raid have been flying around town.

We now see Mr. Whitehead, having lit a kerosene lantern, descending the stairs to the street door in his nightgown, nightcap, and slippers, to see who has been knocking at this unpropitious hour. He is tall and broad-shouldered, and even with his slouching tasseled nightcap and in a sweat-dampened cotton nightgown that reaches below his knees, his bearing is impressive. He is still a young man—in his late twenties—but he is looked up to, as if he were a graybeard, by the townspeople. What counts, of course, is that his family holds a quarter interest in the ownership of the island. His house is on the street—so far barely more than a wide dirt track—that bears his surname. The street was in fact named for his older brother John, who bought a quarter share of the island from John Simonton sixteen years ago, for a price rumored to have been six hundred dollars. John Whitehead no longer lives in Key West—he has gone on to higher flights of finance in New Orleans—and William has taken his place as a kind of proprietary elder (though youngish) statesman in town. William moved here a decade ago, at the age of eighteen, surveyed and mapped the entire island when he was nineteen, and became collector of customs before he had had enough birthdays to be called a man. He still holds that lucrative post.

He opens the door. He holds the lantern high, and its dim light washes a face that is haggard with anxiety. It belongs to Mr. Alden A. M. Jackson, who, besides being the schoolmaster, is a respected, hardheaded town councilman. Tonight, as it happens, his turn has come to serve as captain of the Guard, in command of the rotating land patrol of citizen volunteers who range round the town every night for the security of the townspeople. The Guard has chartered a schooner to fetch arms and ammunition from Havana. For two years the Indian wars on the Florida mainland have had everyone in Key West fearful that the natives would string the wampum of their rage down the necklace of the Keys, and now the recent nearby massacre on Indian Key has brought the town to the edge of panic.

Mr. Whitehead can plainly see that Mr. Jackson, habitually a sobersides, is at this moment wildly a-twitter. He is practically incoherent. "Indians!" he says in a hoarse whisper, looking over his shoulder as if expecting to be jumped and scalped at that very moment. "A raid! They're signaling!"

Mr. Whitehead worms it out of Mr. Jackson that a mysterious drumming has been heard. It cannot be heard from here; it comes from near the burying ground, or perhaps from inside it. Its rhythms are irregular, sometimes syncopated, sometimes agitated and speedy, interrupted now and then by brief pauses and ominous silences. The Guard has so far not dared to close in on the place from which the signals are coming. They fear an ambush, for which the drumming might be designed as a lure. Mr. Jackson urges Mr. Whitehead to come with him to the barracks, to see if the Guard's drum has by any chance been stolen. If it has, a general alarm should surely go out.

In ordinary circumstances, Mr. Whitehead would undoubtedly have been skeptical of this errand. Did it make sense that the Indians would risk stealing a drum from the stronghold of the Guard? But he, too, has heard from the mouths of some of the survivors their reports of what had so recently happened on Indian Key, and he has become credulous.

About two weeks ago, Indian spies evidently observed that the revenue cutters Flint *and* Atrego, *carrying a force of men stationed at Tea Table Key, a mile from Indian Key, sailed north for Cape Florida and Cape Sable as reinforcements for the white men's mainland troops. Only one officer and ten sick men were left at Tea Table—forlorn protection for Indian Key.*

At between two and three in the morning, a night or two after the departure of the cutters, Mr. J. Glass, who lived on the waterfront of Indian Key, happening to be awake, looked out his window and saw in the moonlight many canoes pulled up among the rocks on his shoreline. He ran next door and wakened Mr. J. F. Beiglet, and the two men hurried to give the alarm to Captain Housman, a wily wrecker and more or less the king of the key, but as they crossed the town square, they were surprised by some Indians who were slinking along the fence of Captain Housman's yard. The Indians at once began screaming and shooting. Mr. Glass ran and hid under the Second Street Wharf, and Mr. Beiglet let himself down into a cistern under Captain Housman's warehouse. Those two survived.

Others were less fortunate. Hearing the shouting and shooting, Captain Elliott Smith, on Fourth Street, went down into the cistern under his house, along with his wife and baby daughter and his wife's twelve-year-old brother, and they stayed there, up to their necks in water, for six hours, during which time the house was burned down over their heads, causing them hideous torments. The little brother was suffocated to death.

Just before dawn, the Indians found Captain Mott, his wife and two children, and his mother-in-law hiding in a shed behind their house. The captors shot the grandmother, strangled the baby and threw it into the sea, seized the older daughter, a four-year-old, and dashed her brains out on a porch pillar. Finding Mott and his wife still alive, the attackers beat them to death with clubs and set their clothes and their hair on fire.

A sad loss was Dr. Henry Perrine, a horticulturist, who, on a grant from the U.S. Congress, had been successfully planting, on Matecumbe and Lignum Vitae keys, seeds of many varieties of exotic tropical and subtropical plants, including mahogany and other hardwoods, which he had brought from Mexico and Central and South America, to show that Florida's soil and climate would support all such plants. He had rented Indian Key's largest house, which stood on stilts at the very edge of the sea and had a trapdoor leading down to the family's private bathing place, a walled enclosure that admitted the tides through floodgates. Wakened by gunfire and breaking glass and wild yells, Dr. Perrine hurried his family down into the seawater there. He did not join them, because he felt that for his family's safety he must hide the trapdoor with some bags of flour and corn from the kitchen storeroom. Later, the family heard Dr. Perrine, up above, trying to reason with the Indians in Spanish, but then they heard curdling war whoops and a single shot.

Aware of the hullabaloo on Indian Key, the officer on Tea Table rousted out the ten sick men and loaded them on a small barge with two four-pound swivel guns. The feverish soldiers muddleheadedly put aboard bags of six-pound shot, instead of four-pound shot, and when they simultaneously fired both guns at a crowd of the raiders on the Indian Key wharf, the overloaded guns did back somersaults right off the barge, into the sea. The Indians shot at the vessel and killed one man, and the rescue mission hastily withdrew to its sickbeds.

The next day, only one of the score of houses on Indian Key remained standing. That house belonged to Mr. Charles Howe, who was a Freemason. After the raid, survivors discovered that the Indians had found Mr. Howe's Masonic apron, with its mystical pyramid and all-seeing eye, and they had carefully spread it out on the kitchen table, no doubt in awe and fear, and had skulked away.

With these and many other pictures vivid in his mind, Mr. Whitehead readily agrees to go with Mr. Jackson to look for the Guard's drum. He decides that if there are indeed Indians preparing an attack, he should not leave his wife alone in the house. Soon, therefore, we witness a bizarre march: Mr. Jackson, armed, in step with Mr. Whitehead in his nightgown and Mrs. Whitehead in a quilted cotton pinafore, which she has thrown on over her bedclothes, pacing down Front Street in the pale light of a gibbous moon, to the guardsmen's barracks.

The drum is there; it has not been stolen by the Indians.

What now? Mr. Whitehead is a man who does not like to be puzzled. Unlocking the Guard's racks, he takes out a long gun. Then he leaves Mrs. Whitehead under protection of the barracks sentry and orders Mr. Jackson to lead him to the area where the drumming has been heard. The two men go in a generally southeasterly direction, on unpaved streets at first, and later along tracks to isolated houses at the edge of town.

"Hush," Mr. Jackson whispers, putting his hand on Mr. Whitehead's arm.

Yes. Mr. Whitehead can hear it. The rhythms are strange. Rushed, then slower, then silence for a time, then a slow beat, then again accelerando.

The time has come when a man's mettle must be tested. Mr. Whitehead whispers to Mr. Jackson that he should stay where he is, to provide covering fire if needed. Then he goes down on hands and knees and crawls—awkwardly because of the length of his nightgown—toward the source of the sound. His squirming figure, like that of a fat caterpillar crawling out on a leaf, is all too visible in the half-light from the moon. He is as brave as any Indian brave, and more foolish by far. He recognizes that he is approaching the isolated home of Mr. Charles Schrumm. Have the natives taken the house, killed the owner?

The drumming is louder now. Creeping ever closer, and doing a kind of push-up, the better to see what's ahead, Mr. Whitehead discovers the drummer. He gasps.

The Schrumms' dog, a large crossbred hound used for treeing rats, is perched on the wooden cap of the owner's cistern, scratching fleas. Its hind leg beats on the wood in varied rhythms, responding to the various degrees of torment the fleas are causing. The hollow cistern below resonates the drummed sounds of doom for Key West town.

A Game of Anagrams

Three poets and a novelist play anagrams in Key West every Wednesday afternoon.

You will recognize the poets' names. They are Paladin, Forester, and Drum. Leonard Drum, of course, not Robert Drum the physicist.

The poets are comfortable with each other, because all three have won both the Pulitzer Prize and the National Book Award. Two of them, Forester and Drum, have also won the Bollingen, but Paladin is not envious on this account. He recently sold his translation of *Beowulf* to Universal Studios for a saga film for a sum he commonly speaks of as having had seven figures (though, to tell the truth, two of the seven came after a decimal point), and so he feels able to console himself for that one deficiency and to wear handmade-to-order loafers.

The novelist, Chalker, has also taken a Pulitzer, as readers with good long memories may recall, for his novel *Retorts*. He is very thin and is rather a bad sport. And he smokes.

The other three have given up smoking. No. This is not literally true. What *is* true of one of the three self-proclaimed nonsmokers, Forester, is that he has stopped buying cigarettes. He has been known to strip two or three friends of their entire supplies in the course of an evening's party. Since he has the illusion that he is "giving up smoking," he particularly likes to borrow unfiltered Camels, so as to make his "last few puffs mean something." During the anagrams games he borrows only one or two Marlboros from Chalker, unless he gets ahead. Poor old Drum has read up on the hazards of "passive smoking," but he has much too good manners to ask Chalker and Forester to refrain. For his part, Chalker has noticed that Drum repugnantly turns his head away and holds his breath when a puff of smoke accidentally floats his way, and sometimes, when he, Chalker, is about to make a tricky change in one of his words or is going to steal someone else's and may not want Drum, who is seated to his left and has the next turn, to be too closely aware of the move, he lets fly—perhaps he doesn't even know he does this—with a puff out of the left side of his mouth, and Drum obligingly turns away.

Paladin weighs two hundred and eighty pounds and is, with his left hand, so to speak, a lexicographer. Besides his *Beowulf* and many slim volumes of poetry, he has published three dictionaries, one of Elizabethan English, one of Midwestern U.S. slang, and one of words with seven letters. This definitional avocation tends to make him positive about his challenges of the authenticity of some of the words the others make in the game, and the worst of it is, he is sometimes right. His triumphant demeanor makes those sometimeses so memorable that the others have come to give a bit more respect to his opinions than they deserve.

Readers of Forester's poems will recall the profusion of fauna in them. The critic Bouvier has spoken of this poet's exemplifying the possibility that a person's name may come in the long run to shape his bent, and commenting on the woodsiness of Forester's poems, he speaks of "the moral force of the man's bestiary, set so lavishly among the trees." The other three players have come to expect Forester to purloin their own little prize wordlets, again and again, and to rescramble them into the names of very obscure creatures—extant, extinct, mythical. It takes courage to challenge any of the ditsy zoa Forester trots out.

Lord knows what leaning Drum's name should have caused in him—though, come to think of it, he is rather famous, in his poetry readings, for resonating his stresses, particularly where they fall on plosives in dactyls, and he is sometimes called a latter-day Vachel Lindsay, after that notorious word-thumper of the thirties. Emphatic though he may be at the podium, he is by nature mild and ultrapeaceable; a delicate flinch crosses his face when competitive sparks fly across the anagrams table, as they sometimes do in bright blue heat. But what really matters in the game is that Drum cares about what he eats and drinks, and the other players grow cautious whenever he shuffles the tiles in front of him into arcane names of cordon bleu delicacies, or of recherché mixed drinks, or of highly spiced Asian dishes that have somehow steamed their way into the dictionaries.

For several years in his boyhood, bad-tempered Chalker was dragooned by his conventional suburban yacht-clubby parents into racing in tiny sailboats of the class with the unfortunate name Wood Pussy on Long Island Sound. Drifting in the notorious calms on that body of water, he used to daydream—invariably, therefore, because of inattention, coming in last—to daydream of all the vast lore of the oceans. This has paid off in two ways. Always doing so badly in the races inclined him, later on, toward seeing if he could do a little better in life with the help of some minor cheating; and secondly, the richness of those daydreams, reinforced by bonings up in the *Book of Knowledge* and the *Britannica*, and by later, more sophisticated readings, has made him a big threat to the others in anagrams whenever the remotest nautical or pelagic possibilities turn up: THOLE, DIATOM, VANG, MIZZEN.

Very well. We now know something about the players' specialties, or perhaps we should say their various favorite objective correlatives. Let's sit by and very quietly watch as they gather for a game on a Wednesday afternoon around a card table in Forester's living room, in his modest converted conch house in a compound on Grinnell Street. Mrs. Forester has shut herself in her dressing-room-cum-office upstairs, perhaps to distance herself discreetly from the noisy bonding these games always seem to generate. Paladin spills onto the tabletop a profusion of wooden letter tiles from a frazzled gray flannel bag that obviously once protected a silver something-or-other from tarnish; he long ago assembled the proper anagrams mix of letters by cannibalizing parts of two sets of Scrabble tiles, with their small numbers of valuation incised on them. Still standing at the table, the four turn all the pieces facedown and stir them around.

The first decision that must be made is where the players shall sit. Each turns up a letter; they then take seats around the table in the alphabetical order of their choices. Paladin is well satisfied not to be placed to the left of Forester, who is very good at the game, meaning that whoever plays after him is liable to be on starvation corner. Chalker, for his part, is delighted to have Drum once again on *his* left, or to leeward, as he thinks of it, in case a nicotine attack becomes necessary.

Now the players, flipping their seating-order letters facedown again, divide the mass of tiles into four more or less equal portions and slide them to the corners of the table, leaving the center free as their playground. Then each turns up another letter, to determine who goes first. Paladin draws an A, so he will lead off. The others have turned up R, L, and W. Those four letters remain exposed in the center space, and the players draw yet again, this time cupping the letters out of sight of the others. All is now arranged, and the four men are poised to start.

Before Paladin makes his first move, it may be helpful, for the sake of those of our kibitzing readers who are vague about how the game is played, to give an all too brief description of it (omitting minor quirks some obsessive players occasionally insist upon). Taking turns, picking out one facedown tile at a time and keeping its letter hidden from the other players, and perhaps drawing on whatever letters may be showing in a pool of discards in middle of the table, the players will try to form words of at least three letters and then build longer words by adding one or more letters at a time to change their meanings anagrammatically; they may alter their own words or, much better, steal and rearrange their opponents' words. Thus BUN may become BURN, then BRUNT, then perhaps BLUNTER, and so on. A player who has finished his turn deposits a leftover letter in his hand in the hope-giving reservoir of tiles at the center of the table. There may come a time when a player takes a chance on a complex combination of letters that he asserts (hopes? pretends?) is a perfectly good word; another asserts (hopes? pretends?) it is a perfectly good word; another player—here, as we've said, it's apt to be the huge, didactic Paladin—may doubt its existence and challenge. The dictionary in use on a given day (Forester's this afternoon is the newest *American Heritage Dictionary*) decides the issue, and whoever is wrong loses not only face but also his next turn. The player who winds up with eight intact words wins.

This bare-bones description of the game gives no idea of the interminable ponderings we will sit through with these players, the sighs, the yelps like those of little foxes, and the catacombic moans, and sudden eye-snaps of recognition, and tiles moved into place with trembling fingers, and, after thefts, victims' tightened lips hastily modulating into halfheartedly admiring smiles at inspired outrages of robbery. There are also, it must be said, wonderful bursts of laughter that come from these four, for they do enjoy their follies.

Paladin makes his move. Without a moment's hesitation, he forms the word WAR and places it facing away from him toward the center of the table. We innocent onlookers may wonder, why WAR? Why not a less confrontational word, RAW? Or LAW, for that matter, using the L that lies out there, instead of the R? How Paladin looms and glowers!

Never mind. Forester has drawn a secret E, and he steals WAR and makes it WARE.

Drum hums a brief tune expressive of doubt, and asks, "Shouldn't that be plural?"

A scornful rumble, a sound as of tectonic plates shifting deep.

"Just wondered," Drum says, shrugging.

Forester, not seeing anything more he can do after his next draw, puts an A out in the pool. Paladin will not have failed to notice that Forester has committed a rare goof: he could have changed WARE to AWARE.

When Drum's turn comes, he picks up the A and L from the pool and adds his hidden E to make ALE. That's all for him. Is he planning an Englishy menu?

Paladin has drawn an S, and he slides Forester's WARE his way and makes it SWEAR. Again, we may pause to wonder at the aggression in the big man's choice. Why not WEARS?

As the turns go by, a Q turns up in the reservoir, and surprisingly soon a U, and it is Forester who makes QUA.

In his next turn, Chalker draws another S, takes the SWEAR word away from Paladin, and spells WRASSE.

"Come again," Forester says, outraged. "What's *that?*"

"It's a family of spiny-finned fishes," Chalker of the seven seas rather smugly says. "There's one species, right out here on the reef—you can sometimes see them from the glass-bottomed boat—that have the remarkable talent of being able to change their sex at will. Let's say too few guys around, a female wrasse does a voluntary sex change. Just like that."

"That's what comes from swimming off Key West," Drum says.

Paladin dryly says, "The word 'wrasse' comes from the Cornish, meaning 'hag.' "

"Good God," Forester says, having pulled far back from any thought of challenging.

While Paladin was making his etymological pronouncement, Chalker sneaked QUA away from Forester and made it AQUA.

At his turn, Paladin draws an H, and perhaps somewhat sedated for the moment by having one-upped Forester on "wrasse," he fails altogether to see how the H might be used, along with the ALE sitting out there in front of Drum. He drops the H out in the pool.

Forester's eyes are hooded. He has an S. He reaches, with the absent look of a meditating Buddhist, for Chalker's AQUA, slowly drifting the letters over his way. Half the battle, in this foursome's anagrams, lies in the air of confidence with which a player shapes up a word that is the least bit freakish, and Forester is a master of the sleepy, knowing look. He pulls the H from the middle, reveals his S, and makes QUASHA.

We now see a revealing flush—vulnerability? hesitation?—splotching Paladin's face. He—even he—has often in past games been gored by one and another of Forester's animals. He reads the word in the most noncommittal tone of voice. "Quasha." There does not seem to be the slightest sound of a question mark in his delivery of the word.

"Came across it in *Piers Plowman*," Forester says, with his bland air of the seminar instructor. "A pest in the countryside, as I remember. Something . . . something like a weasel. Stood as a metaphor, seems to me, for a deadly sin. I can't remember exactly . . . covetousness, I think." He stares Paladin straight in the eye as he names the sin.

Paladin has a faraway look; he seems to be riffling through some sort of large memorized pages in a book in his mind, perhaps those of Skeats's *Etymological Dictionary*, in a frantic reach for a clue. You can read on his face that he hasn't the faintest memory of having run across anything like a quasha in the Beowulf legends and that the word is not to be found, either, in his Elizabethan dictionary, during the compilation of which he dredged Skeats till the pages were ragged. Still, with this tricky Forester fellow . . .

"Oh, hell"—Chalker, furious at having lost a word and unable to wait for Paladin to come out of his bulky funk. "I'll challenge that one. Sounds phony as a three-dollar bill."

Drum, made uncomfortable by the bad vibes he feels hovering over the table, reaches for the dictionary. "No," he finally says in a soft voice, not wanting to hurt Forester's feelings. "I can't find it. . . . Not here."

"That's strange," Forester says, looking not the least chagrined. "I could have sworn . . ."

"I do see 'quassia,' pronounced the same way," Drum hurriedly offers, evidently hoping to avert a storm over Forester's shameless invention. "Says it's a drug, taken from the heartwood of some kind of South American tree. Cures roundworm."

Forgiveness does not make a showing on Paladin's face. Chalker, however, is so happy at having got AQUA back, as a result of his successful challenge, that he, too, misses the possible use of the H now restored to the pool because of QUASHA's collapse. He passes.

Gentle Drum slides the H his way and, in the spirit of a peacemaker, changes ALE to HEAL.

In the next few minutes, while other plays are being made, Chalker grabs HEAL and makes it LEACH, and on his next move, Paladin steals LEACH and adds two letters to make CHOLERA. As we who are watching intercept a triumphant look that the big man throws Forester's way, we may wonder again at the malignancy of Paladin's choices. CHOLERA was clever, but why not CHORALE?

Forester, whose turn is next, gets that guru's-trance look again. He has a B, and neatly sliding the brand-new word with his thumb and forefinger from Paladin's stack to his own, he takes his time transforming the dread disease into BACHELOR.

Chalker exclaims, "Hey! That's classy!"—making us wonder a little about his true attitude toward Paladin, for surely he must have noticed that though Paladin may only have lost a word for a disease, he looks now very much as if he'd contracted one. He seems seriously dehydrated.

Soon another interesting progression is unfolding. Forester has formed EKE, muttering, "That won't have a long half-life."

It doesn't. Chalker, of course, makes KEEL, and Drum, his mouth perhaps watering, follows at once with LEEKS. Forester, with another H in hand, then does a rather brilliant SHEKEL.

Paladin, still a little pale but carefully keeping his voice calm, asks with an irony as heavy as his jowls, "What kind of beast is *that?* Quadruped, by any chance?"

"The male of the species," Forester coolly says, "is called a buck, the female goes by the name of doe. I believe its natural habitat," Forester adds, "is in the wilds around Beverly Hills."

Drum, thinking this last crack a bit close to the bone, glances nervously at Paladin, who, however, remains copious in his silence.

The word SHEKEL holds its heat for two rounds, but then Paladin, having drawn a C, and yelping out a delighted "Ha!," takes it and seems to aim HECKLES straight at Forester.

We who are watching have begun to wonder whether the Bollingen has weighed a bit more heavily in the balance of things than we had thought. Paladin, however, has been doing well in other plays we have not noted here, and at present the board stands as follows:

Paladin

FRUMP
BOMB
ROB
HECKLES
BEG

Forester

LAMB
LANGUR
BACHELOR
PAT

Drum

Chalker

AQUA
WRASSE

Forester's LANGUR caused a bit of a flurry when he stole a RANG that Drum had made, but Forester sounded very firm, saying it was a long-tailed monkey with bushy eyebrows, and none of the others thought he would have the brass to invent two whole-cloth animals in such quick succession. The word went unchallenged, and a good thing too, because the dictionary would have made an additional monkey of the doubter.

Poor Drum has been cleaned out, but soon he gets his chance. Forester quite beautifully converts Paladin's BEG (not Paladin's kind of word to begin with, we would have thought) to BEGUM. Chalker, who seems to be catching something of Paladin's virus of hostility, snatches BEGUM and, adding two letters, spells UMBRAGE. We now see from the aim and brilliance of Paladin's eyebeams that he has a strong urge to take UMBRAGE, but in fact it is mild little Drum, with an H in his hand and an

R from the pool, who slides the word his way and finally has something on his plate: HAMBURGER.

At this point, Paladin has a dangerous run of luck/skill. First he steals Chalker's WRASSE and makes it SWEATERS; then he takes Forester's monkey and makes it LANGUOR; and then he turns Forester's PAT into PLAT. This last, he says with an assurance no one dares doubt, is a map of the sort a developer would draw, with land lots sketched on it.

Chalker, furious at the loss of his fish with its gift of ambiguity, points out to the others that Paladin must be stopped: he has seven words, just one short of victory.

Forester says to Chalker, "If you could spare a Marlboro, I might be able to do something." Chalker gives him a cigarette and a light. In a few seconds, wrapped in a turban of blue smoke, Forester recaptures PLAT and makes it PLAIT, and then he robs Paladin of ROB and ducks back among his usual trees with yet another animal—namely, BOAR.

Here, then, is how things now look:

Paladin

FRUMP
BOMB
HECKLES
SWEATERS
LANGUOR

Drum

HAMBURGER

Forester

LAMB
BACHELOR
PLAIT
BOAR

AQUA

Chalker

Chalker, whose face is dark, as we must presume, with bilious envy of Paladin's and Forester's stacks of words, has a moment—but just a moment, as we shall see—of recovered aplomb. He glances at Drum. He pauses then to shoot a big cloud of smoke out of the left side of his mouth, and as Drum turns away, coughing tragically, Chalker slides Forester's PLAIT his way and turns it into TILAPIA.

There was a reason for the smoke screen. An interesting thing that happens toward the end of these games is that the minds of all four players seem to speed up, markedly so after one of them creeps close to victory. Adrenaline flows, just as in a footrace. An alert kibitzer, perhaps himself more mentally alert than usual, will have noticed that just before blowing his smoke screen, Chalker threw a quick glance toward Drum's left hand, in which the latter held his supposedly secret letter rather carelessly. Chalker—who had no business doing this, and probably would not have, had he ever become Wood Pussy Champion of Larchmont Race Week—took note that it was an N. He also saw a second N among the rejects on the table. And with lightning speed he realized that with the two N's, Drum could abscond with the beautiful word he was making. So *poof* went the cloud, and at once Drum's eyes not only were averted, they itched and watered. And Chalker swiftly made TILAPIA.

Forester, all too aware of Paladin's heavy breathing on his right, clears his throat in an interrogatory way. And at the same moment Paladin's next wheeze has the distinct sound of a giant question mark.

"Gladly," Chalker says, as if both men had actually spoken. "It's an African freshwater fish. Amazing phenomenon. The female lays her eggs in Mr. Tilapia's mouth, and he incubates them there."

"My goodness," Forester says, "you *are* frisky today, Chalks."

In any case, no one challenges.

But look here! Drum has recovered with unusual alacrity. Perhaps Chalker fumigated him a little too late. He must have seen something out of the corner of a wet eye. For now, shyly but without hesitation, he takes the letters of TILAPIA one by one from Chalker's array and places another eatable—bland enough it is, but Cubans are said to like it—alongside his HAMBURGER: a PLANTAIN. This is not one of Drum's haute cuisine days.

We can see that Paladin has enjoyed this little drama. It's clear that he is fully recovered from whatever ailed him after he lost CHOLERA. His cheeks are like McIntosh apples, his eyes have not a trace of brutality in them. He reaches across the table and, to the sound of a groan from Chalker, he steals AQUA and forms a word at the bottom of his pile. When he lifts his pudgy hands so the others can read the new word, QUADRAT, there comes a wild "*What?*" from poverty-stricken Chalker.

Forester can count; he sees how many words Paladin has. But he is a gentleman, and he says, "Yes, I'm afraid I know that word. A piece of land—it's usually rectangular, as the name suggests, right, Pal?—that's set aside for ecological or population studies. We could use a few more of them these days. Don't you think, Chalks?"

Chalker swallows hard.

Paladin isn't finished. He changes his own BOMB into MOBBED. He converts Forester's latest animal into BROADS—for playfulness within reason is allowed in the game. The more Forester's stack of words wanes, the more benign he becomes. "Broads," he says to Chalker, "like those fishies of yours—till they change their minds, huh?"

As Chalker splutters, Paladin sweeps up a Z and a T from the pool, and he tucks the I in his hand between those two letters. Paladin's eighth word. So our game has suddenly come to an end, not with a bang but with a pimple.

Paladin releases a huge sigh, in sound not unlike that of a lighter-than-air balloon degassing to touch down in a soft landing after a glorious flight. Chalker is pale. Drum is sweet. Forester is indifferent. He knows they will play next Wednesday, and he'll probably win. He usually does.

Cuba Libre!

Last year Colonel Narciso López, an officer of the Spanish army of occupation in Cuba, a man to whom honor is as sacred as a virgin's thigh, became outraged by the tyrannical cruelty of his own government toward the Cuban people. His agitation on their behalf caused his superiors to charge him with treason, and he fled to the United States. There he recruited an expeditionary force, a motley gang of several hundred norteamericano rowdies and malcontents, who were game for any fracas. "Cuba libre!," *the rallying cry López fervidly taught them, soon became, on their lips, the nickname of a certain kind of rum drink with which, day and night, on the training field and in their tents, they lubricated their bravado.*

In May this year—last week, in fact—all was ready. Four hundred fifty of López's ragamuffin warriors, as elegantly drunk as a crowd of Spanish grandees taking their places in a bullring, filed with haughty heads and rubber legs aboard a rusty old teakettle of a steamer named the Creole, *moored in Key West harbor. The skipper weighed anchor at dusk. All night the great piston rods of the vessel's ancient reciprocating engine rose and fell, clanking and wheezing, as a squad of glistening Negro boilermen fed the fires with cord after cord of lignum vitae and banyan, cut in the Keys, and of live oak, from the Florida mainland.*

Shortly after dawn the old bucket dropped anchor off the city of Cárdenas. López's hope was to capture the important nearby center of Matanzas, and his hung-over force, their bellies growling from a heavy breakfast of thick bacon and Cuban bread and unsugared coffee, landed at Cárdenas. By this hour it has fought its way, a battalion of raging headaches, through town, against light resistance from the small Spanish garrison, and they have reached the depot of the railroad leading to Matanzas.

López now establishes his headquarters in the depot; he sits at the stationmaster's desk. Having received word from his scouts that Cárdenas is secure, he issues a manifesto calling on the Cuban population to rise up against their oppressors. Handbills with his proclamation are posted all over town. Several hired criers roam the city, reading it in loud shouts for the ears of illiterates who yearn for freedom.

López waits for hours at the stationmaster's desk.

Nothing happens. Nothing.

Not a single Cuban patriot volunteers to set the island free. There is an ominous silence in the city. Shops have closed. The streets are empty. Locks on doors click tight shut.

What is wrong? Could it be that the Cubans don't trust these liberators? Is it that Narciso López is known to be a Spaniard? Is it that his cohorts are norteamericanos with a great deal of red in the whites of their eyes—surly men who can't even speak the language, as the Spaniards at least can do, to be sure with a peculiar, ladylike lisp?

López consults with his lieutenants. Once the Spaniards mo-

bilize against him, he will be hopelessly outnumbered if he lacks support from the populace. Chagrined, he decides that he has no choice but to go home—to Key West, that is—with his tail between his legs.

By now his troops have parched throats. "Cuba libre!" they thirstily shout. "Cuba libre!" It might be thought that this heartfelt cry, heard by the locals in a different sense from that with which it is uttered, would rouse the indigenous population. But no. You can hear the dead bolts clicking into place all over Cárdenas.

López learns from the railroad telegrapher that a Spanish force is on the way from Matanzas, and that—worse news—the Spanish gunboat Pizarro is getting up steam at its anchorage off Morro Castle in Havana harbor.

It is now late in the day. In haste, López orders the Creole's furnaces to be fired, and he reembarks his men. As soon as there is enough steam in the rusty boilers to turn over the groaning engine, he orders the anchor raised.

Dawn at Key West. Lookouts are posted in the many tall cupolas along the waterfront, on which wreckers' agents watch for disasters along the reef. See there! Two plumes of smoke on the horizon! In time, two hulls loom up over the rim of the sea. The lookouts focus their spyglasses on the leading vessel, and one shouts, "The Creole! The Creole!" The vessel is being pursued! By a gunboat!

Word runs around town like a mad dog. Soon the wharves are crowded. The cigar factories of William H. Wall, of Estava and Williams, of Odet Phillippe and Shubael Brown, and of the three Arneau brothers—all are emptied of their Cuban workers, who have been thrilled by the thought that their homeland might be freed from the Spanish yoke.

All shouts on the waterfront are for the Creole. But what is *going wrong? As she runs the channel through the reef, the smoke from her tall stack thins out. She seems to be limping like a hurt animal on the gleaming floor of water. The pursuing gunboat is closing the gap. Alas!*

There is hell to pay in the holds of the Creole. *The raucous warriors of Colonel López are not interested in the ship's race with the* Pizarro. *Down in the bowels of the ship they are not even aware that there is a chase going on. Not only have they not had anything except slightly brackish water to drink for many hours; they have not had a bite to eat since the previous morning. The ship's cooks have been preparing to fry many rashers of bacon—the mainstay of the expedition's provender—for the soldiers, when the order suddenly comes down to stop building the fires in their cook stoves. The boiler room is running out of wood; all the cooks' fagots must be taken down at once to feed the ship's fires. The soldiers, unaware of the* Creole's *peril, and seeing that their meal is canceled, raise a curdling battle cry. They have guns. Mutiny seems likely.*

Abovedecks, López can easily see that the Creole *is losing speed and that the* Pizarro *is creeping within range of fire. In less than a quarter of an hour, she will be close enough to sink the old tin can and claim the lives of all of López's men.*

Now the head cook, a Negro named Sam Samson, comes sweating and puffing up onto the bridge from below. The officer of the deck challenges him and orders him to "get down where you belong." But Samson insists that he must see "Mister Cap'un." López hears the ruckus and goes out on the wing of the bridge.

"The bacon!" Samson cries. "Put the bacon!" The chief cook is so excited that it is hard to make out what he is saying. Is he trying to warn of the soldiers' fury at missing their breakfast? Narciso López quiets Samson down.

It comes to this, the commander quickly comprehends: In pro-

visioning the expedition, he loaded onto the ship enough food to last his men ten days—after which he hoped to be sufficiently well established in Cuba to live off the land. Down in the ship's stores there are literally hundreds of sides of bacon, and López now makes out that Chief Cook Samson is shouting, over and over, "Bacon in the steamboat! Make him go fast!"

López understands what the big cook means. He quickly dispatches a squad to the ship's stores. In trotting relays, they carry the scores and scores of big slabs of bacon down to the boiler room, where the boilermen throw the fat meat into the furnaces. First there is a great splattering among the dying embers, then huge flames leap up. The smoke of ten thousand breakfasts belches from the ship's funnel. The steam gauges dance. The wheezing and clanking of the engine's great rods pick up a jubilant rhythm as the ship crowds all steam.

A cheer is heard on the bridge, and a far louder cheer rises from all the docks of Key West. The Creole *rounds Fort Taylor in safety and, trailing its mouth-watering fragrance, runs serenely up the harbor to F. A. Browne's wharf. The happy band of failed liberators, forgetting all about breakfast, pours down the gangways just in time for the nine o'clock ante meridiem opening of the several licensed drinking establishments on Whitehead Street.*

There, shouting, "Cuba libre! Cuba libre!" *they quaff repeated toasts to the hero of the day, Sam Samson the Bacon Man (who, being a Negro, unfortunately cannot join them).*

Fantasy Fest

She heard the flap of the mail slot in the front door drop with a peremptory clank, and she flew from the kitchen to see if the letter that she was waiting for had finally come. She had been making a fruitless dash in response to that sound each weekday morning for more than a month, ever since the inquiry from the California agency, with its flat, blunt wording, arrived like a sudden flurry of wind down the chimney, stirring up ashes that had long lain cold in the hearth.

This time—could this be it?—she saw a legal-size white envelope with an address in a scribbled penmanship, half buried in the usual bouquet of junk mail. She picked it up and tore it open with trembling fingers.

Reading the scrawly handwriting put her through a rhapsody of physical sensations. Goose bumps, first of all, the little puckerings traveling up and down her arms like a million shouts of hurrah. When she got to the part about not wanting to hurt Mom and Pop, she broke into tears. After that, her responses—as she thought about them later—seemed to go haywire. She knew she had always had a full repertory of reactions to excitement, but this letter reached into her for feelings that had been buried and tamped down hard for half her lifetime. Reading on, she began to feel slightly feverish but, as with a fever, chilled to the bone. Guilt had always made her blush, and now she felt the skin of her neck and face blotting up the hot blood of an old and familiar remorse. Her heart had begun to gallop with the most peculiar mix of explosive joy and jolts of uneasiness; she thought she might break out in some kind of rash, or perhaps even faint. By the time she got to the end of the crowded page, she was sweating as if she'd jogged to Smathers Beach and back, yet the ends of her fingers were white with cold, the way they used to get when as a kid she packed snowballs with bare hands in winter up North. She kept trying to persuade herself that she was thrilled, as she would have put it, "to the soles of my feet."

She called Agatha and asked if she could come over, saying that she'd had some wonderful wonderful news but also had a problem like you couldn't imagine; she needed advice. Agatha sighed, sending along the wire one of the sorrowful, indelicate messages that she always seemed to have in stock—such as, this time, Oh, no, not again, Phyllis, not another hang-up. But then Aggie said, "Give me twenty minutes."

This allowed Phyllis time to change into her favorite daytime blue slacks, pale as sea glass, and the silk shirt Aggie had given her the previous Christmas, with hand-painted sprays of pink bougainvillea on it, perfect with those pants. For some reason, she wanted to be smartly dressed for this talk with her most trusted friend. The letter made it an Occasion, she felt. The wild symptoms she'd had while reading the letter had faded away by the time she had changed, and as she drove to Virginia Street, all she felt was a hard lump in her stomach.

Agatha made a shocking sight when she opened the door. She

was wearing a dirty T-shirt with the logo of Key West AIDS HELP on it. Her hair was a mess. She looked to be at the end of her patience. Phyllis felt ridiculous in her festive clothes, as if she had turned up for a party on the wrong day. All the same, just seeing Aggie's bumpy face, her disenchanted mouth, her left eye with that peculiar wedge-shaped fleck of brown in the blue of the iris—just the sight of her friend's face made her feel calmer.

"Hi, sport," Aggie said. "Come on in. Cup of coffee?"

"No, thanks," Phyllis said. "That's the last thing I need. I've got the twitters."

Aggie led the way to the kitchen and waved Phyllis into a chair at the big butcher-block kitchen table. She poured herself some coffee and sat opposite Phyllis.

"So what now?" she asked with the familiar thin edge of impatience Phyllis had so often heard in her voice.

"Oh, Aggie, the most marvelous thing! I got a letter from my son!"

"Your what? Have you lost your mind? Son? What the hell are you talking about?"

"God. I can't believe it."

What Phyllis couldn't believe at that moment was that she'd never told Aggie, but of course it was so. She had never told anyone in Key West. Never, not a soul. Her move down here after the divorce had been a space leap, she had felt, into an entirely new galaxy of existence, and there were some stark memories of the old life that she had sealed tightly away in a back room of her head, perhaps even having forgotten by now where the key to the room was. This was the most securely stored secret of all. She and Agatha had talked often about their divorces, and endlessly about their exes, and freely about friends here in Key West, and also, in their shared lonelinesses, about what a poor place this was for a single woman who wanted to try to shape a new life with a good straight man on the loose. She had always felt there was nothing she couldn't tell Aggie. Yet never a word about *this*. So now she had to pour it all out. Aggie, listening, was as always an ideal friend. The edginess dissolved, her puckish face softened, her eyes filled up, not quite with tears but with deep fascination and empathy.

When Phyllis had more or less finished, Aggie said, "Did you bring the letter with you?"

Phyllis opened her bag and fumbled in it and pulled out the single sheet filled with tiny writing. She flattened it out on the table and reached it across to Agatha. "Here you go," she said.

"Somewhere" in Key West
October 23

Dear Blood Mother:

Surprise! Surprise!

Here is your kid you gave up for adoption when he was six days old. I tell you what. Ive been wanting to know you for a long long time, been wanting to know where my genes came from, who I look like, what kind of person I really am under the skin, if you know what I mean. My Mom and Pop—I hope you dont mind me calling her Mom—theyve been real good to me, theyre a little strict, theyve got a somewhat diffrent idea about whats fun than me, but theyve been wonderful to me. I love them. I couldnt hurt their feelings enough to tell them Im doing this. I graduated USC in June, they put me through which was not easy for them, I majered in psychology because thats the kind of thing interests me, and I did pretty good considering my high school wasnt all that hot, but anyway what Im saying is, is I was scared I would make them think I wasnt greatful if they knew I was looking for my Blood Mother, so I told them I was in classrooms so many years I needed a breather, I wanted to see these United States, I was just going to keep on the move for a few months, then Id come back and settle into a job and so on and so forth. And I will. They even given me the money to go around the country. My Pop couldnt ever do enough for me, he is a ideal father as adoptive fathers go, wants the world for me. But you see, I needed to know where my personality came from, heredity as opposed to invironment.

O.K. So I nosed around and I found out about this outfit, its just called Search, they look for blood mothers for adoptees, I never even knew I was adopted till I was about twelve, one day I overheard my Mom talking on the telephone to her friend Mrs Tarnton and told her the whole story, she had no idea I was even in the house. But right then I began wondering, so that was ten years ago, and I knew I had to be real careful, trying to find out, because as I say I didnt want to hurt them. The people at Search are top quality, I did a lot of investegation and found out that Search is one of the only places that doesnt make you get your adoptives approval, you know, theyll do it totally confidential just for the adoptee. The tricky thing was getting hold of my birth certifacate, I wont go into that, but anyway I got it, and it was remarkable, they found you, your address and phone number and everything, and now *Ive* found you! Practicly found you, anyhow.

Search has enformed me they wrote you asking your permission for me to be in touch with you, and you said yes.

Im here in Key West. Ive been here nearly three weeks. Ive been walking the streets, going in the markets and stores, up and down Duval Street a hundred times, looking at the women just to see if I could spot you. I havent seen you, not the person I imagine you to be. Of course Search gave me your address, but I didnt think it would be right to just go and ring your doorbell, it might be kind of a shock, or I might see dissappointment on your face. I thought it would be better to take my time and write to you first.

Now heres a suggestion, I hope you dont think its too wierd. People in the bars been telling me all about this celebration they have here next Friday, Halloween night. Fantasy Fest. They said its like Mardi Gras, you can pretend anything you want, dress up like a gorilla or like Alice in Wonderland or whatever you can imagine. Well this hit me where I live, because ever since that day when I was twelve Ive been having these fantasies about my first meeting with my Blood Mother. Ive pictured you a million times in fantasyland—and the truly wild thing is that you are always the same. Always exactly the same. Its like I know you. Maybe youve done this identical thing about me.

So this is what Im going to suggest, dear Blood Mother. I suggest we each follow our fantasy on the night of the parade they been telling me about, this coming Friday night. I will dress up as my own particular fantasy about myself, and you do the same. And I have a destinct feeling we'll find each other. Are you game for this, dear Blood Mother?

Look, if it doesnt work, if we don't find each other that way, you and I are no worse off than we are now. I can write you a note and tell you where Im staying, and you can answer, and we can get together any way you want.

But wouldnt it be wonderful if we imagined each other right? Wouldnt it be super if our chromissomes matched right down into our dreams? Id really like that.

So look for me, dear Blood Mother, on Duval Street at Fantasy Fest next Friday night, and I will be looking for you.

God amighty, I realize you don't even know my name. Because they changed it from the birth certifacate one. So I will sign off with the new one.

Sincerely and truly *yours*,
Farnsworth (do you like it?)

Phyllis anxiously watched Agatha read the letter. As Aggie's eyes took in the first few lines, Phyllis thought she saw a look of amusement, blossoming into real delight, on her stubborn, square face, a look that flickered, however, with hints of mischief of a sort she would always expect from Aggie. Certain phrases as Agatha read along made her bounce slightly in her chair, and a couple of times she snorted—not specially unpleasantly—or blew air out between her teeth. Then, evidently when she came to the letter's big suggestion, she guffawed—laughed long and hard—making Phyllis uneasy, because she couldn't tell what was really behind Aggie's hilarity.

But when she had finished, Agatha put the piece of paper down on the table and ran her flat hand over it from top to bottom and said, "What a wonderful letter! He sounds like a darling boy."

"Isn't he kind of illiterate—for a B.A., or whatever he is?"

"Ease up, Phyl. Nobody can spell, these days."

"Maybe he's dyslexic," Phyllis said. "My brother was. Is."

"He wants to know how you like the name."

"Farnsworth?" Phyllis raised her hands and turned them from side to side. "I don't think it would have been my first choice exactly, but if it's his . . . Oh, Aggie, I'm so happy and so scared. What if he's a little monster?"

"The boy who wrote this"—Aggie picked up the letter—"couldn't be. But listen, Phyllis. Be serious. The point isn't whether he can spell."

"I know. I know. Aggie, I was seventeen. The guy was a freshman at Ann Arbor, and I was—I guess you could say I was an idiot. First my father wanted us to marry—you know, shotgun stuff. Then they decided to send me to my mother's sister, get me out of town, I guess so they wouldn't have to be ashamed. To Seattle. It rained every day—oh, Jesus, Aggie, I was so down, I felt so rotten. You couldn't believe the way it rained, day after day. So anyway, when the baby came I had all the feelings you were supposed to have. I had done it, I'd made him, he had the correct numbers of everything . . . and I adored him. I wanted him. And on day six, they suddenly tell me, They're coming to get him. Say goodbye. And they roll the little bassinet out of the room, you know, the thing on wheels, whatever they call it. They'd made me sign a bunch of papers; I hadn't even read them. Aggie, can you understand how awful I felt, the *guilt* I've felt ever since? My son!"

Phyllis hunched over as she said this last, as if there were a very considerable actual weight on her shoulders.

"Part of the trouble was that nobody ever knew. Except of course my mother and father. They always looked at me kind of sideways, as if, you know, How could you have done this to us? And then the next stupid thing I did was after we were married I told Herb. I thought I had to. He never got over it, like he thought I was part whore, you know? But now this letter comes, and I suddenly feel such joy, so clean; this kid with all the bad grammar has given me back a clean heart. It's so good. So *good!*"

What lay in Phyllis's field of vision—Aggie's face, against a background of natural-wood kitchen cabinets above a stainless-steel sink—went all glassy, and she realized her eyes were brimming. She fished a Kleenex out of her bag and blew her nose.

Aggie, meanwhile, was asking, "So what's the big problem? Are you sorry you feel so happy?"

"No, *no*, it's not that. What terrifies me is this idea of his. About next Friday."

"But Phyl! It's a beautiful idea. He's so sure it'll work. That line about the chromosomes spilling into your dreams—what a trusting son! You had to be touched by that."

"You don't understand. It won't work. I never have fantasies. It's a total blank in me. I never fantasize."

"Oh, come *on*, Phyl. You have dreams, don't you?"

"Not that I can remember in the morning. And I never daydream. Never. I don't have fantasies. It's a lack, Aggie. It's a dead place in me. This thing won't work. He won't find me, and maybe that'll turn him off, and he'll just go away."

"You never think about sex?"

"What good would that do?"

Aggie gave out one of her little snorts. A long silence followed. Then Agatha said, "Hey, I have an idea! If you really mean what you say—"

"Yes, damn it, I do."

"—then I'll dream up a fantasy for you. I'll imagine you as I'd picture you imagining yourself if you could."

"Oh, Christ, Aggie—he's looking for me, not you."

"No, Phyl. Think about it. I know you. I think I know you probably better than you know yourself. I can do the real you. Bobby's taking a table again in the garden at The Exile; we'll be right on the street, where the boy can see you. I'll do you, honest. Give yourself some time to think about it. We could pull it off."

For the next two days, Phyllis tried hard to picture herself dressed up as her true self, in a costume so perfectly expressive of her real being that the boy would surely recognize her. But it was like trying to remember a forgotten name: the more she pushed her mind, the more stubbornly blank it remained. Maybe if she put the issue out of her consciousness, something would come to her: her identity would come popping into her head like a temporarily forgotten name. She tried then to shift her thoughts to her son, to imagine what this young man, her flesh and blood—it gave her a slightly creepy feeling that he called her his blood mother—what costume this young man might wear in the Fantasy Fest crowd that would make her know at a glance he was her son. What would he be like? Would he resemble her? What about the other half of the gene pool? She realized with a sinking feeling that she couldn't even remember what Brent Cooper looked like. She remembered his modified flattop haircut, she remembered a sweater that was out at one elbow. She remembered for a shattering moment what it was like to be very young and to be in love and have no doubts. This was not helpful.

Soon the whole idea of dressing up in order to be known seemed absurd to her, to say nothing of frightening. She had watched the Fantasy Fest parade for three Octobers, never dressed up as her true self—or as anything—always with Aggie and the others in Bobby's crowd, always as a spectator safely distanced from the blowout of inhibitions that dressing up would have required. And like all the others in their crowd, she brought a great deal of irony to bear on what she saw in the street; she felt, as well, pity for people who suffered from such volatile wishes. Fantasy Fest struck her as a cross between a joyous Mardi Gras and a birthday party in an overcrowded orphanage. Comical and heartbreaking—everyone (except for condescending bystanders like herself) tricked out as an admired stranger, or as an imaginary doctored-up self, in a demonstration of how blurred the line can get between wild sweet dreams and the utterly shabby and commonplace. She remembered how, on those nights, she had been drawn against her will into the communal yearning for something else, something more, something better. But she couldn't, try as she would, picture an attractive elsehood for herself. To imagine that, she would have had to know clearly what she wanted to be different from. Her essence eluded her.

For one whole afternoon, now, she found herself walking up and down Duval. She almost never strolled on Duval Street, unless she was looking for something specific at Fast Buck's or Assortment. Her place was just two blocks away from Duval, on Elizabeth, and she had often thought that one of the nifty things about this town was that while mobs of tourist types were traipsing up and down that main drag, with its folly of T-shirt shops and its tinkling pedicabs and its high-decibel Sloppy Joe's Bar, at the very same time, just two blocks away where she lived on one of the side streets of the Old Town, there was a zone of total peace laced with palm fronds and frangipani, where you'd never have known that any of the Duval honky-tonk even existed. But on this one afternoon she tirelessly walked up and down the street, looking closely at every man she saw. The boy might be gay, she thought. Of course, thank God, she could rule out all of those derelict homeless characters lounging along the low wall in front of the Episcopal church. There were so few men on the street who seemed young enough. Key West was, more than most places, an eye-contact town, but none of the vaguely possibles seemed to want to glance at her. It finally occurred to her that Farnsworth—that name made him a complete stranger to her—would surely have ceased his search on Duval, now that he had proposed the guessing game for the night of Fantasy Fest. She trudged home, feeling foolish.

Agatha kept phoning her, saying she was getting warm, she had some ideas, she was cooking, though she didn't specify how. Phyllis tried to shake out of her mind an uneasy feeling that Aggie was . . . not exactly manipulating her but somehow arrogating to herself the right to define her, even perhaps to shape her. She was thankful for the warmth of Aggie's concern. She needed it. But she knew Aggie's strength, and she was a little afraid of it.

"I'm still not sure this is such a great idea," Phyllis said during one of the calls.

Aggie shot back, "Got a better one?"

She hadn't.

Bobby called. Bobby called everyone every day. Bobby was the dot at the center of the circle of friends. He had money, and he had style, and he was headlong. A student of Mies van der Rohe, he had shot up like a rocket as a designer of rich folks' houses that sparkled in the Long Island sunlight like a shelf full of crystal goblets from Murano—but then one year, having tucked away a pocketful of money, he dropped everything, wanting, he said, to hurry up and live while there was still time. His lover, a cheerful Argentinian boy named Bichu, who was twenty-three—about a third of Bobby's age—once said that Bobby "was given to all of us as a reminder that clocks everywhere are going tick tock tick tock."

Now Bobby said on the phone, "Honey, this year we're all going to put on costumes. It was Agatha's idea, and I *love* it. I have three tables, right across the very front at The Exile garden. This year the parade will be staring at *us*, not the other way round. What're you going to pretend?"

"I'd like to pretend that I'm me," Phyllis said, taking it in that Aggie's suggestion to Bobby that they all wear costumes was made to provide cover for her as she dressed up for . . . she still found it hard even to think the name Farnsworth. "That I'm me," she said, "in my ordinary street clothes."

"Oh, darling," Bobby was saying, "I can see you—you'll be a luna moth. Promise me that's what you'll be."

Phyllis was thrown by Bobby's blithe assurance. She had no idea what a luna moth looked like. She thought of moths as grungy little things that eat cloth. Was that what Bobby thought she was like?

"You must be sure and have some gold dust on your wings," Bobby said.

Immediately after Bobby hung up, Phyllis was hit by her memory of the terrible sadness tucked into the gaiety of Fantasy Fest. Gold dust on wings said it all. Everyone overcome with the need for hilarity, disguises beginning to slip loose, drinks sloshing out of paper cups, artifice gone tawdry, but look at me! look at my wings! Why couldn't Farnsworth have taken the risk of just ringing her doorbell?

On the third morning after the letter came, Agatha called up and swore Phyllis to keep a secret. Bichu wanted Aggie to help him turn up on Friday night in drag. Bobby wasn't to know. She had a dress all picked out, and panty hose, and she had already found a wig that would go perfectly with that olive complexion of Bichu's. He/she would be stunning. Aggie said it was going to be such *fun* being the costumer and makeup artist for *two* people that evening—three, really, counting herself!

She was still working on Phyl's problem, she said. She was thinking back on a hundred remarks that Phyl had made at various times, totting up the characteristic images Phyl used, and the feelings she expressed, and even the body language she uttered as she moved. As Agatha talked, Phyllis began to feel like a tailor's dummy, on which Aggie was patching together, swatch by swatch, some kind of half-truth dress very much of the dressmaker's own design, if not in her own image. "It's perfect, it's so *you!*" as saleswomen always said.

Hearing Aggie sketching her, Phyllis felt a flare of anger, but all she managed to say was "I find this very embarrassing, Aggie."

"Oh, I know you, dear Phyl, I know you through and through," Agatha said.

Phyllis lost sleep all one night wondering whether she knew how to be a mother. She couldn't think of a trace of the maternal in her life. She guessed she loved her cat, Buzz; she stroked him tenderly, she took him to the vet's, she was careful about vitamins and a fresh flea collar, but there was a streak of enmity in her relationship with him, a feeling of being on guard against something feral burning bright in Buzz's eyes. Herb had said he didn't want children "yet," and they kept putting it off and putting it off, until it was too late; hostilities set in, and a baby would have lived in no-man's-land. She tried many times to conjure up clear pictures in her mind of the room in the maternity ward, of what it had been like to hold that wriggling little life force in her arms, of how joyful the sound of his aerobics of crying must have made her. But it was all dim in her mind. Exactly what had she felt? All she could really remember as if it were yesterday was being furious at the sadistic nurses, who made it all too clear that they didn't like that poor little tot having no visible father.

She hadn't a clue how to become the sudden mother of a college graduate, with not a scrap of nurture or tenderness or discipline or rebellion or kindness or fury or forgiveness ever having been transacted between the two of them. All the same, she began, toward dawn, to feel a coolness, a freshness flowing in her veins. She was going to have an adventure. She felt as if all the sediment that had settled in her personality was suddenly being stirred up again—and perhaps, this time, there could be a new mix; her nature now might turn out to be totally new. She got up and got dressed after that night of restlessness feeling refreshed—at peace with her son's challenge and even with Agatha's offer to help her meet it. She would go through with the game.

It took Friday an awfully long time to reach town, but at last it did. Aggie called and said that Bobby wanted them all at The Exile at seven o'clock. There'd be about twenty of them—all "Bobby's crowd." The floats and bands wouldn't start down Duval until about nine, but Bobby said they'd have some drinks and eats and watch all the dressed-up people who couldn't wait for the actual parade to strut their conceits and fancies up and down the town. Aggie said she'd need at least an hour to get Bichu and Phyl and herself ready. Phyl should come over no later than six o'clock.

"And what am I going to be?" Phyllis asked.

"You'll see," Aggie said. "Just trust me."

"Are you going to make me a luna moth?"

"A what? What are you talking about?"

"Never mind. Forget it. It was just a dumb idea somebody had."

"No later than six," Agatha said.

When Agatha, in a soiled chenille dressing gown, let Phyllis in on the stroke of the hour, she led her straight to the bedroom. Bichu hadn't arrived yet. Phyllis saw three outfits spread out on Aggie's bed. She knew at once which was meant to be hers. It was a dirndl.

"I'm not wearing that," she almost shouted.

"Don't be so skittish," Agatha said. "Try it on. You'll see."

"What is this? You think of me as some kind of wispy freak of a yodeler in *The Sound of Music?* I swear!"

"Trust me, Phyl. He'll know you, I promise."

"You really despise me, don't you?" Phyllis said.

"Hell I do." Agatha suddenly sounded angry. "Want to know what? I wish I were you, Phyl. If I secretly hate you, it's because I admire you too much. I thought, God, to be so perfect and, you know, so damn *Swiss.* So well made, you know, like one of those watches that run under water. Those fantastic chocolates with a bitter edge to them. Best airline in the world. And what about those bank accounts? Total safety like that, that's what you give everyone, Phyl. And I saw, you know, the softness in the dirndl idea. And there's a kind of calm neutrality you have, and—"

"Jesus, Aggie, what *shit* you're talking! You just want me to be some sort of incredible alien mouse."

Before Agatha could answer, the doorbell rang, and Aggie trotted off to let Bichu in. The young man came in breathless, took Phyllis's bleakly offered hand in both of his, and kissed her on both cheeks. He was fiercely ebullient, and when Agatha pointed to the dress he was to wear, he shouted, "All *right!*" and threw his arms around Aggie's neck like a drowning man and hugged her for his life. Aggie looked at Phyllis over his shoulder with a teacherish glare, and Phyllis knew that she didn't have the character to quarrel in front of this little electric Bichu. She was going to cave in and wear the unspeakable dirndl.

She even let Agatha plait her hair in two girlish braids.

Then she felt stupidly grumpy because Agatha obviously was much more excited about dressing Bichu than she had been about Phyllis. Agatha had dug out of her closet a black off-the-shoulder organdy dress which dated back to the last round of very short skirts. She made Bichu take everything off, and they began to giggle and then to laugh hysterically as they wrestled around on the edge of Aggie's bed, struggling to get him into a pair of patterned black panty hose that Aggie had bought. Aggie kept shouting through her laughter, "One size fits all!" When he was finally snugly tucked into the panty hose, Aggie hooked him into a black strapless bra over some reasonably moderate falsies—"I didn't want you to be Wonder Woman," Aggie said—and then she slipped the dress over his head. She settled the wig and made up his face. She had found a mask with large eye holes, and when she had put it on him, the purple eye shadow and sooty lashes made his eyes mysterious and wicked. Phyllis couldn't help thinking him a breathtaking woman. He had magnificent soft shoulders and the neck of a pale dove.

Next Aggie threw off her dressing gown and put on her costume. She turned out to be Columbine, in a loose soft dress of garish diamond-shaped patches. She put on a pink tricorn hat and a mask with upswept wings. "What do you think?" she asked Phyllis.

What Phyllis thought in a leaden mood was that if Aggie imagined herself a soubrette, a heartthrob for some Harlequin who would come dashing to her out of the desperate tide on Duval, she sure as hell had another guess coming, and—this was an even worse thought—if she was so miserably wrong about herself, how much more mistaken she would certainly have been about this hideous dirndl. "You look just great," Phyllis halfheartedly said.

By this time it was already past seven. They decided it would be impossible to park anywhere near The Exile; they'd walk the five or six blocks. Bichu said he wanted to make a gala entrance, to tease Bobby when everybody else had arrived; he'd see them later.

"No pickups, now, cutie," Agatha said.

"Mind your own business," Bichu said, then shaped his carmine lips in a pert moue beneath the black of his mask. "Trick or treat!" he called, falsetto, and went off laughing.

Most of Bobby's crowd had already arrived when Phyllis and Agatha, masks in place, fought their way across Duval to The Exile through the stream of revelers already milling and eddying in the street. As Phyl stepped up into the garden, she felt like an utter fool in her white mutton sleeves and suffocating bodice and fussily gathered skirt.

Great confusion under the tree at the front of the garden, to her relief. She might not be noticed. It seemed that only two tables had been saved, and as usual, Bobby had invited more guests than he had meant to. Dressed as a Venetian grandee, in a squashy cloth hat and an embroidered jerkin and puffed velvet knickers and crimson tights, nervously pushing an anachronistic pair of horn-rimmed spectacles up the bridge of his nose now and then, he was in a shouting match with the owner, who finally threw up his hands and agreed to dislodge the half-dozen young men at a third table; the young men, however, already raucously drunk, had a notion to stay where they were. It would take a long time, and a great deal of hectoring on Bobby's part, to drive them away.

A woman done up as a clown pushed her extravagantly painted face close to Phyllis's mask and asked, "And who would this be?"

Phyllis recognized the clown at once despite her lurid makeup—a casual friend, Diana Benton—and she said, "It's me, Dine. Phyl."

"You?" Diana said. "Heidi? Good God!"

Agatha came and took Phyllis's hand, saying, "Come on, Phyl. I want you to be right out front. Over here." And she led Phyllis to a seat beside the sidewalk railing at the table nearest the bar, which the young men were finally giving up, but not without a hailstorm of obscenities. "Dry up, you fatheads!" Aggie, still holding Phyllis's hand, shouted at them over her shoulder. Then, to Phyl: "We'll all be standing, later. You'll be right here in front. He'll see you. Don't worry."

Scanning the faces of the milling revelers in the street, some masked, some not, Phyllis was struck by the hopelessness of her search. A faun, a London bobby, Venus and Adonis with linked arms (but which was which?), a Frankenstein monster, Brunhild with a horned helmet, a topless mermaid pushed in a little boat on wheels by a scuba diver, slopping along in his flippers. The only thing she could be fairly sure of was that her son wouldn't be one of a pair. A baseball player, a bride, a handsome fellow in a wig and body tights and a tutu. Could *his* name possibly be Farnsworth?

"God help me," Diana's husband, Bryan, standing next to Phyllis, feelingly cried. "There's my *dentist!*" He was pointing at a beautiful creature wearing nothing but a flowing black net cape, a dozen bracelets, and a jockstrap sparkling with sequins. "Spare me! I have an appointment with him for root canal work on Tuesday!"

Bryan had to be making that up. It was a relief to be able to laugh. Then, trying to dig down for a grip on some common sense, Phyllis decided that there was one other thing she could be sure of: Her son would be a person who was eagerly searching the faces of women. Most of the people in the street were in fact looking hungrily at others, but all they seemed famished for was a momentary flicker of admiration. Farnsworth, unlike them, would be looking carefully for his long-lost Blood Mother. For a woman in a dirndl?

Bobby, as always a hectic host, was near Phyllis's table, trying to get all his guests seated and to rally a couple of waiters to take drink orders, when here came Aggie holding another woman's hand. This woman was Bichu. "Bobby! Bobby!" Aggie was shouting. "Be civil, dear. I want you to meet my friend Cynthia Barrow. I hope you don't mind my having brought her. I tried to call you—that she was in town."

Bobby was distracted, half listening, obviously a little annoyed to have to greet one more freeloader, when this Cynthia said, in a fluty contralto Louisiana drawl, "Mistah Worth, I'm jus' so *thrilled*. My late husban' was a architeck, he was ol' enough to be my daddy, passed away las' Febwy, but you see, 'cause o' him, I knew every single creation of yours. I'm *such* a admirer."

Bichu's overdoing it, Phyllis thought, though there was joy in his mimicry. But Bobby was thinking of other things; he turned away from this pest and spoke to one of the waiters. The Cynthia woman, however, unwilling to let him escape, plucked at his sleeve and said, "You know, Mistah Worth, my husban' had pitchers of every one of your fab'lous houses? Could I tell you my favorite one of 'em all? My very favorite one? It'd be the Billin'sly house, you know, Eas'hampton? Minded me of a shootin' gall'ry at a country fair? It's just *scrump*tious."

Bobby shouted, "Oh, God, I loathe that house! That house is from a hundred years ago in my life! Please!" Then, rudely: "Look, forgive me, I'm busy right now." And again he turned away.

And again Cynthia tugged at his sleeve, saying, "Sure, honey, you go on 'bout your bus'ness. But first off, you better polish yo' little ol' eyeglasses." She took off her mask and stuck her face up near Bobby's.

Amid the loud laughter all around him, Bobby recognized

Bichu. "Why, you little rascal," he said. He rallied then, joining the laughter at himself with apparent good grace, but Phyllis noticed that the lover's pinch he gave Bichu's face had some bite to it. Though she laughed with the others, she realized that this lighthearted byplay had made her feel uneasy. It seemed that the game of recognitions carried some risks for the players; there might not be any winner.

At last the actual parade began, and Bobby's crowd all stood along the railing of The Exile's garden to watch. In between gaudy floats and loud bands, the stream of merrymakers, all now heading to the south with the flow of the march, meandered on and on. Phyllis assumed that Farnsworth would not be on a float and would not be in a band, so she tried to concentrate on the mobs of independent roisterers in costume. She couldn't possibly take time to stare. All those around a samba band whirled and whirled, throwing their hips to the winds. Surely not there; a Californian would be more laid back than that. She could only get glimpses of faces and forms: of a geisha girl, a chef in a tall white hat, a tall black caveman with fur slung over his shoulder, Uncle Sam waving the Stars and Stripes, and a boob in bathing shorts that Phyl had seen in a Duval shop window, with an elephant's face built into them and a long, swinging trunk sticking out from the crotch. It was like watching a commercial on the tube—a swift series of flashing hints at the possibilities of comfort and love, firmly embedded in schlock. She wanted to be thrilled; she wanted a wild moment of recognition, reconciliation. She felt more and more forlorn.

She began to think she might drown in a sea of noise: klaxons of the flatbed trucks of the floats; blaring saxophones, trumpets, trombones; the deep heartbeat of drums; even, in passing, a whining complaint of bagpipes; maddeningly shrill whistling; and the clicking of hundreds of little metal finger-crickets, tossed from one of the floats to the crowds of bystanders along the sidewalks.

She tried to be alert for the face of a hunter—a face eagerly scanning the crowd of onlookers along the street. She imagined, in fact, that she saw several. One was a boy dressed up as an old-fashioned tar, in white bell-bottom pants and a white cotton pullover with a blue-striped bib at the back of the neck and a round white cap cocked on his head. Another wore the habit of a priest, but with a heavy sommelier's chain around his neck; his nose painted a winy red, he staggered as if very drunk. A cowboy twirling the loop of a lariat. A youth in white tie and tails, waving a baton, conducting music only he could hear. These all seemed to be taking in every face along the way with a pathetic, yearning care. But none of these—nor of any other possibilities she thought she might be seeing—took so much as a second look at her.

Here came a most astonishing figure, dancing down the middle of the street to the West Indies beat of a band that was marching along behind. This was a man all in black under a magical fanlike construction, a huge peacock's tail ten feet high and even wider, with each feather independently sprouting, it seemed, from his shoulders, each gossamer plume rigged to tremble and shimmer as he rhythmically played at a harplike system of controlling wires with his hands, each feather winking brilliant iridescent eyes in all the colors of the rainbow, the entire dream of beauty swaying and shaking in time with the music. The sight made Phyllis draw in her breath, and then she began to weep. My son! My son! Why couldn't this be you!

And now the high-stepping band that had animated that vision swept into view on a wave of throbbing island music—the blacks of the famous Bahamian Police Precision Marching Band, dressed in all-white uniforms with sparkling brass buttons, their faces shiny with the heat of their exuberance under helmet-shaped white topees. They were playing "Mary Ann," very fast. Just before they reached The Exile, they broke their rectangular ranks and began to snake back and forth from curb to curb in single file, pumping their knees waist-high, triple-tonguing their trumpets, their drums like the utterances at the heart of a huge engine of joy. The crowds on the sidewalks broke into cheers, and Phyllis into happy sobs.

Gripped and shaken by the pulsing energy of that music, feeling as if she was finally coming to her senses, she broke away from the railing, jostled her way through the press of Bobby's guests, stepped down from The Exile's garden onto the crowded sidewalk, and, shoving hard and hoping the tears on her face would serve as apologies, rudely fought her way into the street and across it, dodging as best she could the celebrants dancing to the receding beat of the band. One whirling woman almost knocked her down. Once through, she ran along Angela Street the two blocks to Elizabeth, never stopping to catch her breath, and turned left toward home.

Half a block before reaching her house, she began unlacing the bodice of the dirndl. Inside her door, she tore it off and was no sooner in her bedroom than she was out of the shirt and skirt. Opening her closet, she reached at once for the hanger on which she had put away her pale-blue slacks and the blouse printed with the sprays of bougainvillea. This outfit would be her talisman—the clothes she had chosen without a moment's hesitation the morning the letter came, to celebrate its arrival. She thought that maybe she had had a mild fantasy, after all, that morning—one in which she saw herself, for better or worse, as just the kind of mother who would wear those clothes. She tore out the ribbons that held her silly braids, and she brushed out her hair as well as she could in haste.

A few minutes later she was back on Duval. She felt completely free. She veered away from The Exile, and, an active searcher now herself, she made her way down the street. By now the parade proper was spent, and all the revelers were milling about in disorder, still wanting to see and be seen, walking slowly up and down Duval. Now that she was immersed in the stream herself, she was aware of being stared at occasionally—

perhaps just for her surprising ordinariness, but perhaps *that* stare . . . or *that* one . . . ?

She encountered, again, the boy who had rigged himself up as a drunken priest, and he did, indeed, look closely at her as they passed each other; but no, she thought, no self-respecting son would look for his mother in such a foolish getup. Here was a young man dressed as Charlie Chaplin, who stopped in front of her and peered at her—but then he snapped his fingers in her face and twirled his cane with his other hand. And here was a sad boy with a guitar, who seemed to want her to listen to a song but who drifted aside when she paused to do so. And here was a half-naked skinhead, with an Iroquois topknot, who shouted, "Hi, Mom!" and chucked her under the chin, and reeled away laughing.

She struggled to keep her spirits up, but it was hard. If only she could have had some hints of what to look for. She walked slowly on, hoping that the intentness of her own scanning of faces would be a clue for her son, who must also be seeking, as she was, for a seeker. Having passed La Concha and The Bull and Sloppy Joe's, she began to worry that Farnsworth might have been farther down Duval when she turned downtown. She faced about and started up the street.

There seemed to be a looseness in the crowd now, an enervation with the setting in of anticlimax. The fun was pretty much over. She herself struggled against the letdown. Having so vigorously shaken off the feeling she had had at the railing of The Exile, that life was something that just happened to her from minute to minute, that like sand on the shore she was a receiver of whatever flotsam the tides might bring—having thrown that off and having taken her search for her son into her own hands at last, she had felt fiercely exultant as she first plunged into the crowd on the street. Had she truly had a fantasy at last—that she was a vital person? She did not want to admit to feeling downhearted, but she had to face a suspicion that she had let herself be lured into playing a game meant from the start to fail.

Still she hung on. She searched. She saw the sailor boy again; he looked hard at her, and she smiled. His expression didn't change; he passed her by; he must have been looking for someone else to be loved by. Phyllis soon realized that she had gone right past The Exile again without even noticing whether all the friends were still there. If they were, had they seen her? What did they think she was doing?

Up ahead, a flash of something white caught her eye. She was in front of the French bakery to which she often came for croissants for breakfast. Yes, she noticed that white something again, a rectangle, waving above people's heads. Half a block more, and she saw what it was. The young man dressed as a cowboy—one of the hunters whose pleading eyes she had noticed back at The Exile—was now no longer twirling his lariat but was standing still in the middle of the roadway, holding a placard over his head, like a limo driver waiting for a passenger at an airport arrival gate. On the placard she saw, as she came closer, a single word scrawled in cramped letters with a Magic Marker. The word was: PHYLLIS.

Her first thought, which came to her before her heart even jumped, she realized later, was: He's going to want to call me by my first name. Then she saw that he was short, that he had a sad little mustache that seemed to have been put there to prove something. And then her heart did jump in a big way, and she fought an impulse to rush to him and throw her arms around him. Instead she stepped in front of him, three feet away, and stood there.

He looked at her with a blank face. Then she saw him see that she was not moving on, she was staying planted in front of him. And he gaped and then said, "Is it *you?*"

She pointed at the sign, unable yet to speak.

"I'm sorry," he said. "I panicked. Gee, I thought you'd be older."

"It's okay," she said, unsure exactly what she meant to excuse. She couldn't help looking at him from head to foot. She saw that he was wearing cowboy boots with high heels.

He held the sign behind his back. "I lost my nerve. I got scared it wasn't going to work. I didn't know there'd be so many people."

She wanted to ask whether he would have recognized her if he'd had a good look at her this way. Was this the Blood Mother he had seen so often in fantasyland? Had he always, from the age of twelve, been a *cowboy* in his imaginings of meeting her? Could he still believe, now, that he and she might have had matching dreams of each other's reality?

"I was afraid if it didn't work," he blurted out, "you'd be disgusted with me, you might not want to ever see me."

"Oh," she said. "No. I'd want to see you."

He was such an odd-looking little person.

She had a moment of remembering the wild sensations she had had last Tuesday—ages ago!—reading this person's letter. Now all she felt was an inward shrug; she couldn't tell whether her shoulders actually moved. Trying to tell herself that she'd be happy sooner or later, Phyllis reached out for her son's hand and said, "Where are you staying? Let's get your stuff. I'll take you home."

Just Like You and Me

Mr. Asa F. Tift has a tough mind. Mrs. Asa F. Tift has a tender heart. Both have sharp tongues. They have been quarreling into the night.

This is the reason for their dissension. Ten days ago, the gunboats USS Mohawk *and* USS Wyandotte *escorted into Key West harbor two slave ships they had captured in waters north of Cuba, the* Williams *and the* Wildfire, *carrying altogether three hundred candidates for slavery, both male and female, including numerous children. A party of the Engineer Corps based at Fort Taylor, under command of Captain E. B. Hunt, has fenced in a barracoon to hold the Negroes until it can be determined what to do with them; and with remarkable speed, after that, Captain Hunt's carpenters have thrown up a crude dormitory, comprising nine rooms twenty-five feet by twenty-five feet in size, in each of which approximately thirty-five Negroes, sorted according to age, are, as Mrs. Tift will have it, incarcerated.*

Mrs. Tift early became aware of the pitiable state of these "human souls, just like you and me," as she keeps referring to the captives, to her husband's annoyance. Recently Mr. Tift learned that his wife, without asking his permission, has banded together with the wives of Messrs. Stephen R. Mallory, Winer Bethel, and Henry Mulrennan, and perhaps others, to press the engineers to build a hospital shed, which the army workmen have now, in fact, brought to completion; it measures one hundred fourteen feet by twenty-one feet, and it is already crammed with one hundred eighty patients suffering from ailments ranging from pinkeye and fungus of the scalp to far more serious illnesses, such as scurvy and typhus and even, in two cases, an unmentionable venereal disease. The ladies have also managed to persuade Drs. Skrine, Weedon, and Whitehurst to care for these sick folk and generously to defer until later the question of how much the United States Government will be obligated to pay them for their services.

The issue between this husband and wife is embedded in the fact that Mr. Asa F. Tift, who came here years ago from Georgia, considers himself a Southern Gentleman. So, it goes without saying, do Messrs. Mallory, Bethel, and Mulrennan, the husbands of Mrs. Tift's meddlesome cohorts; and so, for that matter, do other good solid citizens of the town, such as Messrs. William Pinckney, Joseph B. Browne, William Curry, and Peter Crusoe, to name only a few of Mr. Tift's friends. These are men of substance, culture, and refinement, with mercantile and other business interests. In summertime they scrupulously wear fresh-laundered suits of white linen duck, and in winter, on the Sabbath and all holidays, frock coats and tall silk hats. Some moved here from St. Augustine, some came from Virginia and the Carolinas, and some from the Bahamas. They are all firm states' righters, and they are dead set against the federal government's practice of intercepting slavers. They are scornful of the "riffraff" in town who celebrated with such vulgar obstreperousness, just last week, the news in the Gazette that the Republican convention in Chicago had nominated to run for President the darling of the antislavery states, Mr. Lincoln.

Mr. Tift says to his wife that these Negroes are property, which the United States Navy is piratically stealing from rightful owners.

Mrs. Tift says to her husband that he is mistaken. These are not chattels but "human souls, just like you and me, my dear Asa." To Mr. Tift's ear, the modifier "dear" is, at this moment, supererogatory, if not actually provocative.

Mrs. Tift and her friends have been visiting the barracoon every day. They have been shocked to see the way Captain James M. Brannan of the First Artillery, who is now in effect the commandant of the barracoon, is feeding the Negroes. The captives get only one meal a day, seated on the ground in circles of ten around crude tin buckets containing boiled rice and chunks of fatback. That is all they are given. Each Negro has a spoon and must dip into the common pot.

The aforementioned ladies, under a dark cloud of their husbands' disapproval, have gone out into the town and have rallied the women of Key West, no matter what their husbands may think of Lincoln or states' rights or abolitionism, to tasks of mercy. Already scores of women have begun flocking each morning to the enclosure, carrying nutritious foods—fruits from the trees in their yards; eggs that have been laid in innumerable bosky places by the town's many chickens; and spinach greens and lettuces and plantains from their kitchen gardens. They have also been contributing armfuls of clothing, appalled as they have been by the lack of modesty of the captives, who wear nothing but skimpy clouts. Indeed, a delightful entertainment for a fairly large audience of idle men and young boys, as well as members of the Corps of Engineers equipped with spyglasses on the parapet of nearby Fort Taylor, has been afforded by the daily washdown in the sea taken by the captives, men and women *alike, quite unashamed, in their birthday suits. These poor ignorant people* must *be covered!*

As the Tifts' disagreement wears on, tears spring into Mrs. Tift's eyes. This afternoon, she tells her husband, she dropped in at the hospital shed in the encampment, and there she saw "a sight that would break even your heart, Asa *dear." The patients have no beds or cots, as in a normal infirmary. They lie, many of them groaning in pain and fear, on a bare wooden floor. Huddled in a seated position against one wall, Mrs. Tift says, she came across a mother with a sick baby. The mother was herself a mere child. Dr. Skrine, who was showing Mrs. Tift around, estimated her age as "twelve or thirteen, at most." The infant was probably suffering—"I can only guess," Dr. Skrine said—from some typhus-like ailment. Also probably starving, since the mother was obviously ill-equipped to nurse.*

"Asa, the young mother was so proud of her baby, and so delicate in the way she brushed away the moisture on its face with her fingers. You can't tell me that those two poor sick defenseless little creatures are just boughten things."

"No sign of a father within a hundred miles, I'd wager," Mr. Tift scornfully says.

Mrs. Tift, weeping now from both pity and frustration, tries to tell her husband how pathetic the baby's tiny head was, limply declining onto the mother's childish, fruitless breast.

"Revolting," Mr. Tift says.

The baby has died, and Mrs. Tift has made it her business to have this, the first death among the captives, announced in the Gazette. *The morning after her altercation with her husband—in other words, two days ago—Mrs. Tift went straight back to the hospital shed in the barracoon, carrying a jug of milk and some soft cloths to serve as nappies. She found the mother sitting on the floor exactly as she had been the previous day, leaning against a stud of the wall, hugging her baby and gently caressing its cheeks. Mrs. Tift saw at once that something was amiss. The mother seemed not to be able, or not to be willing, to see her as she leaned forward, offering the milk. Mrs. Tift hurried off to find whichever doctor was on duty.*

Without even touching the infant, Dr. Whitehurst said, "It is no longer with us." He leaned forward to take the baby from the mother's arms, but the child-mother clutched the tiny corpse to her bosom and began to scream. For six hours, she fiercely refused to give it up. Then, Mrs. Tift heard later, it was taken from her forcibly.

The baby's funeral is this morning. Much to Asa F. Tift's disgust, Mrs. Tift has taken the lead in arranging everything. The article in the Gazette *roused great sympathy among the women of the town. Mrs. Tift took up a subscription for a decent deal coffin—so very small!—to be hammered up by Solomon Bertal, one of the ship's carpenters at the waterfront. She overcame the most stubborn sort of resistance on the part of Captain Brannan to her proposal that armed men from his artillery company should escort the entire boodle of captives to a plot at some distance from the barracoon, out on Whiteheads Point, which could serve as a burial ground for Negroes, for the infant's funeral.*

That march is now in fact taking place. At the head of the procession, escorted there by the committee of ladies, is the child-mother, decently covered by a white shift that Mrs. Tift has borrowed from the youngest daughter of Mrs. Mulrennan. Next comes a foursome of Negro men, dressed in new white denim trousers that Mrs. Tift has bought for the purpose, bare-chested, carrying the little coffin on their shoulders. Then come the mass of captives, most of them, unsuitably for a funeral, nearly naked. They are flanked by soldiers with guns. A large number of curious townspeople follow behind.

The captives gather around the six-foot-deep grave, which was dug yesterday by a squad of able-bodied male captives. Reverend Simon Peter Richardson of the Methodist Episcopal Church South stands at the head of the pit, and he sonorously says, "Brothers and sisters, we are gathered together here—"

Now he pauses, evidently feeling that he is not being given due respect by the Negroes, for some female voices have begun to make a strange wailing sound, which soon takes a curious turn toward melody. Men's voices join in. Some throats cry out with prolonged moans. Reverend Richardson is looking aghast. The singing grows louder and louder. Bare feet rise and fall, slapping the ground in time with the insistent repetitious throbbing of what would sound to the townspeople's ears like a chorus of irrepressible joy were it not for the unearthly moans that punctuate and underlie the song. There is a terrible radiance in the pulsating music, and we see the captives dipping, turning, stamping, their limbs resonating to the sounds that thrum from their chests.

The emotion in their song and in their swaying is palpable, soaring, ferocious, but to the people of Key West it is deeply enigmatic. To Reverend Richardson, it appears to be blasphemous, and with wild gestures he commands that the coffin be lowered forthwith into the pit. The four bearers, themselves singing, pick it up—it is a light thing—and, with Reverend Richardson waving his arms over them almost as if he were conducting the unbearable heathen music, they literally throw the box into the hole.

At that moment, as if cut by a huge machete, the chant stops. There is complete silence. Without a word, without a whisper, in appalling stillness, the Negroes turn and start walking back to their captivity.

Page Two

"MANDARIN" TAKEN INTO CUSTODY

Police yesterday arrested Marly Francis, 26, and charged him with having committed a robbery three nights ago at 23 Charter Lane. On that occasion, James Whitlow, occupant of a second-floor apartment at that address, told police that an intruder, having somehow climbed to the balcony fronting the apartment, had cut a screen at an open window, had entered while Mr. Whitlow was asleep, and had stolen $300 from a wallet, a wristwatch valued at $250, three silk shirts custom-made in Madrid, an enameled and jeweled Russian Easter egg, and three pairs of elaborately embroidered blue satin cloth shoes, said to have been made for members of the Chinese imperial family in the Forbidden City, Peking, in the nineteenth century, which Mr. Whitlow reported he had purchased six years ago from a smuggler in Hong Kong. One pair of these remarkable shoes bore the faces of tigers over the toes; a second pair had slender upsweeping forms at the front like swans' necks; and the third were pricked in gold thread with the character *fu*, meaning happiness. The arresting officer, Warren ("Bull") Johns, who happened to have taken the description of the stolen goods from Mr. Whitlow the night of the robbery, was driving his own car while off duty yesterday when he saw a man whom he at once suspected of being the perpetrator walking debonairly along Duval Street wearing one of the Spanish silk shirts, pink chinos, and the swan's-neck shoes. Officer Johns parked his car, accosted Mr. Francis, read him his rights, took him to the Monroe County Jail, and booked him. Mr. Francis cheerfully confessed the thefts and asked the duty officer whether he had ever seen such beautiful shoes.

MAN'S BEST FRIEND

Willy Simpson, 42, was arrested last night on Roosevelt Boulevard for driving while intoxicated. The arresting officer, James Burns, said he saw Mr. Simpson's 1977 Plymouth Volare cutting erratically back and forth across lanes in the 2300 block and gave pursuit, stopping Mr. Simpson in the vicinity of the Ramada Inn. Officer Burns reported that Mr. Simpson, though not at all obstreperous and in fact seeming eager to please, had sufficient difficulty with a walking-straight test to justify a breatholator test. He showed a blood alcohol level of .19. When he said he had left his driving license at home, Officer Burns radiotelephoned the 24-hour Motor Vehicles Alert and learned that there was no record of a license in Mr. Simpson's name. Mr. Simpson was adamant that he had a license back at his house. Leaving the Volare where it was, Officer Burns took Mr. Simpson to his residence at 1073 Leon Street. "Don't be afraid of the dog," Mr. Simpson told the arresting officer. Mr. Simpson was greeted at the door by an enormous gray-and-white Great Dane named Tiny. There followed an extensive search for his license by Mr. Simpson, who in his urgency threw clothing out of drawers, scattered papers from his desk, and even rattled pots and pans in his kitchenette. He then said, "Tiny, you're a bad bad dog!" He backed the Great Dane, which now had its tail between its legs, into a corner of the kitchen, and he shouted, "Bad! Bad! You're *naughty!*" Officer Burns asked, "What's he done?" Mr. Simpson said, "Obvious what he's done. It's obvious. Ate my license while I was out. *Bad* dog!"

COMPLEAT ANGLER

James Boomer, 34, one of the best-known fishing guides in the "backcountry" of the Keys' flats, who is said to be able to cast a fly fifty feet to within six inches of a bonefish's chin, was arrested at 3 a.m. this morning shortly after committing a robbery at the home of Mrs. Matilda Prockett, a widow who lives alone at 1302 Esmeralda. Mr. Boomer, who made away with $650 in cash and some not-yet-evaluated jewelry in the theft, was apprehended quite by chance, as Robert Ransom, a neighbor of Mrs. Prockett's, walking his dog at that unusual hour, saw the perpetrator duck out of Mrs. Prockett's fence gate and run north on Esmeralda. Mr. Ransom got a close look at the perpetrator under a streetlight, and he noticed that he was carrying a fishing rod and a woman's purse. The witness promptly ran into his house and telephoned 911, and very soon thereafter Mr. Boomer was taken into custody as he ran south on Petronia Street. Examination of the premises and interrogation of the perpetrator revealed that Mr. Boomer, aided by the light from the street lamp, had cut a foot-square hole in the screen of the glass-louvered window to Mrs. Prockett's ground-floor sleeping quarters. The window was protected by burglar bars, so Mr.

Boomer would not have been able to slip louvers out and crawl inside, as robbers customarily do, but it served his purpose that the louvers were wide open. Mr. Boomer inserted his seven-foot Isawa casting rod, which he had rigged with a treble-hooked Yellow Cockle Streamer fly with a six-pound tippet, through the hole in the screen and between two louvers of the window. With a sidewise flicking motion, he was able to cast the fly approximately ten feet to Mrs. Prockett's bureau, hooking the handle of her purse on the third try. With a cautious, slow retrieve, he "fought" the catch to the window, at which point he reached through and lifted it out. Mrs. Prockett slept through the entire operation.

AN ADVENTURE IN THE SKIN TRADE

Felicity Branden, 23, of 729 Sarah Street, filed a complaint yesterday at the Monroe County Sheriff's office against Stephen Timmity, who operates an all-night tattooing parlor, Skin Sketches, at 1023 Caroline Street, alleging that she had entered his premises at approximately 2 a.m. Wednesday morning and had requested that he tattoo a monarch butterfly on her left buttock. Mr. Timmity completed his operation at about 2:45. He offered her a mirror to examine the result, but she told the police that she was by then too embarrassed by being half undressed, and she covered herself and went home. Not having a hand mirror with which to check the results of Mr. Timmity's work, she retired to bed and slept until three yesterday afternoon. Then, after drinking three cups of coffee, she went to Eckerd's and bought a vanity mirror, returned home, and, she said, discovered that Mr. Timmity had imprinted on her posterior not a butterfly but instead a large, hairy tarantula. Officer Mary Cox took Ms. Branden to a rest room and examined the artwork. She confirmed Ms. Branden's assertion. "The guy's a genius," Officer Cox said. "It scared the shit out of me. I thought the damn thing would bite me." Police picked up Mr. Timmity on suspicion of malicious mischief. Mr. Timmity professed outrage. He said "this cockeyed-drunk idiot little bird" had come in his shop in the wee hours and had said she wanted to spook her boyfriend. Mr. Timmity claimed he had no memory whatsoever of her having asked for a butterfly. He said he is very proud of his butterflies. "I am at heart a philatelist in skinwork," he stated. "I *hate* spiders. But this one said she wanted to make her boyfriend's hair stand on end. I think she said his name was Oscar." An argument between the complainant and the accused ensued. Ms. Branden admitted that she had a friend named Oscar, but steadfastly maintained that she had wanted a butterfly, which Mr. Timmity just as stubbornly denied. When asked if she desired Mr. Timmity, as a penalty for his alleged mischief, to remove or obliterate the tattoo, she suddenly smiled and said no, she guessed she kind of liked it. Police then released Mr. Timmity for lack of proof of complaint.

MR. GOLDILOCKS

Mr. and Mrs. Morton Forum returned to their home at 804 Burroughs Street at about 11 p.m. last evening and discovered that the front door, which they thought they had left locked when they went out to dine at the house of friends, had apparently been jimmied and was standing open. Fearful that they had been robbed, they hurried into their living room and, turning lights on, were relieved to see that the television set was still there. They noticed, however, that the soft, down-filled cushions of the sofa had been disturbed, as if someone had been stretched out on them. They went upstairs to their bedroom and were distressed to see, not only that drawers had been rifled and clothing from them thrown about, but also that the coverlet of their king-size double bed had been removed and the sheets and blankets were in disarray. The bed had obviously been occupied. While Mrs. Forum telephoned the police, Mr. Forum conducted a further search of the second floor, and entering the guest room and switching on the lights there, he saw a man tucked under the covers of one of the room's twin beds and sleeping so soundly that neither the sudden brightness in the room nor a shout from Mr. Forum wakened him. Mr. Forum saw that one of the sleeping man's hands, on top of the sheets, had hold of the strap of a small backpack. He was able to remove the pack from the man's grasp without waking him. Inspection revealed that the pack contained Mrs. Forum's jewel box, with items valued at over $3,000 in it; ruby-studded cuff links belonging to Mr. Forum; as well as a number of valuable small objets d'art, which the couple had not noticed as missing in their excitement and confusion in the living room. When the police arrived, an officer was finally able to waken the sleeping man, who was identified later as Mr. Shawn Gilligan of 57 Gumbo-limbo Trailer Court. On being questioned, he stated with a heavy south Georgia redneck accent, yawning frequently as he spoke, "Ah was jes' so daggone *tahred*, couldn' hep mahseff, *had* to cawnk out." Then, speaking to Mr. and Mrs. Forum, he said, "Thet sofa of yourn downstars so fucken sof' Ah couldn' git to sleep on the thang, and hell, thet big ol' bed in thet other room thar's jes' lak a fucken slab a concrete. But this yere other'n, thass a *good* ol' bed. Ah thanks y'all fer the nap." Mr. Gilligan was arrested and charged with breaking-and-entering and aggravated attempt of grand theft.

THE DOMINO EFFECT IN WARFARE

At 1:30 a.m. last night, Officer Allen Cramp was dispatched to a reported altercation in front of The Blunderbar on Roosevelt Boulevard. There he found Arthur Almond, 22, and Willy Thrumm, 24, in a free-for-all fight. A bystander, Kurt Simpson, 58, said the young men had come out of the bar arguing about an alleged insult one of them had offered the other's girlfriend. Two young women, overcome with what seemed inappropriate giggling, were in fact watching the fight. They were later identified as Jill Franklin, 17, and Pelagrina Carlson, 19.

When Officer Cramp attempted to separate and subdue the combatants, they at once made common cause, transforming themselves from enemies into allies and teaming up to box the officer. The scrapping men—including the policeman, as the bystander Simpson later reported—set up a wild hullabaloo of blue swear words as their fists flew. Added to that noise were repeated loud calls on the radio in the policeman's patrol car, parked nearby, asking whether Officer Cramp would like some backup.

At this juncture, Manuel Suarez, the owner of the bar, emerged from the front entrance and began shouting at the three contestants, ordering them to "knock off that goddam noise," making the reasonable point that the disturbance was bad for his business. It should be added that he did not stint on *his* epithets, which he directed equally at the young men and at the arm of the law. Hearing some of this extravagant profanity aimed at him, Officer Cramp lost his temper and turned and attacked the owner. With alliances thus altered once again, Almond and Thrumm went back at each other.

Just then Baxter Williams, 36, and John Klickstein, 42, customers of the bar—evidently first-rate customers, to judge by their condition—emerged from the front entrance of The Blunderbar and, seeing owner Suarez under attack, joined the officer in the assault on him, shouting that he had overcharged them and was, as Klickstein put it, a "swamp rat and a damn swindler."

With Suarez accordingly outmanned, Officer Cramp turned back to deal with Thrumm and Almond. But Mr. Simpson, the bystander, protested that the two were having a fair fight over a woman and should be left alone. The officer did not agree. At that, Mr. Simpson, despite his somewhat advanced age, lit into the officer with impressive vigor.

This was now an extremely active three-ring fight, but more was yet to come. When one of the young men of the original fracas, Mr. Thrumm, appeared to be getting the worse of it from Mr. Almond, both Miss Franklin and Miss Carlson entered the fray, attacking Almond and shrieking at him as their fingernails dug in, even though it was Thrumm, not Almond, who had been alleged to have delivered the insult in the first place.

Now two backup patrol cars arrived. Officers James Burns and Warren ("Bull") Johns, rushing into battle and flailing right and left with nightsticks, succeeded in restoring order, but not before having received some serious bruises and scratches from both male and female combatants.

All eleven casualties of these cumulative hostilities were taken to the emergency room at Florida Keys Memorial Hospital to be patched up. The eight participants in the affair who were not in uniform were then transported to the Monroe County Jail. Duty Officer Frank Taylor has told the *Citizen* that it took two hours, in the booking process, to untangle the rights and wrongs of what had happened.

PROFESSOR HOUDINI

James Higgins, 54, a resident of The Beachcomber, was surprised red-handed some time after midnight last night in the act of committing a robbery at Wilhelmina's, the novelty and jewelry store at 1502 Duval Street, when Procter Wilson, the store's proprietor, chanced to return to his shop at that late hour because he had realized he had forgotten to set the burglar alarm. Mr. Wilson stated to the police that he was mystified by two things. First, the man was very well dressed, in a sporty Hawaiian shirt and white slacks of a fine duck material, pleated at the waist. And second, more significantly, the intruder had been able to penetrate two doors—one the entrance from the street and the other the door to the small back room where Mr. Wilson nightly locks up his stock of valuables—both doors being secured by Marlis Super-Unpickable Barrel-Bolt Locks, said to be the most sophisticated burglarproof devices in the world at the present time. Upon getting this information, Detective Sergeant Wallace Brown recalled three other recent Key West robberies, in all of which state-of-the-art pickproof locks had in fact been ravished. Procuring a warrant, he therefore conducted a search of Mr. Higgins's quarters—a surprisingly elegant condominium in The Beachcomber complex. In a closet he found all the goods stolen in the three previous unsolved robberies, which Mr. Higgins had obviously not taken the trouble to fence, leading Sergeant Brown to entertain a sneaking suspicion that the crimes might have been committed by an enthusiast, simply as bravura exercises of skill, for the sheer pleasure in the difficulties. In the course of the search he also saw, on the wall of Mr. Higgins's study, a framed diploma, certifying his graduation from the William Burford Jones Security Academy and Institute of Locksmithing, in North Miami. A telephone call to the academy brought this statement from Dean Michael Frawley: "Higgins? Oh, my heavens, yes. He was the most brilliant student we ever had, and we were extremely fortunate in being able to attract him to our faculty, where he was a distinguished professor for fourteen years. Please give him my very warmest regards. We miss him. That man is an artist!"

Amends

"Should we invite Colonel Maloney?" Mary Browne asked her husband.

"Sometimes, Mary," the Honorable Joseph Beverly Browne answered, "your charity verges on frenzy. The man was a Unionist through and through."

The Brownes were planning a dinner party that they were to have the honor to give the following fortnight for Jefferson Davis, ex-President of the Confederacy, who, freed not long ago from his two years of unspeakably degrading imprisonment in Fort Monroe, Virginia, would be stopping off in Key West on his way from Baltimore to Havana. It was hoped that the benign December weather in Cuba would help to mend his broken health.

There could be no more suitable host for the ex-President than Joseph Browne. He came to Key West from Virginia thirty-seven years before; he attended the St. Joseph Convention and helped write the constitution on the basis of which Florida was admitted to the federal union; he was state marshal under three presidents and served as clerk of the district court; he had been chosen several times as mayor of Key West; and he had been elected the previous year to the state legislature. His bearing was noble; his oratory, often called upon, was Ciceronian. But most to the point on this occasion, he had been a staunch secessionist all through the War Between the States, in a city of the farthest South that never managed to break away from Union control.

"But he's so charming," Mary Browne said. "You're an unforgiving man, Joseph."

"What makes you think Colonel Maloney has forgiven President Davis? Or will ever?"

It was inevitable that Colonel Maloney would soon hear about the Brownes' plans for the Davis dinner, because the Negro domestics of Key West knew everything worth knowing and Colonel Maloney's houseman, Jobel, told his employer about the dinner before Mistress Browne even knew what she would serve that night—though Jobel knew, because his friend Sara, the Brownes' cook, had already settled her mind on a pit-roast shoat. Colonel Maloney realized, absolutely without regret, that he would not be invited to what would probably be the most elegant affair of the winter.

The Civil War had torn Key West bitterly asunder, and of all the substantial men of the town, Colonel Maloney stood apart as the most steadfast, the most outspoken, the most irascible leader of the Union wing of the rift. A tall attorney with an astonishing toucan nose, haunted blue eyes, and a beaver streaked with gray on his cheeks and chin, he wore a frock coat all winter long, even on weekdays, and he carried a rather dangerous-looking buckthorn walking stick, almost a shillelagh. He came to Key West in the thirties, taught school for a while, and eventually took up the law. He was the clerk of the Southern Circuit Court and also mayor before Joseph Browne was either. No one knew exactly where he got the title of Colonel. He seemed a bluff, jovial Irishman most of the time, but it was not considered wise to cross him. Sometimes he was thought to have tucked a pistol under his belt. He once said to a man who had, he believed, insulted him, "If you will step outside and repeat those words, I will put a buttonhole in your weskit that no seamstress can ever mend." He could be insulting himself; once he said, "Sir, I shall beat your brains out with a sponge." And in a debate on the war, he said to an infuriated opponent who had raised his fist, "When you strike me, Daniel, you strike the United States of America."

In December 1860, eight days before South Carolina seceded from the Union, the largest meeting ever held in Key West was convened at the Monroe County courthouse to choose delegates to a state convention in Tallahassee, where Florida's withdrawal from the Union would be discussed. Among all the leading citizens of the town, Colonel Maloney was the only speaker who argued for Florida's staying in the Union. A month after the war broke out, eighty-six men marched from the St. James Hotel to the Union stronghold, Fort Taylor, offering themselves as a volunteer company for the Union cause; Colonel Maloney was put in command. With few exceptions, the volunteers were "common folk"—carpenters, clerks, wreckers' crewmen and divers, and workers in cigar factories. "Respectable folk"—the gentry, attorneys, town elders, and business leaders—were on the other side, and it took some grit for Maloney to go against the grain of his class and, indeed, to oppose so stubbornly many of his warm friends. One of them, Henry Mulrennan, having hoisted a rebel flag at his place of business, wrote to Major William H. French, commander of Fort Taylor, demanding that he surrender, or he, Mulrennan, would come unarmed with friends to take possession of the redoubt; an ultimate consequence of this quixotic act of gallantry was that Mulrennan found himself firmly locked behind bars in Fort Lafayette, in New York harbor. William Pinckney and Judge Winer Bethel, likewise former friends of Colonel Maloney, were arrested for treason and shipped north to be imprisoned at Fort Monroe. William H. Ward, pro-Confederacy editor of the local paper, *Key of the Gulf*, threat-

ened with the same fate, fled and joined the Rebel army. The cruelest twist of all for Colonel Maloney came when his own son, Walter junior, sneaked away by night in a small sloop with a man named Pacetti, eluding the sentry vessel in the harbor, and sailed all the way to Tampa to enlist with the rebels.

This defection from his father's stand by Walter junior had a most ironic sequel for Walter senior. Among the many paranoiac directives issued to the defenders of Fort Taylor during the war was one, by the Union commander of the Department of the South, ordering that "you will immediately send to this post the families (white) of all persons who have husbands, brothers, or sons in rebel employment . . . in order that they may be all placed within the rebel lines." Six hundred Key Westers—including Colonel Maloney!—were told to be ready to be hauled off to Hilton Head, South Carolina; thence to be dumped in the Confederate wilderness. The rebel sympathizers who were affected by the order were appalled by the thought of being snatched from their comfortable homes in Key West and tossed at random into the chaos behind the rebel lines in the war zone. Colonel Maloney and the local federal district attorney rallied the Unionists in town to send a vehement protest to Washington against this monstrous order, and soon Colonel T. H. Good of the Fourth Pennsylvania Volunteers was sent to relieve the previous commander of Fort Taylor. His first act was to suspend the deportations. The citizens of the town, supporters of the Blue and the Gray alike, gathered in Clinton Square to present Colonel Good with a gold-hilted sword. And whose tongue uttered the beautifully crafted presentation speech? Colonel Maloney's, of course. And when he had closed his peroration with thanks to the deity, the good people of both loyalties all joined hands and sang:

Colonel Good has got the sword.
Bully for that! Bully for that!

And now the night of the Brownes' dinner for Jefferson Davis is fast approaching. The Brownes can accommodate no more than eighteen at table, and the satisfaction of those "respectable folk" who have been invited, and the galling envy on the part of those who have not, are acute. The dinner is very much on Colonel Maloney's mind too, though not because he wishes he could be among the guests. There is a quality in Walter Cathcart Maloney, Sr., which he does all he can to hide from the world. Deep beneath his bad temper and his swagger there lies a layer of generosity, of tender conscience, of which he is both proud and ashamed: proud because he secretly thinks it makes him fair-minded, ashamed because others may consider him soft—"mush-souled," he would say—on account of it. It is to this quality that the impending visit of the hated Jeff has been making its appeal in recent days.

The Colonel has made it his business, ever since the end of the war, and with special fervor because of the assassination of Lincoln, to inform himself about the fate of Jefferson Davis. It gave him great satisfaction, at first, to learn, a month after Lincoln's death, that the "other president" was locked away in formidable Fort Monroe, on the Chesapeake not far from Washington, with its granite walls thirty feet high and, in places, ninety feet thick. Old Jeff would never escape from that fastness. Later, however, as Washington friends sent the Colonel exultant reports of Davis's imprisonment from the capital's newspapers, he began to suffer from unwelcome qualms; the spirit of vengeance, it seemed to him, had grown morbid. Davis, a man of great learning in the classics, a former U.S. senator and secretary of war, was being subjected to vile humiliations. Suffering from painful neuralgia, he was housed in the former gun room of the fort, where windows had been walled up, leaving a suffocating damp smell of fresh plaster. More than seventy soldiers with loaded muskets were set all round to guard him, and by day and by night two sentinels had been ordered to pace back and forth inside his cell in their *heavy boots. A lamp was kept lit all through the dark hours, right at the head of his cot. He could not sleep. He was fed boiled beef in a bucket covered with a dirty towel, his only implement a wooden spoon. One day, an officer entered the cell with a blacksmith. Davis, seeing that he was to suffer the hideous disgrace of being put in irons, asked the officer to shoot him. The blacksmith approached with fetters and chains and knelt to go to work. Davis, in a rage, grappled with the man and threw him across the room. The blacksmith ran at the prisoner with his hammer raised; the officer blocked him from killing Davis. A sentry cocked his musket. The officer ordered him to hold his fire and summoned four men to subdue Davis. They held him down on his cot while the blacksmith riveted the leg irons to the ankles.*

This was too much. All through the two years of Jefferson Davis's imprisonment, as news came that he suffered from constant pain, his body wasting, his eyesight growing dim, nothing could erase from Colonel Maloney's mind the picture of that distinguished gentleman (no matter how much you wanted to hate what he had stood for) being pinned to his cot by four strong young men while he was put in irons, like a deranged murderer or rapist.

At the long table, the merry twinkling on the glassware of the light of thirty candles does nothing to dispel a feeling that the dinner has not been the success everyone had hoped it would be. All through the meal, Mary Browne has doggedly flirted with the great man seated to her right—alas, to no avail. He stared at the turtle soup without tasting it, nibbled at the chilled crayfish, pushed bits of roast pork, fried plantain, and spiced turnip greens back and forth across his plate, and he is now picking at the edges of a slice of pecan pie. He is pallid and dull. Mary Browne risked her husband's displeasure by emerging for the occasion, in honor of the Hero of the Lost Cause, most daringly décolleté. She is habitually self-confident, she is ripe, she is ample. She evidently hopes the ex-President need only take one look at her to feel that he is among bosom friends. At the other end of the table, Varina Davis, who, everyone knows, fought so gallantly to have her husband set free from his humiliating imprisonment, has eaten heartily but sullenly. Not even the Honorable Joseph Beverly Browne's eloquent toast to the Davises has brought anything like a smile to her face. The couple have been exhausted beyond the farthest edge of enjoyment of life by the ordeal of the last two years.

Now all at the table can hear a loud knocking at the front door of the house. There are sounds of commotion in the vestibule. What unpleasantness is this, to cap the failed evening? An insistent bass voice. A flurry of sounds of doubt. The fractious noises trail roundabout into the kitchen.

And here, through the servants' swinging door, bursts a tall, robust Negro, resplendent in a butler's uniform with gold braid at the sleeves, wearing white gloves and holding high a silver tray. He grins; his bearing is cocky and borders on the insolent.

Mr. Browne, who has his back to the servants' door, can't help noticing that the Key West gentlemen at the table look shocked and angry. He swings around and sees over his shoulder that the man standing there is the one called Jobel, Colonel Walter Maloney's manservant.

His face flushed, Mr. Browne looks at his wife at the opposite end of the table, and obviously making an effort, for the guests' sakes, to control his voice, he says, "Mary, is this your doing?"

Mrs. Browne has barely begun to shake her head, to defend herself, when in a deep voice Jobel says, "Colonel Maloney wishes to pay his respects—and make amends—to Mr. Jefferson Davis. He wishes for me to tell you that he gathered these gifts from his own garden and arranged them for your pleasure, sir, with his own hands."

Jobel steps around the table to the ex-President's place. A pantrymaid hastily clears a space for the tray on the table in front of the guest of honor, and Jobel sets the tray down.

At the center there is a white-fleshed, bowl-like half of a coconut, immediately surrounded by blooms of half a dozen varieties of orchid. Around them are placed, on a bed of variegated croton leaves, an abundance of brown, rough-skinned sapodillas; pale-green anones; mangoes of three different varieties, yellow, orange, and red. And scattered here and there, all through the display, are pink West Indian cherries, well known by the Key Westers at the table to be Colonel Maloney's special object of pride, so often has he boasted about them without ever offering to give a single one of them away.

Mr. Browne's face is scarlet. "Mr. President," he says, "if I were you I would not touch anything on that tray. Those things come from a bitter enemy of yours. This Colonel Maloney opposed you, Mr. President, all through the war, with the most violent and abusive intransigence. I would not think it safe for you to eat any gift of his."

As Browne speaks, Jefferson Davis, for the first time all evening long, brightens, looks up into the faces of the guests, and is alive. He reaches forward and picks up one of the ugliest of the fruits, and after curiously examining it for a moment, he turns to Mrs. Browne and says, "What is this? And how does one eat it?"

Mary Browne says, "It is called the sapodilla, sir." For a moment she seems not to know what to do. Then, throwing a defiant glance at her husband, she takes the fruit from the Hero, picks up a knife, cuts the sapodilla in two, and hands the halves to Mr. Davis.

There is palpable consternation around the table. One of the men blurts out, "No!" But Davis, suddenly looking excited, and almost mischievous, takes a bite from one of the halves. He chews. And he chews. After a longish hesitation, he swallows. Then he carefully reassembles the two halves of the sapodilla and puts them down on the tray.

The Hero's lips are puckered by what must be a sharp aftertaste, but his face is otherwise unmarked by pain of any sort, as he looks, triumphantly now, at Mr. Browne, then around the table at all the others. His expression seems to say, "Ah, you people in this safe haven, far from the war, did you see that? I am quite used to putting myself in harm's way."

"Do you like our Key West fruit?" Mary Browne asks.

His mouth still wry, the ex-President says, "I can't say I care for it particularly."

It seems as if everyone in the room, the room itself, the whole heavy-timbered house, lets out a sigh of relief. Not only is Jefferson Davis entirely safe; he is frank to say that he dislikes this Unionist colonel's gift.

Then, in haste, evidently not wishing to be seen as having been outmannered by the hostile giver, and perhaps mindful that Mrs. Browne has seemed rather proud of "our Key West fruit," he adds, with good grace, "But I fancy some *people might be right fond of it."*

Piped Over the Side

The first sight Lieutenant Commander Robert Selden gets as he arrives is of some thirty guys—pals and gals, different ranks—*They didn't have to come; I really think they like me*—standing at ease in a split formation on either side of the walkway up to the flagpole, all of them dogged out in their summer whites, as crisp as typewriter paper. He approaches them from their rear. The flagpole, in its little parklike space, has always seemed to him to stand at the heart of the naval air station, and as he steps toward it now, very likely for the last time, unsure of his feelings, trying to distance himself from anything maudlin, he hears the executive officer, at the podium, call out, "*Ten . . . hut!*" and at once the uniformed figures stiffen, feet together. In his honor. There's nothing he can do to stop the rush of blood to his face.

He goes forward between the halves of the formation to the little low platform on which Captain Peckham and the executive officer and the chaplain are standing, and moving toward the seat that the XO points out to him, he half turns and takes in the gathering of civilian guests in flanking rows of folding chairs at the front of the audience. A few empty seats. He winks at Ginny, in the front row, to the left. She is pale. There is his mom, down from Philly, and next to her the two boys and their girlfriends. He can't believe some of the other people who have made it down here to see him shot out into the world. His best high school friend, Russ. Dear God, fat cousin Bart, Frogface. The whole Simpson family. He is too excited to check everybody out.

Ginny looks as if she doesn't want this to be happening. She has been worried. About finality. About having him around the house all day. Most of all, about money. How can a family of four live for a year on twenty-one five these days? His pension will be only half his lieutenant commander's pay, O-4 grade, twenty-year level. But he tells her the boys are both earning paychecks, good long-range construction work in the Truman Annex, and they're living at home—that saves money right there. They've promised to chip in for now, and he can start in on a civilian job even during his thirty-day terminal leave. Smart to take that option. They can all stay on in the navy house this extra month and look for a place in the Old Town to live. Key West is his piece of pie; he wouldn't think of moving away. He'll go on with his night job at Scotty's that he's already been doing to earn enough extra money beyond his pay to give the family some leeway, and he'll also scout around for a permanent full-time day job. He's told Ginny that lots of retirees take two jobs, on different shifts, and how about that guy Clifton—rakes in his pension, rent on a house he owns, and pay from two jobs: a quadruple dipper! Everything's going to be fine. Ginny wearily says, "You're unreal." He winks at her again, and this time she manages a halfhearted smile.

The XO steps to the podium, and orders the colors to be

presented, and says, "Please remain standing afterward while the chaplain gives the blessing." The color guard, off the edge of the grass to Bob's right, start marking time. They've chosen his clerk, Lizabet, who just made yeoman second, to command the colors detail and carry the American flag. The group is a comedy-club sight, because Lizabet is barely five feet tall and pouts in concentration, holding the flag straight up, this duty heavy on her mind as if this were a funeral, while the two fellows and the other girl in the detail are all six feet tall and mixed ethnic, with shining faces, recruiting-poster material, proud to be American. Lizabet gets the four up to the platform somehow, and when the national anthem comes up on the speakers, sounding far away and tinny, the air station colors dip but not the Stars and Stripes. The chaplain has the mercy to get his part over quickly, and Lizabet marches the detail off again, with just a bit of raggedness in the wheeling process. No matter. To him, on this particular day, these customs—the detail's order of march, the angle of the flags during the anthem, one saluting, the other saluted, everything straight out of the Big Book—these are the sorts of things that tell him he's lived for twenty years in a zone of comfort. Where you do what you're supposed to do, and do it right. You can get good at that. That part's been easy. Everything's going to be hunky-dory.

Off to the far side of the podium from where he is sitting, there is a low table holding a pile of what look like picture frames. The exec, with the CO now standing beside him, asks Ginny to come forward. Although she knew this was going to happen, she looks surprised, taking quick sidelong glances at Bob's mom and the boys—as if to convey, "I had no *idea!*"—and she gets up and with one little stumble steps up to the platform. Ginny has put on weight, and she has developed a habit of sadness, which she wears like a uniform; he feels a stirring of uneasiness, watching her come forward. She doesn't look at him. The XO picks up one of the framed items and reads out the Certificate of Appreciation of the retiree's wife. A boilerplate job, you can tell, but Ginny's face reacts to each phrase, as if: Yeah, that's me. Yes. Okay. I'm glad you realize. *Cut it out, Gin; this is getting embarrassing.* But he also feels a kind of ache for her, looking so gloomy in her delight. The exec hands the frame to the CO, who hands it to Ginny and kisses her on the cheek. Then Chuck Stone—*my guy, the one person in the service I can tell anything to*—comes forward from the formation in back and gives Ginny a bouquet of roses and baby's breath. Ginny's sadness under the blush of her pleasure really shows at this point in time. She doesn't seem to have a clue how appropriate her long face is for a retirement ceremony. Bob can see plainly enough, though, that her mood doesn't really have anything at all to do with the occasion. That deep look isn't dedicated to him as a gift. Something is going on in her head that is privately hers, something inward, something maybe locking into place in the back of her mind that he'd better hope he'll never hear about.

Yeah, there'll be times, he knows. That woman in the three-day course on retirement at the Family Service Center, a j.g., thinking she's motherly at age about thirty, saying, "You'll be a different person, sir. You tell me you've been close, but one morning pretty soon your wife is going to wake up in bed next to a stranger. Two and a half stripes? The enlisteds've been saluting, it's 'sir' to you all the way down the line, and when you say hop, they fly right up off the ground with pointy toes. Then you retire and find yourself out there in a job with some squirt who got out of graduate school about two weeks ago, you know, smart-ass little M.B.A., suddenly your boss, and he tells you you got a lot to learn, mister, do it my way. You're going to be taking this stuff home to supper, sir. You'll have a whole new identity. You'll be a person your wife didn't necessarily think she was marrying."

Captain Peckham is at the podium, clearing his throat. His

face has a caved-in look; his hat always seems, because of this, to be tilted too far forward. "We are gathered," he says, "to congratulate our good friend Bob Selden on his retirement from active duty. This is a sad day indeed for me." Bob accepts this, as he does much that the CO says, at a discount. Peckham wears wings. Bob doesn't. Bob came up from the ranks. The CO sure didn't—he graduated from Annapolis. There has been a gaping empty space between them, always a hint on the CO's face, no matter what Bob has said, of maybe yes and maybe no. But Bob has always done his thing on time, and whenever he has handed papers to Peckham, the CO has glanced at them and then nodded to him, in a very low-key code, if you wanted to take it that way, for "Well done." But to hear his speech now, you'd think that if this particular paperwork pilot hadn't flown his desktop in such perfect formation on the CO's desk's wing, the whole naval air station would have slid right off the Keys into the Florida Straits. High praise, but a not too subtle reminder that Lieutenant Commander Selden hasn't ever flown anything but a desk. Never mind. *I've done my job.* One thing that the CO points out is written in stone: A man can't come all the way up through the ranks from raw seaman to lieutenant commander without having gotten whistle-clean performance ratings every step of the way.

But Bob is grinding. The nerve of that cocky little j.g. lecturing him in the retirement course. Social-worker *bull*shit. He knows damn well how not to be an officer. In the job at Scotty's, working nights—perfectly legal—in jeans and an apron, stock-clerking, putting stuff on shelves, waiting on customers, whatever, he's been with several guys from the air station from different ranks below him, four or five seamen first and second, a petty officer, couple of chiefs, a warrant—no such thing as "sir" there on the job, they're all just guys, first names, you're who you are in your bare bones to the rest of them. Every one of those friends from Scotty's is standing at attention back there in the formation. Isn't a single one that didn't voluntarily show up for the ceremony. No one was ordered to attend.

I'll never *be a stranger to my Ginny. She's got every corpuscle in me tagged and labeled, and if a single one looks like it's mutating, she'll let me know.*

No question about that. Just two days ago, Saturday morning, there Bob was in his hammock, off duty, slung between a royal palm and an Australian pine, on the water side of his house on Trumbo Point, watching the parade of charter boats and yachts on their morning run out the channel through the overpass from Garrison Bight, his own smart little Mako twenty-footer dancing in their wakes at his private dock at the foot of the lawn, and he was thinking, *Oh, brother, what a good-luck guy I turned out to be. It'll be hammock time whenever I want.* Starting Monday, he'd be on the loose. Free from the cluttered office in the admin building at Boca Chica. From all that hassle of the regulation drill for every single move of his little finger. Thirty-eight years old, healthy as a hammer, free as the air. Free as that frigate bird he saw soaring overhead, trailing its sassy long tail feathers, the whole sky its personal backyard. *Imagine me,* he was thinking, *imagine me every day, if I want, in jeans and an unironed work shirt, like right now, flat on my ass out here in my hammock at zero nine hundred hours in the damn morning! Every day a Saturday.*

Just about then he heard Ginny call him from the kitchen. He held his breath for a few seconds, then let it all go and rolled out of the hammock and went in.

"I'm going to the commissary," she called when she heard his footsteps in the hallway. "Be back sometime. I'll pick up the *Herald.*"

In the kitchen door, he said, "I'm coming with you."

She gave him a long straight look. "To the store? What for?"

"Thought I could, you know, help you carry stuff."

There was a long pause. Her back was turned to him. Then she said, "Let's go. I'm driving."

"Suits me."

Inside the commissary, Ginny backed a shopping cart out of its nest. Bob reached for the handle, but before he could grab it she was already off down the soups-and-condiments aisle. She knew what she wanted. A can of Progresso minestrone. Then around to whole wheat bread. Cornflakes for him. A couple of rolls of toilet paper. Some virgin olive oil. Sardines . . .

Bob hung back. He began lifting rolls of toilet paper off the shelf, checking the labels. Carrying two of the rolls, he hurried to catch up with Ginny. "Look, hon," he said. "This kind has fifty more sheets to the roll than them"—pointing to the rolls she'd tossed in her cart. "Eleven cents cheaper the roll too. Don't you think?" He leaned over to reach into the basket and exchange the rolls he was carrying for the ones Gin had chosen.

"Get your hands out of my cart, Commander," Ginny sharply said.

"You're the one who's been fussing about the money," he said.

Ginny took a deep breath. "This I do not need, Bob. This is something I can live without. I don't need this. I appreciated your wanting to carry the bags for me. That was real nice. You were rehearsing, right? You're planning to be a helpful husband, beginning immediately after the ceremony day after tomorrow, right? Things'll be different, right? But when you think about it, I've been carrying grocery bags for nineteen years. Haven't I? Was it such a horrible life? Tell me."

Bob takes a quick look now at Ginny in the front row—she's sniffing at the bouquet—as Captain Peckham calls him forward and holds up another of the picture frames. The CO explains to the civilians in the audience that this is President Clinton's reply to Commander Selden's letter asking the Commander in Chief for permission to be allowed to retire from active duty and be admitted to the Fleet Reserve. "Permission granted," the CO says. "Reserve for the next ten years," he adds in a slightly triumphant tone, as if this were a punitive sentence Bob deserved—and then, to make it worse, "Subject to recall. Two hitches possible. Total four years maximum." He rotates the framed document for everyone in the audience to see, and he says, pointing at a place in the text, "Right here President Clinton sends his personal thanks to Commander Selden for his twenty years of loyal service to his country."

Now, while the civilians all clap, the CO hands the thing to Bob, and Bob gives it a quick once-over. The President's signature looks printed to him, but what the hell.

He looks at Ginny again. She has lowered the bouquet into her arms and is holding it like a baby. She is glaring at the framed document in Bob's hands. On the whole, she has been like a rock during his climb all the years up the ranks, but this kind of rigmarole—request to the Commander in Chief; permission granted; personal thanks—always strikes her as childish, as if it all came out of the Boy Scout manual. "You and your 'regs,' " she said one night not long ago when they were discussing the ins and outs of the retirement pay he'd be getting. "I'm sick of your 'regs.' It's a pretend life you lead. This book that you say it all comes out of . . . You know what? It's all like from a make-believe story, like you could buy it in paperback for twenty cents at that secondhand-book store on Truman Avenue. Bet there's a whole chapter on the salute. I've seen you salute that retard Captain Peckham. You don't have your heart in it, Bobby. Plenty times I've seen guys salute you like they were giving you the back of their hand. There's a thousand and one meanings in that business of the salute—all depends how you make the move, doesn't it? Every time you salute, you're playing a dangerous little game in your guts, aren't you?"

"Come on, Ginny," he said. "There has to be a right way of doing things. There has to be, when you may be asking people to put their lives on the line."

Ginny knew how to bring a conversation to an end. "Because they might have to make the supreme sacrifice? Did anyone ever ask you for anything like that? You never had a war, Bob," she said.

Now Captain Peckham goes over to the little table and picks up the largest framed object of all, a strange contraption in the shape of a triangle fastened atop a rectangle. Bob has looked forward to seeing this, the "shadow box" that they told him he'd be getting, a wonderful memento for him to hang on a wall at home. Under glass in the upper part there is an American flag, folded in the ritual way into a compact small triangle. "This flag," the CO says with a straight face, "has been flown over the dome of the Capitol in Washington in honor of Commander Selden." Bob doesn't dare look Ginny in the eye after this whopper. How many navy men all over the world are retiring on this very day—in other words, how many domes does the Capitol have to fly all those honorary flags to give away? The CO is holding the shadow box upright for the civilian guests to see. "Look," he says. "You can see here, in these three compartments"—they are in the rectangle beneath the triangle—"first off, here on the left, a flag anchor for every one of the pay grades Commander Selden has gone through . . . let's see . . . mmm"—he laboriously counts—"sixteen of them. And over here on the right, the rows of his ribbons. And here, in the middle, the really important thing, the list of all his duty stations. The story of his life." The CO puts his glasses on, heavy horn-rims, which help to fill out the weird concavity of his face, and he bends over and reads them off.

Duty stations, God. Yes, Ginny was right, that night. He never had a war. He entered boot camp just when 'Nam was petering out. He was on the beach down here at Boca Chica during the quickie in the gulf. The closest he ever came to a war was that time during one of his hitches at sea, not far offshore at Lebanon. He can see in his memory the sparkling sweep of waves under the Mediterranean sky and, on the beach, clouds of dust and smoke rising from the shelling of the forlorn city. He had no wish for combat. He preferred a distant view of it. That hitch in the Mediterranean was surely his best duty of all, for as a chief warrant officer he had thumbscrew sway over all the enlisted ranks and had, as well, the warrant's delightful sense of superiority over all the officer grades at least as high as full commander. Could look 'em in the eye and read their minds: This guy, they're thinking, has come up the hard way, he's had grease on his hands, knows the men, *is* one of them but he's above them too; has the phantom authority, over all of us, of a hard-butt uncle. But now Bob suddenly thinks of Ginny's letters back then. Reached the ship in bunches. The boys had grown into full-blown hellion territory. Sometimes she wondered whether she had the strength. Worried about him all the time, with those crazies over there, terrorists. Money awful tight. His letters were so happy. How come?

Wait a minute. *Was* that the best duty of all? It had to be the time right here, right here with Gin. This has been like a two-year vacation under the sun. He remembers a beautiful Sunday with Ginny at Fort Zachary Taylor Beach—she really shouldn't have been wearing a bikini—she was rubbing sun-screen lotion on his back, and she said, out of the blue, "It's pretty tough cookies, this life, isn't it, Bobby?" And then she added, in a quiet voice, "You're good company." Then quickly said, doubtless in order not to seem a pushover, "I mean, you're good company the few times you're around home and not doing some of your damn sea duty." By which she meant, of course, going out fishing.

Out in his sweet little Mako. Lots of tarpon in May and June. Never actually caught any bonefish or permit out on the back-country flats, but what great Saturdays and Sundays with Chuck Stone out there, poling along in the shallows, a beer now and then to neutralize the blazing sun, maybe hard-boiled eggs or a salami sandwich Ginny's made up, and close-in talk, lot of belly laughs—and, suddenly, *there!* See over there? Big son of a bitch. Hooo. Spooky fish—*ffft*—gone. Enough just to *try* for them. And now, any damn day of the week, think of it, he can go out. Any day. He'll have to find somebody else to go with on weekdays, but a deal as tempting as that shouldn't be hard. Chuck'll still be there on weekends. Bob could wish Ginny didn't hate going out on the water so much. She makes a face—thanks, she'd rather get her fish at the Waterfront Market. He thinks of her pinched little sigh, as if she didn't want him to hear it or see it—trying to be decent—when he says he's going out in the boat. "What time'll you be back?" You don't know what's out there; how could you say exactly what time you'd be back?

There was that time out there when he and Chuck got talking about wives. Chuck's Esther was a whiner. The worst thing, Chuck said, was in bed. She was a whiz between the sheets, really she came after him like a nympho, but the trouble was that as soon as they finished, when he was thinking how great that had been, she'd start complaining: something he'd forgotten to do around the house, or he never talked to her, or, what really hurt, why had this gone so flat?—wasn't fun anymore, he was like a cold fish.

Bob said thank God it wasn't like that for him. Bed with Ginny couldn't be better; the two of them almost always arrived at their destination at the same moment, and the afterwards with her was very warm, lots of laughing. "She's such a natural person," he said. But then he felt a sudden little shiver of a mood change, as he remembered something that had happened a few nights before that, and he added, "I have to admit, Chuck, sometimes I don't know. Sometimes, when I think about retiring, I feel like she's going to have me on a leash." In a sort of advance celebration of his getting out, he and Ginny had gone to a night spot called Two Friends to listen to some music. He was in civvies. The place had a pretty good trio, they seemed to like requests, and Ginny mellowed out a lot. They had a big nostalgia going, all the good years. Remember this? Remember that? They even held hands for a while, like kids. But there were these four guys sitting at the next table and talking at the top of their voices and giggling—high-pitched—very loose at the wrists, that kind of thing, you could tell what they were. Pretty soon he began to get the feeling these characters were laughing at the way Ginny and he were, heads close together, murmuring, so sentimental. So in the middle of one number he turned and said, "Would you cut down on the volume, you guys? We came to listen to the music." One of them said, "Oooh, sorry!" but then they went right on like before, louder maybe. He was about to get up and punch a nose, but then he saw Ginny's face, and she had a look he didn't think he'd ever seen before. "It was like," he said to Chuck, " 'If you do that, I'll . . .' You couldn't tell exactly what she had in mind, but it was as if I had to be reminded I was about to be sort of a nobody, pretty soon I wasn't going to have stripes anymore. Other words, I was going to be fresh out of substantial authority. Over anyone. Including her. She's always been so tender with me. It was a real shock, that look on her face."

"Ease up, Bob," Chuck said. "She just didn't want you to make a damn fool of yourself."

"Maybe. Maybe that's all it was."

Now Captain Peckham turns and nods to Bob. It's the cue for his farewell speech. He is bothered by how nervous he is as he steps up to the podium. He has written it all out, but when he starts talking he doesn't even glance at the paper. To begin with, a few little white lies are strictly required. "I want to thank you, Captain, for the kind words you said about me a few minutes ago. I feel real lucky to have been working with you these last couple of years. You always made my duty seem . . . I won't say"—Bob grins—"I won't say exactly a pleasure, but anyway real easy." He sees his friends in the formation chuckle at his dig. He is surprised himself at his nerve. He sees rhythmic bulges begin to work in the CO's jaw. You never can tell, when Peckham grinds his teeth, whether he's mad, or in a hurry to get things over with, or maybe nothing, maybe just digesting his breakfast. "I also specially want to thank two people who've helped keep my desk from looking like Mount Trashmore"—Key West's huge hill of half a century of garbage disposal over by the hospital—"and who've done plenty to help keep the whole station on an even keel: I mean Chief Wilkins and Yeoman Second Allend. Thank you, Tom and Lizabet."

So far so good. It seems to be going over okay.

But now he comes to another obligatory part of his speech—the retiree's passage of thanks to his wife—and he suddenly feels as if he is in free-fall. His mind has gone blank. He has entirely forgotten what he wrote down to say about Ginny. He swallows twice. After a long silence, he manages to say, "Quite a few of you know my wife, Virginia." And now, all at once, some of what he wrote comes back to him. "I couldn't've got here without her," he says. "Not in a million years. She is the most considerate person I know, the kindest, the most loyal." Every word of what he is saying is honest and true, and his heart was full when he put it down on paper, but the terrible thing now is, it sounds hollow, it has no feeling in it at all. He doesn't feel a thing. He can't look at Ginny; he talks straight at his friends back there in the formation. "However," he says—but now he has forgotten his lines again, and there is a long, excruciating pause, until his intention suddenly comes back to him. "However, the main thing is," he says, "she has a mind of her own. She never lets me blame anybody but myself. I'll tell you a little story. It was when we were stationed one time at Norfolk. I had just made j.g.; I was a bit older than most of the greenhorns that had come half baked out of OT school. One of these was this lieutenant, one rank up from me in the same section, who I couldn't stand. We were in base ops. He'd graduated UCLA, and he was always pulling this stuff of 'If you had a bit more education' on me, not necessarily in those words, but he made it clear—he had a long nose to look down—and one day he says . . . I'd made some mistake, it was minor, a nothing, and he says, 'You're going to have to learn,' he says, 'to think a little faster on your feet.' I wanted to say, excuse the expression, ladies and gentlemen, 'Up yours with a twist of lemon peel,' or something, but you couldn't. So that night I was telling Ginny about the guy, how rough it was to be stalled in a slot lower than him, with him on my back, and she said something that has stayed with me ever since, it's come to me anytime I thought I was going to lose it for keeps. 'Honey,' she said, 'you chose the navy. You signed up of your own free will. It was your choice,' she said. 'You looked into it, you knew the risks, you made the choice.' "

Now comes the queerest part, when he tries to say what it means to him to be leaving what he chose. Because just the opposite happens. His voice breaks. When he wrote this down, last night, he felt absolutely nothing and kept thinking, *This is what I'm supposed to say, this is royal b.s., this is out of Ginny's Big Book of Make-Believe.* In the act of writing about what wonderful years the navy time had been, he caught himself thinking, as if it were the marrow of truth, that he couldn't be gladder that those years were finally going to be over. But now as he speaks his voice begins to quaver. He looks to Gin for help, and looking in her eyes, he gets a surprise. He sees that she sees that he's scared. He realizes that he was miles off base last night. That the real truth is he's spooked out of his mind by what may be waiting for him outside the zone of comfort. That squirt of an M.B.A.—"Do it my way." He is suddenly furious with himself for having wasted a thought on that snippy little bitch of a j.g. . . . "The great thing about our regulations," he is saying in his speech, "is how they pave the way, how they make the tough decisions so much easier, because, you know, when you come down to it, there's only one right way. . . ." But what he hears in his memory's ear is Ginny's voice on that subject. And he almost loses his place in the speech again as, with a little mental lurch, he wonders: How far *will* twenty-one five go?

No, there's something much scarier than any of that. It's the truly basic thing: After all these years, he doesn't know where he really stands with Ginny. He has always counted on her to be his gyroscope in rough waters, but he gets no steadying help now from her eyes. He hears in his mind the raw edginess of her voice, in the aisle at the commissary, the day before yesterday, gripping the handle of the shopping cart with white knuckles: "You're planning to be a helpful husband, right?" Suddenly self-conscious, afraid of getting even more choked up, he looks away from her. And he can see that his friends back there in the formation really like it that he's so deeply moved—as they must think from hearing his words and his shaky voice—at leaving their ranks.

When he turns away to go back to his seat, he gets a big, big hand from all present, in uniform and out.

The CO is up, telling the civilians that what is to come next is a venerable and precious custom of the United States Navy. "It symbolizes Lieutenant Commander Robert Selden's leaving the ship," he says. "This little ritual of ours is called Piping Him Over the Side. He will have an honor guard, as he leaves, of eight of his closest friends, and he will have the gratitude and respect of all who have worked with him over the years."

The CO raises his head—the peak of his hat is still slanted forward in that goofy way—and he calls out, "Post the Side Boys!"

Eight of them. Chuck Stone, of course. Treadwell, Banton, Furr, Pollowicz . . . *yeah, they really are friends*. He had to pad out the other three, to make it eight. *Eight is a heck of a lot of best friends to have. Who has that many? Codder, he's more or less all right. Lawson. But why in hell I picked Franklin, I'll never know. I've never really trusted the guy.*

There they are, the eight of them, forming up on either side of the red carpet that is laid out at the end of the path to the curb, to where the navy car is waiting. He's made sure that Chuck would have the first spot on the right. The eight stand there on either hand of the red carpet, his Side Boys. They snap to attention when the CO barks the order. Then the CO shouts, "Prehent *harms!*" and eight swords flash in the sun and swoop up to form inverted vees high over the red carpet, a glistening arch of esteem to guard a valued person as he leaves the ship for good. Now some more tinny music comes on. The retiree can choose what music they'll play, and he's picked "Anchors Aweigh," as if: This is a celebration, it's a game, we're going to win, cheer up.

The CO nods toward him, and he steps down off the podium and goes over to the civilian chairs and takes Ginny on his left arm, and they start down the path and get to the red carpet and involuntarily duck both their heads on account of the sharpness of the swords. As they go along, Ginny is trying hard, without much success, to be military and keep in step with him. They're about halfway down the red carpet—the thin music back there in the speakers is still going—when a bosun's whistle splits the air. Over the Side. This is when it begins, at last, to be real, but it's hard to say whether he's thrilled or alarmed by the familiar sound. Goose bumps start on his behind and travel up his back and all down his arms. And then, on top of that, when he and Gin are just two steps away from the curb and the car, the door of which the driver is holding open, *dang!*—a single stroke from behind them of a ship's bell. How many times has he heard that sound in the past twenty years? It hits him like a blow. That's it. That is the end. He is out.

He almost stumbles. He feels numb.

He more or less shoves Ginny into the car, and he scrambles in after her and says to the driver, "Peel outta here."

The driver doesn't say, "Yes, sir." "Sir" is for officers. He says, "Trumbo Point?" Like a goddam taxi driver.

Ginny quietly says, "That's right, driver. We're on the bight side, near the upper end," and then she takes her civilian husband's hand and presses it hard, and it's as if what she means by the squeeze is just *Cool it*, but what she says is something entirely different. "It's all right, Commander," she gently says. "It's over now. It's all over." For a long time she has always, always seemed to aim the word Commander at him with a barb on it: "So you think you're the wheel around here, do you?" But not this time. This is different. She sounds as if she were far away, in an unfamiliar countryside, on some surprising, unexpected terrain of regret and dim hope. He is certain that she will never use that word in connection with him again. But this time, for once, she has given it every bit of its full value. She lets go his hand.

To End the American Dream

Here he comes. Along Green Street, from the direction of Whitehead, rolling like the Pilar *in a beam sea. Wearing shorts and a grimy T-shirt fouled with gurry and blackish stains of blood. He turns into the door on the street floor of the clapboarded white house on the left side of the alley. Dimly lit within, but enough light, as he bellies up to the curving bar, so anyone can see that he looks pleased with himself. Watch out, if you know that look.*

"What you say, Josie?"

"Not much," Russell says.

"Hello, Skinner."

"All right," the bartender says.

"Did you fix me a coconut?"

"Yessir."

Skinner leans over his ice cooler and lifts out a coconut with a hole bored in it.

"When did you put the gin in?"

"Five o'clock, like you said."

"Let's have a try."

Skinner puts a straw in the hole and hands the coconut to him.

"This coconut fresh?"

"Yessir."

"Tastes like piss."

"Which of course you know the taste of," Josie Russell says.

A charming laugh. Watch out.

"My friend Charlie Thompson tells me you're quite the amateur." This comes from a big guy sitting a couple of stools down the bar. Legs crossed. Wearing a Brooks Brothers cotton shirt with a button-down collar and immaculate white flannels with wide cuffs.

"You can't be much of a friend. He hates being called Charlie. Amateur what, by the way?"

"He says you split your finger on his punching bag."

"Who is this, Josie? Some more of that Matecumbe trash?" The CCC workers from Matecumbe Key, bottomed-out war veterans, who used to come in here before the hurricane drowned them all. Always asking for trouble.

Last night he was on his first drink, talking with Russell at the bar, when the middle-aged St. Louis woman came in with her two grown kids. Said they were curious about the name Sloppy Joe's. Girl, Marty, long blond hair, a hoity-toity accent with fake Englishy r*'s; turned out of course she'd gone to Bryn Mawr. The boy, Alfred, very handsome. They called their mother Omi. Marty did a thing with her nostrils when she saw the blood on his T-shirt. He talked softly. Said both his wives had gone to school in St. Louis; he knew the city well. Marty got around to saying she, too, was a writer. You could see she was impressed; she'd caught on who he was. "I used a quote from you for an epigraph* *for my novel," she said. He didn't ask what it was. Just the one book? No, there was a collection of stories,* The Trouble I've Seen. *"Good title," he said. Before they left, he said he'd show them the town. "Like you to meet Pauline," he said. Where were they staying?*

"My name is Apramian," the big man says.

"Sounds Armenian," he says. "You sell rugs?"

"I see you're the kind of guy gives his sparring partners bloody noses," the big man says, aiming his chin at the stains on the T-shirt.

"Only if they misbehave."

"Like pop you too hard?"

"Oh? You talk like you think you can box."

"Heard of Farnham's gym? In Queens. I work out there a little."

"You trying to give me a message?"

"Charlie said you have a short fuse."

"Wrong. I'm fast at calculating the odds. On Bimini I offered two hundred fifty to any Negro on the island who could win against me. This monster named Saunders, they said he could carry a piano on his head. Wanted to go without gloves. I said yes right off. He only lasted a minute and a half."

"Oooh," the big man says. "No; I sell commodity futures."

He's had the T-shirt on for two days. Fact is, the blood is from that opalescent sailfish yesterday, wounded when he'd had to use the gaff or lose it. Sacker was trying to get it up over the roller at the stern. It wasn't huge. It had taken only twenty minutes to bring it alongside. Six glorious jumps. The sail erect—the pride of an aroused peacock or wild turkey. Sacker had ahold of the bill, tugging at the trembling weight on the roller. It thrashed out of control and threw the hook too. He'd had to resort to the gaff. Had to. Fast. He hated doing that. Such beauty should be given back to the sea intact.

Now he has his arm around the broad shoulders of the man in white flannels. "Sure," he says. "How about three rounds of four minutes each, two minutes between?"

"If that's what you want," the big man says.

"My gloves are on my boat. We can walk over. Josie, would you bring your Reo around? We'll need the headlights."

Russell gives the man in white flannels the once-over. You can tell he's thinking, That guy is big. "You go along," Russell says. "I'll be there with the car."

The Pilar *is tied up stern-to. "You wait here," he says to Apramian. "I don't like strangers on board at night. I'll get the gloves."*

He jumps down on cat feet, goes forward to the con, and turns the lights on. He drops through the hatch into the engine room and switches on the overhead light there. The submachine gun is up there on its slings, in its oil-soaked case. He reaches up and pats it. That's all he wanted to do. Just pat it. He turns out the light and climbs above. He decides to call the girl Marty after the fight. The gloves are in the upper starboard locker, in the passageway to the head. He hangs both pairs around his neck on their laces and heists himself up onto the wharf.

He spent nearly three hours on the one paragraph this morning. He makes it a rule to quit the day's work while it's going well. So he can always pick right up the next morning and move along. Standing, working longhand at the tall podium, in the almost empty second-story room in the guesthouse in the place on Whitehead surrounded by its fortress wall made of the paving stones left over from when the streetcars were junked and the tracks removed. It was sunny out this morning. He took his time. He's pretty much finished up the have-nots; Harry Morgan is mortally wounded. Now it's back to the haves. Here's this grain broker in his bunk in the master cabin of his elegant black brigantine, thinking—but not really worrying—about the people his greed has ruined. Some made the long drop from the apartment or the office window; some took it quietly in two-car garages with the motor running; some used the native tradition of the Colt or Smith and Wesson; those well-constructed implements that end insomnia, terminate remorse, cure cancer, avoid bankruptcy, and blast an exit from intolerable positions by the pressure of a finger; those admirable American instruments so easily carried, so sure of effect, so well designed to end the American dream when it becomes a nightmare. . . .

Yes. Yes, indeed. Good place to stop for the day.

The important thing is to keep the headlights mostly behind him, to have as much light as possible full on the other man. Those pretty flannels are going to be soiled when he goes down. Josie Russell has the stopwatch. The fellow's big, all right, probably got three or four inches' advantage in reach. If he tries a haymaker, duck and get in under there with an uppercut. Give a jolt to the Armenian-American dream. A kayo is a miniature death. Must be careful on the uneven footing.

"Are you ready?" Russell asks. "All right. First round. Start!"

It doesn't take long to find out he's strong. A cruncher on the cheek. But it doesn't take long, either, to find out he's . . . oh, God, he's so slow. This should be easy. His shoulders relax, and even though he's paying attention to the moves the slowpoke is making, a line comes into his head for tomorrow morning. Somebody has to lose, *the grain merchant could think*, and only suckers worry.

The Wedding Dress

On the blank white wall on both sides of the door of Universal Cleaners, on Elizabeth Street across from the Monroe County Library, there are twin paintings of big, white-footed black cats, facing each other, maternally licking the fur of their kittens with pink tongues, with the legend GENTLE CLEANING wrapped around each of them. A cardboard sign, YES, WE'RE OPEN, is clipped with wooden clothespins to a wire coat hanger, which is slung on the front doorknob. If you're picking something up, you walk in to the counter in the anteroom and shake a length of harness strap with sleigh bells on it, which hangs down from the end of a shelf.

You hear Libby, inside the shop, call out, "Be right there!"

To your left is the wide doorway through to the bright, high-ceilinged main room of the shop, where you are used to seeing rows on rows of racks, with clothes that have been cleaned hanging in thin plastic wraps. Each item has its distinct personality; you can almost see the people the clothes belong to, wearing them right there, as if they're lined up at the Cobb, waiting to get into *Postcards from the Edge*. This time, though, there is an unusual sight. Just beyond the doorway, where customers can't fail to see it, a long tube of that plastic sheathing, about a foot in diameter, is lapped around something cream-colored. It hangs from a pipe near the ceiling, and it reaches almost all the way from there to the floor; the tube and its contents must be twelve feet tall. At eye level, a placard is pinned to the tube, with big letters:

UNCLAIMED—FOR SALE—$25

And you remember, and glance at, the notice on the wall beyond the counter, warning customers that garments left for more than thirty days will be sold for the cost of cleaning.

Cheerful little Libby comes out to wait on you.

You ask: "Is that a dress?"

Libby bobs her head yes.

"Gosh, she must be tall."

"It's a *wedding* dress," Libby says, smiling at your silliness. "It has a long train."

You realize the seriousness of its being for sale. "What happened? Was the wedding called off?"

"Oh, no," Libby says. "The wedding was four years ago. That's what the woman said, anyway. She said she had a three-year-old daughter; she was finally getting the dress cleaned to save it for her. I thought there was something fishy, though, 'cause she looked kind of off center when she told me that."

"And she's never come back? You must have had her name on the slip. Didn't you try to get in touch with her?"

"The number's been disconnected. Elsa even went to the house. For sale. No one there."

. . .

On that morning in May, Monique was on top of the world. It had been wonderful with Farrell the night before, and while she had been getting Tricia out of bed, he had fixed breakfast: he set up the coffeemaker, squeezed the juice, burned the toast—the whole works. Unbelievable. She didn't realize until later that he was conning her. He was so nice when he kissed her cheek and patted her on the behind as he left for work. She didn't give a second thought to seeing him back out of the carport with his board and his new 5.5 sail on the rack on top of the Camaro, the sail carefully folded and lashed under the mast and boom. This was Monday, and he'd just been lazy and left the gear up there when he got back in, the previous evening. That often happened. He liked to tool around town with the board showing.

Little Trish was so sweet and pliant in the kitchen that morning. Monique, feeling a surge of amazement at the marvel of this little person's trust in the world, hugged her hard, and Tricia squealed. It was at the height of Monique's joy that she looked out the window, over Trish's head, and saw the driven fronds of the areca palm on the front lawn. The good feeling suddenly drained away. She *hated* the wind. She went to the counter and flicked on the tiny NOAA weather box. Small-craft advisory, the voice said. Winds increasing to fifteen-to-twenty-five. Monique slammed her hand down on the lip of the box to turn the damn thing off. She had too much to do to waste her time worrying. She'd let Trish's room go; it was a pigsty. She had to go to Fausto's to shop for dinner. She'd promised to go to Latitude 24 and pick up the Ronny wet suit that Farrell had ordered for days when cold fronts would come through. She had to phone her mother. She'd have to call Sweetie's for a cake for Trish's third-birthday party on Wednesday. And what all else? God!

An hour or so later, after giving Tricia her breakfast and after reading about the local crimes on the second page of the *Citizen*, she started putting the breakfast dishes in the dishwasher. The phone rang. She picked up.

An angry voice, saying, "Mrs. Johnson?" Oh, God, Mr. Katchen. "Where the hell is that stud of yours?"

She guessed where he was. Fifteen-to-twenty-five knots. It figured. "I have no idea," she said. "He left for work about half an hour ago. At least that's what he said he was doing."

"This is, I don't know, the sixth time. I've had it with this stuff of his. We have things to do here. When you see him, Mrs. Johnson, you just tell him for me that he's unemployed. Understand what I'm saying?"

"Oh, come on, Mr. Katchen, give him a break. He can't help himself. A real wind blows, he goes out."

"So too bad. I have a business here. I don't live on whims."

An hour later, with all that she had to do, she was lying flat on her back on her bed. For some reason, she couldn't stop thinking about the happiest day of her life. The reception, that was just about the highest point. They'd rented the big room at the Officers Club. Beside the entrance to the hall, on a metal stand, there was a full-length prebridal portrait of her in her wedding dress, a picture four feet high "exclusively created for the bride," a little notice beside it said, "by Sassoon of Boca Raton." Her best friend and maid of honor, Bunny Slippa, had decorated the place with heart-shaped silver balloons that had inscriptions written on them with a Magic Marker, like EVER MAKE LOVE IN A BARREL, FARRELL? and IS THIS GUY UNIQUE, MONIQUE? Bunny also had charge of getting people to sign the wedding guestbook. Monique felt she was floating. She didn't even mind all the ancient Romeos, fat old friends of Farrell's rich old fat old father, trying to, like, French-kiss her in the receiving line.

When the line broke up, and before they all sat down to eat, Farrell's ushers—the whole sailboarding gang—started horsing around, using a lot of windsurfing terms in a suggestive way. There was nothing actually dirty; it was real nice how respectful the guys were of her parents and all. It was super. Monique knew that Farrell was way out in front of the other guys in his skill on the boards, and she was proud of him; of course, they were all just beginners back then.

After they were seated and the food had been served, the champagne began to flow. Some of the toasts were comical, some made her want to cry. She soon climbed up on the most beautiful high. There wasn't a thing in the world to worry about. It wasn't as if Farrell was going to drag her away afterward and make off with her cherry—something he'd done, with wonderful gentleness, eight months before. But after this they weren't going to have to sneak off up Route One to any more of those seedy motels. Cool cozy tiny house on Georgia Street. Farrell's rich old fat old father had helped with the mortgage. Whenever Farrell ran low, old man Johnson wrote him a check, which was mighty convenient. Or so it seemed to Farrell.

Now her father, who looked kind of sheepish—he hadn't bothered to rent a formal wedding getup like Farrell's old man, but so?—was asking her to dance. She gathered up her train in a double loop over her right arm, and all by themselves out on the floor they did an okay waltz, and the clapping was like a delicious welcome downpour on a tin roof in the dry months. Then, when she had cut the cake—a "Steps Up to Heaven" creation by Bambi Lott—with Farrell's hand on top of hers, and when she was back at the table, giddy from the bubbly and all the flickering camera flashbulbs, she finally had the courage to stand up and do a toast of her own. How could she have known, in her haze of pure delight on that day of days, how truly stupid what she said was going to turn out to be?

"Happy sailing on the seas of life, Farrell."

Everyone clapped like crazy, and the guys stuck their fingers in their mouths and whistled to split your ears.

She was still flopped out, with nothing done, at about eleven, when the doorbell rang. Tricia was napping. Without bothering to fix her face or her hair, Monique went to the door and looked through the peephole. It was Bunny Slippa. She thought at first she just wouldn't open the door, pretend she was out. But then she realized her Toyota was in the carport, and besides, Bunny might have heard her coming to the door. So she opened up.

"Bunny! My God, am I glad to see you! I've had such a shitty morning."

"Hi, sweets," Bunny said. "Thought you might be ready for a coffee break."

"Break from what? From sitting on my lousy tailbone? I don't know what's eating me, Bun. I've just got zero energy."

Monique led the way to the kitchen. She set up a new batch in the Mr. Coffee machine, and the two friends sat down at the kitchen table to wait for it to brew.

Bunny said, "What's the trouble? Farrell been acting up?"

"No. Certainly not. What makes you think that?"

"I don't know, he just struck me as kind of antsy lately."

"What the hell do you mean by antsy? Not with me he hasn't been. Come on, Bunny, what are you saying?"

"Nothing. Sorry. My big mouth."

"It's never been better between us. I don't like you trying to cook something up like this, Bun."

"Hey. I said I'm sorry. I take it back. He's a model husband."

"No, God damn it, Bunny, I want to know what you're saying."

"Isn't he a little bit off the edge of the page on this windsurfing stuff? Jesus, it's all you ever hear."

Monique got up and went over to the coffee machine. She

felt as if the floor were moving under her feet. As if the strong wind outside that she hated so much had come right into the kitchen. Her hand shook as she poured. She turned with the two cups in her hands and said as flatly as she could, "There's no one better than him out there."

The bride, entering on the arm of her father, wore an ivory bridal gown of ecru peau de soie by Priscilla Carnegie, with a deep sweetheart neckline, leg-of-mutton pouf sleeves, and a basque waistline. The sleeves and bodice were appliquéd with cutouts of alençon lace and embroidered with scattered seed pearls and iridescent sequins. A large bow with a white silk rose at its heart adorned the bustle, which cascaded down to a cathedral-length train. This in turn was accented with the same alençon lace cutouts and seed-pearl-and-sequin decor, and all along the edges of the train were miniature bows leading up to the large pivotal bow at the bustle.

Her veil, decorated with seed pearls and lace, was suspended from a crescent headpiece of ivory-colored silk roses.

She carried a bridesmaids-delight bouquet, which, within a mist of baby's breath and bridal illusion, featured delicate umbels of spiraea prunifolia, accents of dendrobium, miniature pink and white roses, and three sprays of boat-shaped cymbidium orchid blooms.

The groom was attired in a gray-pinstriped white tuxedo with tails from the Baron Rouge Collection. His boutonniere, echoing the bride's bouquet, was a large white rose with a whisper of baby's breath.

The mother of the bride wore a simple aqua-colored body-shaping tea-length dress with a belling skirt. One shoulder had a lift of fine-meshed stiff netting in the shape of a butterfly.

The mother of the groom wore a peach-colored satin spaghetti-strap dress embellished with a handkerchief-length multi-layering of pale peach flowered lace.

Randolph Johnson, brother of the groom, who flew in for the ceremony all the way from Madison, Wisconsin, to stand up as his brother's best man, wore a pale-gray-with-blue-pinstripe tuxedo with tails, likewise from the Baron Rouge Collection. On his arm going up the aisle was the maid of honor, Marion ("Bunny") Slippa, the bride's closest friend, who wore a fuchsia taffeta dress with a twin-tiered drop waist of lighter fuchsia tulle. Her bouquet featured a "love knot" of pink and white ribbon.

The bridesmaids were Belinda Figueroa, Roseanne Briggs, and Susan Fuller-Jones, friends since childhood of the bride. They, too, carried bouquets with "love knots." Joy and Regina Manley, younger sisters of the bride, were flower girls.

Groomsmen were Thomas ("Tom-tom") Parker, Roberto Cuellar, and Simeon Grund, close friends of the groom, all said to be, like Mr. Johnson himself, enthusiastic windsurfers. The ring bearer, Manuelito Sanchez, cousin of the groom, carried the twin rings on a white satin heart-shaped pillow dotted with seed pearls and sequins, matching those which beautified the bride's wedding dress.

It never gets better than this. It's blowing up a pisser out of the northeast, the white is being knocked off the waves like beer head. He does a series of six wave jumps, letting out a "Yahoooo!" each time he gets into full flight. Tom-tom Parker is with him, to leeward. He phoned Tom "on the way to the office," and Tom said sure, why not, he'd call in sick. Best to have someone with you on a wild day. The only thing that was a little bit unfair to Monique was that when he got dressed—she was in the other room with Trish—he put his bathing trunks on under the jeans that he always wore to work. He'd known right off that he'd be going out. He'd seen the wind in the trees when he brushed his teeth.

On a day like this, he can push his board and himself to the limit. This is what life is all about. Part of his joy is his pride in his sensational gear. All new. State of the art. An 8′6″ Robby Naish roundpin board with a 22-inch beam; a carbon mast; a 5.5 Gaastra sail with hollow battens to set the draft according to the wind, and with a low-drag "twisted" head. As he rips along on a close-hauled reach at something like thirty knots—Jeeee-zus!—he feels like . . . like what? Like, he thinks, like he's doing it for the history books! He tries to nail it down from things he's read about or seen on the tube. Like Lindbergh out there at the edge of his luck in the pea-soup fog fifty feet above the water? Going to get there, going to get there. Babe Ruth, pointing to the upper deck in the dim old black-and-white film, watch me hit one up there, and then he does? Petty, throoming dangerously close to the wall under the checkered flag at the Indy? Joe Montana, looping it sixty yards in the air, for six more than ever before, just as seven hundred pounds of linemen crunch him to the carpet? No way to even compare. There's nothing like this. Nothing. Oh, man, glistening along like a fucking cigarette boat over the spindrift. Whooo-eee! Tom-tom can't keep up with him, so he carves off a lay-down jibe and sails back toward him for a couple hundred yards, then jibes again and trims in once more to full speed.

Bearing down close to Tom-tom, and a little ahead of him, he shouts back, "How about let's go out to the Stream?"

Tom-tom looks doubtful, but what can he say? "Yeah, man!" he shouts.

It only takes them about an hour. It's sloppy over the gap in the reef but not too bad. Then! The waves out in the Stream—current running against the wind—are twelve feet high. Even Maui never could have been like this. First it's rock-climbing up a sheer face, then—whoo!—it's down to death valley. Then again. And again. From the top of one of the ramps, Farrell rips off a huge big cheese roll, and when the board is well up in the air he actually lets go of the boom with his hands for a half second, clapping once for sheer gladness and grabbing hold again. Lands a little flat on the down slope but loops off on a reach under full control without any trouble. At all.

It had become famous as Farrell's "big joke" at the wedding, and in her anger at its suddenly coming into her mind—she couldn't seem to shake thoughts of that day—she heard herself shouting, "For Christ's sake, Trish, would you stop that god-awful *noise?*"

After Bunny had left, she had calmed down a bit from her annoyance at her friend's busybodying, and she'd begun tidying up Trish's room. Trish was happily but absentmindedly helping, making chirping sounds, off in some enchanted aviary of her mind, when her mother let fly.

The child looked at Monique with huge eyes, which slowly filled with tears.

"Oh, honey, I'm sorry," Monique said, sitting down with a heavy thump on the edge of Tricia's unmade bed. "I'm all ragged this morning. I'm so sorry, dumpling. Come here." She took her daughter in her arms.

Tricia wiggled out of the embrace and perfectly cheerfully resumed what she'd been doing—but silently now.

Monique leaned forward with her chin cupped in both hands, her elbows on her knees.

The Old Stone Church had never been fixed up prettier. Up on the altar, on either side of a bank of white gladioli peppered with red carnations, there were eight tall candlesticks, with enormous hybrid hibiscus blooms, instead of candles, propped in the holders and slanted forward to be seen in all their radiance. Their petals' dazzling colors, in the thin noon light coming down from the stained-glass windows, were enough to make you believe in God—or, in her case at that moment, to think of Farrell, despite all his pranks and tricks and games, as one of God's better pieces of work. Those flowers were the first thing she saw, as her father, murmuring "Let's go, baby," started her up the aisle. She waited a few seconds to let her little sisters pick up the train. Then slow, slow steps like in the rehearsal, no way of keeping time with the jumpy Mendelssohn from that weird Wanda Medzuska creature at the organ. I'm shaking, she thought. I've got to focus. So she focused on those huge disks of color balanced on the candlesticks up there on the altar. The people on both sides of the aisle were standing and looking at her like she was a banana split with extra whipped cream.

She made it all right up to where Farrell and the minister and the groomsmen were standing. Farrell had a world's-record shit-kicking grin on his face. In her eyes, though, seeing him in a fog through the veil, he looked beautiful, even with that toothy grin. Beautiful. She was still shaking.

The minister—she tried to think of his name but couldn't—had a voice like an afternoon nap, and soon her trembling eased up. It all went along fine then, till it was time for the vows. The preacher looked Farrell in the eye, and he said, "Farrell McAlister Johnson, do you take this woman to be your . . ." and the rest of it. When he finished, silence. Farrell wasn't saying anything. So she turned her head and looked at him. He was standing there, with his hand working at his chin, sort of like that statue of *The Thinker*, and he had this expression of "Let's see about this, do I really want to get into this mess, give me time, ummm, wait, I just don't know . . ."

The groomsmen broke out in loud guffaws. Right out there in the most solemn part of the ceremony. Farrell must have told the guys he planned that little act. At the time, she laughed too. What else could she do?

. . .

At Fausto's she asked Trish to wait in the car in the parking lot while she shopped. She left the engine running, with the air-conditioning on, so it wouldn't get too hot for Trish in the locked red Toyota there in the sun.

She wheeled a shopping cart into aisle four. She dropped in some raisin bran and a can of Chock Full o'Nuts coffee and, at the back, a plastic gallon bottle of Crystal drinking water. She was standing by the packaged-meats counter, trying to think what Farrell would want—he'd be hungry after being out there in such a strong wind—when she had the feeling again of the wind coming right indoors and pushing, pushing at her.

What had really hit her was the thing about after the reception. He'd told her the day before that the only plane they could get for Miami—they were taking their honeymoon in Aruba, where everyone said the waves were so perfect that they seemed to be raised from the sea on the backs of dolphins—their only plane would be an American connection flight that wouldn't be leaving until five in the afternoon, so there'd be several hours to kill. She had thought there'd be a storybook getaway, with her trying to make sure she tossed her bouquet to Bunny Slippa, and then showers of rice, and tin cans tied on strings behind the Camaro, JUST MARRIED written with soap on the rear window of the car, then he'd take her only as far as Georgia Street and pick her up and carry her across the threshold of the house—even though they'd already been in it a hundred times, fixing it up. And *then*, she'd thought, there'd be some kind of Wedding Day Special on that big double bed!

Not on your life. It's toward the end of the reception. Farrell is on his feet, tapping the edge of a glass with a knife to get attention. "Okay, folks! Listen up!" he says. "You're all invited to come out to Smathers Beach to see an exercise in formation sailboarding that us four guys have planned in honor of the bride. I promise you you won't regret it."

So about fifty cars drove out to the beach. Earlier in the day, Farrell and the guys had decorated one of the picnic shelters with a zillion colored balloons, and she was given the seat of honor there. All the other people stood around getting sand in their shoes. In those days Farrell was still just renting boards from the guy named Slim—primitive recreational boards with deep daggerboards in slots. These crazy nuts just took their shoes off and waded out in their wedding day outfits, Farrell in his white tuxedo with tails, and got up on their boards and began doing their stuff. There was a pretty good breeze. First they just eased back and forth in a diamond-shaped formation. They really didn't know how to do much in those days. They had only begun to do a little simple hot-dogging. One short tack rail riding. Then back again in a rail ride on just one foot. Then all four doing a head dip—leaning way over backward till the tops of their heads skimmed on the water. And finally a "helicopter" in formation, each one swinging the sail 360 degrees, so the boom swept out over the bow of the board and around back again to make a full rotation, whirling around that way two whole times. And then, at a signal from Farrell, they all got clumsy at the same moment and fell off the boards, screaming and throwing their arms out and making a huge splash. In their wedding suits. All the guests died laughing.

To her surprise, she loved the whole thing. Farrell was so original.

Back then that was what she'd thought.

The wind in the store died down just enough so she could pick up a cellophane packet with six pork chops in it for him. Breaded pork chops, his favorite. He'd be famished.

. . .

He came breezing in, a personified wind, at a little after four. He looked as if he had just made a down payment on the whole world. His face was like pink satin from the salt and the sun. He came right to her and threw his arms around her, and even though she was almost choking with the anger that had been building up all day, she put her arms around him and held him close. It was as though she had no idea what she was doing. She could smell the beer on his breath. She put her cheek against his. She was on the edge, the very edge. Trish had come running from her room, and Farrell broke away and turned and picked Trish up and tossed her toward the ceiling, three times, her sexy little shrieks rising, with her body, higher and higher.

"You can't believe how good it was out there today," he said, holding Trish in his arms. "It was like, I don't know, like the palms of your hands were wings. You could fly just waggling your hands. Think about it."

"You've been fired," she said. "Katchen called. He fired you."

"We went out to the Stream," Farrell said. "Oh, shit, I've never seen it like that. It was every single amusement-park ride you ever took—the Whip, the Looper—remember the Killer Coaster at where was it? St. Pete? Only, it was different, you know, it was different, *you* were in control, you were the one defining the limits."

"Farrell. Did you hear what I said? You booted your job."

Trish wriggled in his arms. He put her down, and she ran off to her room. He turned a bland face to Monique.

"Who cares about the frigging job?" he said, shrugging. "I've got better things to do than kiss ass to a lot of insurance freaks."

"God damn it, Farrell, you promised me."

"I don't *need* the job. I don't need the money, I don't need the hassle, I don't need you sticking it to me like this. Come on, Monnie, get human."

"You have to have something to do on dry land, Farrell. You're going to drown yourself."

"Oh, no, not that again. Don't you realize I'm a grown-up? Jesus! I know what I'm doing out there."

"Every time the wind blows, I get terrible shakes."

"I was going to quit the job, anyway," Farrell said. "Actually, tomorrow. I was going to do it tomorrow."

They were still standing in the front hallway. Farrell turned and walked into the living room. She followed. He said back over his shoulder, "I'm going to Hawaii."

A gale had come into the room. Monique dropped into a chair to stabilize herself. She just managed to say, "You're what?"

"I was going to tell you. I have a reservation on Thursday to go out. I got to try Maui. I have to have that. I need some better competition than I can get with the jokers around here."

The wind was howling around her ears. "You tell me this three days before you leave? Do you remember what happened last night, Farrell? Are you telling me that you could do that and you knew this? And how long is this . . . this . . . Just how long do you plan to be on this little vacation?"

"I don't know, Monnie. I have to see."

Monique sat silent for a long time. Farrell didn't seem to have anything more to add, either. Finally she heard herself shouting into the teeth of the hurricane, "It never occurred to you to take us with you? I mean, Tricia and me? That never crossed your mind?"

"Look, Monnie, I'm sorry, I have to go out now. I promised to meet Tommy Parker. He was out there with me today. I'll be back."

Now in the tumult it was as if someone else, some total stranger, were speaking through her throat. "I got pork chops for supper for you."

But he was at the door—and then he was gone.

. . .

Ten minutes later, she was driving across Southard, a little too fast. She had laid out the wedding dress on the back seat, folding it back and forth to try not to crush too many bows. Trish was strapped into her car seat on the passenger side.

"Honey," she said, "don't rush it. Find a guy, you know, that you're really sure. I mean really. You'll be able to tell. The whole thing is to remember that the day you get married . . . well, it's just a start. To everything. It'll all be right there to see, right in what happens. You'll be wearing the dress there in the back. It's for you, Trish. What a *day*, honey—wait till you see. You won't be able to believe some of the things. . . . All I ask is, take a good look. At the surprises. And the main thing is, don't let yourself forget the dress was a present from me. It's the one your mother wore. Think about that, hon."

Monique darts a glimpse at Tricia and notices that her head is turned away; she's looking out the window on her side.

"Trish, are you listening to me?"

The little girl swings her trusting face toward her mother and says, "Can I have Jennifer over tomorrow?"

Monique lifts both hands from the wheel and pounds the heel of her hands down on it three times, then grips it tight. She has begun to weep.

Tricia sees this and says, "Mommy?"

"Nothing, honey, nothing. I just talk too much."

Monique has no idea where she is, but she makes the correct turns—right on Simonton, right again on Fleming, and right once again on Elizabeth. She parks in the loading zone in front of the cleaners. "You wait here, sweetie. I'll be right back." She goes around and takes the wedding dress out from the sidewalk side and carries it into the anteroom. No one is there, and in the fury that blows through her mind just then, she shakes the strap with bells on it so hard she almost tears it off its fastening.

In a minute, a peppy little woman comes out from in back. Her eyes light up at what Monique is carrying. "Isn't that gorgeous!" she says. "Were you just married, dear? The *Citizen* carry it? I don't remember seeing your picture."

A Little Paperwork

"Thank you, Mr. President." This from Merriman Smith of United Press, senior gun in the White House correspondents corps, who has the right and duty of bringing news conferences to an end.

Truman is sitting bolt upright in a white wicker chair on the carpet of Bermuda grass in front of the "Little White House." He's resplendent in his tropical mode: a white linen suit over an open-necked Hawaiian shirt splashed with a lurid print of passionflower blossoms. He nods to Smith, accepting the adjournment, and the reporters surge up from the arc of folding chairs on the lawn and scramble off toward the annex gate on Whitehead Street, racing to phones.

Truman stands. His face, pinked by the sun, is a palimpsest: a slightly cocky defiance is newly scribbled now over what had been, half an hour earlier, a quite different text, written in taut facial muscles and pressed lips. Word came in midmorning of a bleak Gallup poll. At the endless hearings in the Senate Caucus Room in the Capitol, Senator Joseph McCarthy's hectoring nasal tones have zeroed in on Owen Lattimore as "the top Russian espionage agent" in the country. Recently the McCarthy uproar has turned nasty. In the Senate, Styles Bridges, whom the President regarded as a friend, and others—Mundt, Wherry, Capehart, Taft—have been openly egging McCarthy on. And now, according to the poll, McCarthy has won a favorable rating—as one who is helping the country—from more than half of a sample of the citizenry. The rating of the President, on the other hand, has fallen to a horrendous 37 percent, nearly as bad as at the nadir, two years ago. When Matt Connelly relayed this news to the boss, Truman at once ordered the press conference—a rarity during Key West vacations.

The reporters have all left. Charlie Ross, who has been standing with other staffers behind the President, steps forward now. The circles under his eyes are little purple balloons of stored stress and heart-weariness. He manages a smile. "That was very good," he says to the President.

"It was?" Truman's hugely magnified eyes behind his glasses take on a rogue glint. "In that case," he says, "it must be time for a little paperwork."

The press secretary knows what that means, and so do the other staffers, who have overheard. All now turn to go into the big ungainly box of a house, which breathes the soft March air through many rows of lifted white wooden louvers.

The group makes its way onto the spacious veranda. At one end, a large round table is all set up for paperwork: There are eight chairs. On the tabletop in front of one of them lie the "papers" that must be dealt with: two decks of cards. At all eight places there are equally apportioned stacks of blue, red, and white poker chips.

"Well, gentlemen?" says the President of the United States. "What would you say to a jigger of Old Grand-Dad? Looks as if we're in for some awful hard work"—gesturing toward the table.

This is, after all, a vacation. The day's official business has been done—one could say well done. A pick-me-up is in order.

A Filipino mess attendant brings a tray with a bottle, some glasses, and a pitcher of water. The President is served first, a couple of fingers neat. Bill Hassett and George Elsey, who won't be playing poker, decline. So do Charlie Ross and Harry Vaughan, who will be in the game, the latter looking heart-broken at having to go without; he's on strict orders. Others help themselves: Matt Connelly, Charlie Murphy, Dave Stowe, Doc Graham, John Steelman.

"Top of the afternoon, gentlemen," the President says, holding his glass high. "Sit you down."

It is understood that the President is entitled to the first deal, and he takes the chair by the decks of cards. He shuffles. He likes fluid, wide-open games. "For starters," he says, "let's have five-card stud with deuces and one-eyed knaves wild." He has often called jacks knaves since he tried to teach Winston Churchill the game at the time of the iron curtain speech. As the deal goes around the table, some of the players cater to the loose tastes of the boss, asking for Texas, or Spit-in-the-Ocean, or a freewheeling deal the President calls "Papa Vinson." Charlie Murphy, however, confrontational to his lawyerly bones, always asks for "poker," by which he means straight draw, pair of jacks to open. As usual, the President is a gamer. He stays and stays in the pots, often well beyond the worth of his holdings. "I'll see you in hell," he keeps saying, tossing chips in. Now and then a bluff of his works, and he scoops in the pot with a radiant delight.

The chatter is cheerful. The press conference has obviously given Truman a chance to let off steam, and he looks more relaxed than he has been for a long time.

"What was that gobbledygook you and Bill Hassett were talking at breakfast this morning?" Harry Vaughan asks.

"We were just saying that 'The Walrus and the Carpenter' could have been written about Congress. You know. 'The time has come,' Senator Taft says, when a bill I want to get passed

reaches the floor, 'to talk of many things'—everything but the bill. Shoes. Ships. Cabbages. Kings. And the Carpenter, he's a Republican, all right, sitting there eating the poor little oysters. 'Cut us another slice,' he says, and then he turns around and complains—as if it's the fault of the White House—too much butter."

Later, the President says, "To take my walk this morning, Nick and the others rode me out to the pathway by that long beach near the airport." It was peaceful out there as the sun rose. The President and the Secret Service agents were moving along at his habitual brisk pace—the army marching speed, one hundred twenty steps to the minute, two miles in half an hour—when, he says, "here was this little lady taking her constitutional at six a.m. One look at me and she said, 'Gracious sakes, it's Mr. Truman.' 'Morning, ma'am,' I said. And she said, 'You keep after 'em, sir. Keep 'em hopping.' It was remembering her saying that, later in the morning, that made me decide to have the press conference."

The deal moves around the table. The President is playing more and more loosely, taking foolish chances, losing and not caring. At one point he says that after he told Charlie Ross to summon the reporters, he took a dip, to calm himself, off the Fort Zachary Taylor Beach. Those who were nearby would have seen him swimming in the dead-still water in his ungainly style, a hybrid of dog paddle and sidestroke, designed to keep his glasses dry as he moved slowly through the water. He talks now about how bracing the swim was. "The water's warmer here than in the pool at the White House"—the pool built for F.D.R. with pennies donated for the purpose by schoolchildren—"but the saltiness buoys you up." And he drifts off into one of his beloved historical anecdotes. "I was thinking out there, you know," he says, "about how old John Quincy Adams used to like to walk along the Potomac early mornings—Washington was just a small town in 1825—and sometimes he'd stop and shuck off his clothes and take a dip. There was this hoyden of a newspaper-

woman named Anne Royall—she was later fined by a court for being a common scold. She'd been trying to interview old J.Q., but he refused to see her. So one day she followed him on his walk, and when he was in the water she sat on his clothes, and she wouldn't let him out till he answered her questions."

Charlie Ross asks, "Did you feel as if some of those reporters were sitting on your clothes out there this afternoon?"

"Not for a second," the President says.

"You really ticked the senator off," Matt Connelly says. "What was that line?"

"It was time somebody rebuked that low-down skunk," Truman says. "What I said was—and I meant it—I think Senator McCarthy's the greatest asset the Kremlin has."

"And about whether Lattimore's a spy," Ross says, "that was fine. You didn't hesitate for a second. 'Of course not. Silly on the face of it.' That was what had them running to the phones."

"Don't gloat, Charlie," the President says. "That reprobate isn't going to care what I say."

All the same, there is an expression on the President's face that looks very much like gloating, premature though it may be. It has come around to be his deal. He shuffles a deck, and then he says, "All right, gentlemen. A new game. I'm going to call this one 'Key West.' Seven-card stud, with deuces, sevens, and all four queens wild. And of course the jokers, if you happen to catch 'em."

"Doesn't that hand out an awful lot of free tickets?" Charlie Murphy, the purist, grumbles.

"Yes, sir," the President replies. "You could say that, Charlie. A person could say Key West does that. Where else could you get such good advice from a little lady at six o'clock in the morning?"

ALSO BY

JOHN HERSEY

Available from Vintage Books

Antonietta

Fiction/0-679-74181-X

A Bell for Adano

Fiction/0-394-75695-9

Blues

Fishing/Sports/Nature/0-394-75702-5

Life Sketches

Journalism/Essays/0-679-73196-2

Hiroshima

History/0-679-72103-7

Available at your local bookstore,
or call toll-free to order: 1-800-793-2665
(credit cards only).